OFF THE CHARTS!

Off the Charts!

A Novel

Kevin Scott Hall

iUniverse, Inc.
New York   Bloomington

Off the Charts!
A Novel

*This is a work of fiction. All of the characters, names, incidents, organizations, and dialogue
in this novel are either the products of the author's imagination or are used fictitiously.*

iUniverse books may be ordered through booksellers or by contacting:

iUniverse
1663 Liberty Drive
Bloomington, IN 47403
www.iuniverse.com
1-800-Authors (1-800-288-4677)

*Because of the dynamic nature of the Internet, any Web addresses or links contained in this book
may have changed since publication and may no longer be valid. The views expressed in this work
are solely those of the author and do not necessarily reflect the views of the publisher, and the
publisher hereby disclaims any responsibility for them.*

ISBN: 978-1-4401-9469-6 (sc)
ISBN: 978-1-4401-9467-2 (dj)
ISBN: 978-1-4401-9468-9 (ebk)

Printed in the United States of America

iUniverse rev. date: 02/1/2010

CHAPTER ONE

▼

A twenty-first birthday is supposed to be a momentous occasion, but I had no idea just how momentous mine would end up being.

I was out with a couple of buds celebrating my coming of age, and we ended up in a dive called Fat Bo's. We stumbled into the place a little after seven, laughing about I don't know what. The hoped-for big celebration didn't look promising.

I bet it hadn't changed much since the miners had been in town. Three walls were a peeling, faded red paint and one wall was brick. It was dimly lit with a few swinging overhead lights with red bulbs, and crooked sconces haphazardly lined the walls, many hanging by one screw. It was a neighborhood bar with older guys wearing Steelers caps and flannel shirts and drinking beer, and hardly a woman in sight. A few guys clacked balls around the handful of billiard tables scattered around the large room. The bar itself was long, the entire length of the back wall, and curled around to a dark corner where, sipping a beer, one larger-than-life woman—big blonde hair, big tits, big round ass on the stool—caught my eye.

We took in the scene for a few seconds before I turned to Rick Puccio, my ridiculously bulked up friend and fellow wrestler on the University of Scranton team. "What exactly is the attraction of this place?"

"It's still early, don't worry," Rick said. "Trust me, after the girls are out dancing with their guy friends who don't yet know they're gay at the Copper Penny, they'll come over here looking for action."

"University girls come in here?" I found it hard to believe. So many of the college girls, although not angels, were from strict Catholic families and dressed the part, and I couldn't imagine them in here being hit on by these Cro-Magnons.

"Oh, yeah, and from the other schools, too. Probably even Baptist Bible College," Rick snorted.

"Not to mention the locals," Pete Trueblood chimed in. "They love to get laid by a university guy." Pete was blond and six-foot-something, taller than both Rick and me. His life seemed pretty charmed to me and he was already looking at a job offer in Florida through some family connection.

"Yeah, probably like to get pregnant by one, too," I said.

Rick and Pete were trying to cheer me up because Amy, my girlfriend of a year—and, my mother hoped, a nice marriage prospect—had just dumped me over semester break. I mean, you have to understand my thinking at the time: *She* was dumping *me*? Okay, maybe my grades weren't so great, but I was in line for the Bounder fortune, my father being head of Bounder & Lightning in Philadelphia. What's more, on that particular birthday, I was getting access to a half-million-dollar trust fund left to me by my grandfather. Another reason to celebrate! With my family connections, I could have been Ivy League, but I was more of an entrepreneur than a student, so I never worked too hard on the grades. But the University of Scranton had a good marketing major and it left me close enough to Philly to remain under my mother's thumb. So anyway, our attitude that night was *Fuck Amy, let's party!*

I'd been out to a few Scranton bars before, mostly downtown near school, but not this part of town. This was further west on Lackawanna Avenue, past the river and up the steep hill. The poorer part of town. "Let's drink," I said. "What are you having?" Unimaginatively, we settled for Heinekens and I headed to the bar.

The bartender, maybe late thirties, had trimmed, thinning blond hair and looked like he worked out—an exception to the rule in this place. After he got our drinks, he went back to the blonde in the corner. She somehow looked familiar to me, but I couldn't place her. "Do you guys recognize her?" I asked Rick and Pete. "Does she work on campus or something?"

"Shit, dude, can you wait a bit? I know you're on the rebound, but are you gonna pick up the first old skag you see?"

"I never seen her," Pete said. "If she's your type, you really are ready to get over Amy." Amy had short brown hair, was smartly dressed, and had a fawn-like manner—on the surface. When you got to know her, she could be needy and demanding. This woman at the bar seemed to be kind of the anti-Amy.

"I'm just trying to figure out who she is, that's all." I couldn't admit to them that I was strangely attracted to this woman. She must have been forty, maybe older, and she was a little out of shape in her tight clothes, but I liked her no-nonsense manner with the bartender and the occasional smoky chuckle that she let out every once in a while. She habitually turned over a cigarette pack in her hands—Scranton had recently passed a no-smoking ordinance in the bars—and shifted her attention from the bartender to the overhead TV, where a game of Celebrity *Jeopardy* was being played.

"Let's go shoot some pool," Rick suggested, and we found an unused table several feet away. We didn't really play a formal game or anything, just sipped our beers and went on about school, calling shots and aiming balls at pockets.

"So, yo, man," Pete said to me, "You got all this money and shit coming in now. You don't even have to worry about what you're gonna do in June."

"You think my mother is going to let me sit on my ass and collect?" I asked them. My father, Martin, at eighty, still doddered into the office every day. He had an amazing work ethic but pretty much left me alone. My mother, Doris, was boss. She was about sixty and very active in Philly society. She had had me late in life, but my birth was not an accident. See, when my brother Marcus was about eighteen and a freshman at NYU, he came home for Christmas and at one of my mother's big parties, stood under the mistletoe and proclaimed, "Come kiss the Christmas fairy for good luck in the New Year!" That's how he came out.

After that embarrassment, only weeks into the new year, my mother had happily announced to all her friends that she was pregnant. The way I look at it, she already knew Marcus was a lost cause to inherit the business, so she had to give it one more try while her eggs were still good.

She had kept me under her protective care ever since. And boy, was she pissed when Amy broke up with me—but she blamed me. "She was such a nice girl, but you don't take your life seriously, Greg. Now you have the means to provide for a wife, and you don't appreciate her." My mother only had a few months until my graduation and I figured she was already plotting Plan B.

"You're twenty-one now. You need to cut the cord," Pete said.

Nothing would have pleased me more, but it's a hard thing to do when you've been brought up since Day One to be next in line to the Bounder & Lightning Inc. throne. My father had already been carving out an office for me in the Walnut Street headquarters. "You guys are the lucky ones," I told them. "You can map out your own course. Your parents will be thrilled with whatever you decide to do." This was especially true for Rick. He was on the soccer and baseball teams, as well as wrestling, and fall, winter, and spring, his parents would come over from the outskirts of Pittsburgh to catch as many games as possible. Unbelievable! His parents actually *encouraged* him in his career choice, sports management! My mother would go apeshit if I had told her I wanted a career in sports management. Pete, in addition to his job offer in Florida and part-time accounting job at the *Scranton Times-Tribune*, was also looking at graduate schools all over the place—he got As effortlessly. Yet all they could focus on was my pile of money, like that made my life easy or something.

"Shit, you just came into all this money and you're going back to Philly to work for Bounder & Lightning? That is whack, man!" Rick smacked a fresh triangle of billiard balls to emphasize his point.

"For real," I acknowledged. "I'd like to go to New York, meet the movers and shakers, do my own thing." I took a sip of my Heineken. "But not Wall Street. I've been around the corporate world my whole life and I do not want to be working my way up to line someone else's pockets. Fuck it, Amy's gone. Why do I need to play it safe? I need to find my own business."

"Maybe Bounder & Lightning isn't so bad. You can start out on top," Pete reasoned.

"Can you imagine me in downtown Philly going in there for the next fifty years? No way. I'm gonna talk to my brother, see if there's something I can do in showbiz. Marcus is unbelievably successful."

This was a pipe dream at the time because the truth is I was not that close to Marcus, a well-known deejay not only in New York but all over the country. It was not only the eighteen-year age difference, but he was all caught up in the gay lifestyle of New York and beyond. I did visit him for a weekend once at the end of my freshman year, and had a blast. He took me to one of his gigs at a place called Twirl and I sat in the booth with him while he spun records. He introduced all his friends to me and many of them kept hitting on me. Marcus laughed and told them I was only eighteen. I'd have appreciated it if he'd also told them I was straight. Anyway, Marcus foolishly told my mother about the trip and she was furious. That probably explains why whenever I went back to New York for the occasional day trip he was always too busy or out of town and couldn't see me.

I should explain something here. As a kid, I ended up listening to the crates of promotional CDs and twelve-inch vinyl records that Marcus would send to me back in Philly. I grew to love the stuff and became quite an expert on all the artists. So, while the other kids were listening to Puff Daddy and Alanis Morissette and the Backstreet Boys, I was becoming addicted to urban dance music. As a college student, I had to keep that passion in the closet. It was a weird thing, I know, but the bottom line is that I was not then and never have been gay. Period. I just liked their music. What can I say?

Pete shot me a doubtful glance. "And your mother is going to go for that?"

"Fuck, no!" We all had a good laugh and drained the last of our beers. "You all want another? My treat."

"Damn right it's your treat. For the rest of the semester," Rick said. I gave him the finger and headed back to the bar.

The bartender was leaning on the bar listening to the blonde, who was commenting on *Jeopardy*. "You see that guy? He used to be on that courtroom show—what was it called—that was real big back in my day. Now he's doing this." She downed a shot of something. "There are no guarantees in this business."

I smiled and turned slightly to look at her more fully. "Holy shit," I said out loud. I couldn't help myself.

She turned her head towards me. "Got a problem?"

"You. I mean, not you! I mean, you're not a problem!" I was making a complete ass of myself. "What I mean is, I think I know you!"

"Is that so?" She regarded the bartender. "Rolf, get me another Jameson, please."

"It's true, you're Sally—excuse me—Miss Testata!"

"If you insist," she answered, lifting her beer and clinking her bottle to my empty one, which I was still holding aloft. "I actually go by Teskewicz now." I remained motionless. "Rolf, the guy's in shock. Get him another Heineken. On me."

"I'm sorry, it's just that I was—am—one of your biggest fans," I stammered.

"No, no, *was* is the right word. As you can guess, I haven't done shit for years. I didn't know I had any fans left, thank you."

"Come on Sally, *we're* your biggest fans," Rolf said, setting down my beer and motioning around the room.

"No, you guys are family. Big difference."

"I just loved 'Bombs Away,' of course, and I have some of your earlier records from when you were with Pillow Talk." "Bombs Away" was her one big solo hit from several years before, and then she was never heard from again. But there she was in front of me. Sally Testata.

"You've got to be kidding me. I thought that shit hit the recycle bin years ago."

She gave me a long look up and down. Sally was checking me out! I mean, she was a little rough around the edges there in Fat Bo's, but back in the day she was *hot*! And never wore much, either. "Quite frankly, you don't look like the type to be one of my fans. You don't even look old enough to be in here. Rolf, did you check his ID?"

"Oh, yeah, I'm old enough. Just turned twenty-one." I fished around my wallet for my license, even though nobody was asking for it.

"Happy birthday, uh," Sally said without emotion. "What's your name?"

"Oh, I'm so sorry. I'm Greg. Greg Bounder." While I was fumbling with my wallet, I pulled out a business card and gave it to her.

"Are we doing business?" Her eyebrows arched up.

"Oh, yeah, always doing business, even if the business is pleasure," I said, extending my arm for a handshake. Could I have been any cheesier? "I'm a marketing major at the university."

She looked down at my card. "What the hell does this mean? 'Greg Bounder—Rocket Scientist?'"

"That's part of the marketing. If I put 'Greg Bounder—Marketing,' nobody would notice or care. But you'll always remember me now, right?" I'm glad there was no mirror around because my smile must have been goofy as hell and so fucking wide it felt like it would split my face.

"Uh-huh." She stared right into my eyes. "We got a real pisser here, Rolf," she said, without shifting her gaze. Shit, she made me uncomfortable.

"Thanks for the beer," I said, and lifted my bottle to toast hers. "So, uh, what do you do now? Do you still sing?"

"Hell, no. Those days are gone."

"That's too bad."

"No, it's not," she said. "It's a blessing. Life is much easier now."

"So I guess you made your fortune and got out."

Sally almost spit out a mouthful of beer. "Yeah, right! My big fucking fortune!" She took another sip. "Actually, I clean houses," she stated matter-of-factly.

"You what?" I protested. It seemed inconceivable. "No, that can't be. You're too talented, too big a star for that."

"Look, my friend," Rolf interrupted. "Why don't you leave the lady alone." It was more of a threat than a question.

"Rolf is very protective of me," Sally said, putting her hand over his on the bar and giving him a wink. "Thank you, sweetie, but I'm okay with this. Greg here is young and it's as good a time as any to teach him the facts of life: dreams don't always come true."

"But yours did. You had songs in the clubs, on the radio. You were going up, up, up!"

"And then it was down, down, down," she said, and then downed another shot.

"But how did that happen? 'Bombs Away' was a big hit."

"For a minute," she sighed. "2001, that was finally going to be my big year. First the song hit in July, then the video in August. Do you remember the video?"

"No," I said, puzzled.

"I'm not surprised. Let me refresh your memory while Rolf refreshes my drink," she said, sliding the glass across the counter. "The video was an expensive shoot, it was a retro look based on an old film called *Attack of the Fifty-Foot Woman*. I was the new fifty-foot woman, dressed in a bikini, throwing kamikaze planes into buildings while singing, 'Don't mess with me, I'll make you pay, I'll take no prisoners, bombs away!'"

"It sounds great. I wish I had seen it." I was still not getting her meaning.

"Very few people saw it. It was yanked after 9/11, along with the song. At the end of August, I had the number one dance song and was climbing the pop chart. A month later, I couldn't get arrested." She took a gulp of her beer. "The irony is, if it came out today, it would probably be a hit for exactly the same reason. Fucking warmongering country."

"Wow. I had no idea. But it must have been around that time that I was blasting it on my stereo when my mother came in and yanked the plug out of the wall, saying, 'How dare you play that garbage at a time like this?' I thought she meant I shouldn't be having fun at a time like that. I wasn't paying attention to the words, I guess." I felt the need to explain further. "I mean, *she* called it garbage. She hates all my music."

"Maybe it was garbage," she said. She looked me over again. "Are you gay?"

"Me? Gay? No way, no way," I assured her. "I know it seems kind of weird that I listened to dance music, but my brother was—and still is—a deejay in New York and he used to send me all the leftover promotional CDs, so that was my musical influence."

"No wonder I didn't make any money. They were giving the shit away," she said with a wry grin on her face. "What's your brother's name?"

"Marcus. Marcus Blonder. He changed his name slightly to match his hair, which he dyed this ridiculous shade of yellow. It's kind of his trademark."

"I remember Marcus Blonder. I never met him, but he was known on the circuit."

Just then, Pete and Rick came over to the bar. "I guess we're gonna have to get our own beers, huh?"

"Oh, I'm sorry, guys. Pete and Rick, I'd like you to meet Sally Testata. She's a famous singer. I told you she looked familiar."

"Oh, wow," Pete said, as they took turns shaking her hand. He was such a bullshitter, I could tell he didn't know who she was. "What brings you to Scranton?"

"I actually live just outside of Scranton in an old farmhouse. Same house I grew up in." That statement seemed more frightening to me than cleaning houses. "Your friend Greg here is being awfully nice, but the truth is I haven't sung for a while."

I ordered two more beers for my friends. "I'd love to hear you sing again, Sally—Miss Testata—"

"You can call me Sally,"

"Thank you, Sally. So, yeah, I'd love to hear you sing again."

"Well, you have my CDs, so listen anytime."

"Maybe a little show here in town." I looked around the room. "Here?" The room was spacious and a small stage could be set up easily.

She let out a big, throaty laugh that became a smoker's hack. Finally, she dabbed the tears from the corners of her eyes. "Rolf, what do you think?"

"Nope," Rolf answered. Who the hell was he to say?

"See? Ain't gonna happen."

"You know," Rolf began, "You guys know her club music from her New York days, but back in high school she won talent contests singing the classic songs."

"Rolf, shut your damn yap. Don't give away our age." She smiled at him.

"What kind of songs?" I asked, genuinely curious. Pete and Rick looked at each other like they couldn't have been more bored.

"Oh, I don't know," he considered. "'The First Time Ever I Saw Your Face,' I still remember that one. Like it was yesterday." I wondered if he was messing with her, or if he ever did. It seemed like he was still in love with her.

"Yeah, if that was yesterday, that was one long, fucking night," she said dramatically.

"Well, hey, it was nice to meet you," Pete said. "We're going to go back to our game." He looked at me. "You coming, Greg?"

"In a few minutes. Sally bought me a beer, so I'd like to finish it with her if I may." I looked at her to make sure it was okay, and she nodded her head in agreement.

The two turned and headed back to the table, Pete shaking his head while muttering something to Rick.

"They're wondering what the hell you are doing with me," Sally observed.

"They're good guys," I said. "But to meet you is a dream come true." Jesus, I was ridiculous!

I stood in silence for a few moments, not knowing what to say. She was watching the TV, not exactly encouraging me.

"So, uh, Sally, how did you get started cleaning houses?" Could I have asked a more stupid question?

She didn't seem to mind my lack of tact. "I had a tough few years after my music career ended. I needed something that allowed me to work by myself, quietly."

"Didn't you have enough momentum after 'Bombs Away' to do something else?"

"Nah. When a record company has spent a lot of money promoting you and you go belly-up, they'd rather cut their losses and let you go. It's not like I was your age. They didn't want to take another chance on me." She paused, perhaps remembering something unpleasant. "And Eddie, my manager, listened to them. Cut me off at the knees after ten years."

"But it wasn't your fault."

"Do you think they give a fuck? It's all business to them and I was a bad risk. They were probably right."

"Their loss was our gain," Rolf said from a few feet away while rinsing glasses. Was he going to listen to our entire conversation?

"You said you lived in the house where you grew up. Do you take care of your parents?"

"No. Well, not anymore. My mother died a couple years ago. Cancer. That's what brought me back to Scranton. And if it had to happen, I suppose the plus side of it is that it got me out of New York once and for all, out of the music business and away from Antonio, my ex."

"Wow, you really did have a couple of bad years."

"You don't know the half of it," she said. "But this last year, I've been about as calm as I've ever been in my life. I'm getting used to it and it's not so bad."

To me, it didn't seem so much calm as numb. I couldn't figure out how someone with all that talent could be happy cleaning houses and living in an old farmhouse outside of Scranton.

"So you never hear from anyone in New York?"

"Of course not. In that town, you leave a room for five minutes and everyone has forgotten about you. You're only as good as what you can do for someone else."

"But don't you get curious about what everyone is doing?"

"That's why we have newspapers and television and Internet. If any of my old gang is doing anything important, I suppose I'll hear about it." Sally gave me the once-over again. "But enough about me. What about you? What do you want from life?"

I could feel the heat rising to my face and hoped the lighting was dim enough that she wouldn't see me blush. I tried to sound sure of myself. "I want to finish off the year and maybe move to New York or Miami or LA. I want to start up my own business."

"Doing what?"

"I'm not sure yet, but I'm very ambitious. I can't see working for someone else for very long."

"Oh, to be young again, and have those kinds of ideals." She spoke up to Rolf, who was nearby pretending not to listen. "Rolf, we were like that once, right? I was going to be the next Madonna and you were going to own golf courses all over the northeast."

"Yes, that's right. But then life happens. But you did okay for yourself, Sal," he said.

"Yeah, I had my day in the sun."

"You act like it's all over," I protested. "Look at Eric Clapton, Bob Dylan, Neil Diamond. They're still recording big hit albums."

"Men," she cursed. "All men. How many hit albums by women over sixty?"

"You have a long way to sixty," I said, all the while admitting to myself that she wasn't exactly young.

"Too much work. I don't have the patience for all that again."

"More work than cleaning houses?" I couldn't imagine …

"Hell, yeah!"

Suddenly, like a freight train approaching from the distance, a big idea was taking shape in my mind: Sally could be my post-graduation project! Wouldn't that be something, to engineer a comeback for Sally Testata? "I can't wait to tell Marcus I met you."

"I'm sure he'll be thrilled to know I'm living in Scranton and cleaning houses."

"Maybe he'll have some ideas."

"For what?"

"To get you back in the studio making music!"

Sally glared at me. "Did I miss something here? Did I say anything about wanting to sing again?"

Rolf butted in. "She's not interested."

I'm the nicest guy in the world, but I'm not a championship wrestler for nothing. My aggressive side will come into play when it needs to. "Are you her manager? I'm not asking you," I told him. I caught Sally smiling out of the corner of my eye.

"Look, punk, don't disturb my customers. You and your candy-ass school chums can head back downtown where you belong. We don't need your kind."

I would have said something that definitely would have gotten me kicked out, but Sally chimed in just in time. "Lay off, Rolf. He's not disturbing me. We're having a conversation."

Rolf nodded and muttered, "Whatever you say," then headed down to the other end of the bar.

"Thank you, Sally. I can take care of myself, though."

"I see," she said, and gave me the once-over again. I don't know if it was the booze or what, but she was definitely coming on to me big time.

"Anyway, as I was saying, Marcus has connections and maybe it's no accident that I'm meeting you here. I might be able to help you get back into the clubs."

"You're kidding me, right? Do you have any idea how much all that costs? Not to mention the work."

"What if I could get you into the studio and it would cost you nothing?" I was hatching a plan with the trust money that would launch both of our careers.

"There isn't anything that costs nothing." She pulled a cigarette out of its pack. "I need to go out for a smoke. This ban on smoking is going to kill me." She nodded towards Pete and Rick who were quite involved in a pool game. "I think your little friends have forgotten about you."

She stood to go and I boldly grabbed her by the elbow. "Wait, Sally. I'm not kidding. I'm looking to start a business when I graduate in a few months and I admire you so much. I could be your manager."

Sally smiled at me like I was a lost four-year-old. She even patted my head, for Christ's sake. "Honey, I don't think you want to go down that road. And I *know* I don't."

"But we could do this, I know we could."

"We, huh? You and what army? Believe me, it takes an army because it's a fucking battle. I have the scars to prove it."

"I have a trust fund," I answered, laying all my cards on the table. "I could start the business with that money."

She paused for a quick second. Did I see hope in those eyes, a remembrance of past glories that might yet come again? "I have your card. I'll give you a call."

"Can I have your number?"

"You can always find me at Fat Bo's every Friday," she said. "Thanks for being a fan." And with that, she strode out the door and I returned to my friends at the pool table with a plan and a purpose behind my big grin.

CHAPTER TWO

▼

If you're like most people who have never been there, you probably have an unfavorable impression of Scranton. I mean, simply saying the word "Scranton" kind of scrunches up your face and the sound honks through your nasal passages. Not a pleasant word or sound, resembling words like *skank, rat,* and *scram.*

You might be surprised to learn that Scranton is a pretty nice town. Yes, it did have industry back in the day—coal, iron, textiles, and railroad—but that brought in the bankers and investors. Downtown has been taken over by the university, but it retains the charms of a bygone era: stone churches, Victorian houses, stately banks, and the like. The famous Board of Trade Building stands right in the center of it all, with the orange "Scranton: The Electric City" sign on top, lighting up the sky for miles around. In addition to the university, Scranton pushes tourism for its trolley museum, a coal museum—for anyone who's turned on by a coal mine—and its proximity to the ski slopes of the Poconos. There are small pharmaceutical companies and ammunitions plants and a few smaller colleges, but, all in all, it's not a place someone with my ambition would want to call home after I graduated.

Meeting Sally right after losing Amy set my mind in motion for bigger dreams and a firm purpose to do my own thing, to hell with my mother's expectations or Amy's dreams. I realized at that moment that I had been appeasing my parents by staying in college for four years, getting by on Bs and Cs, but I viewed college as a stepping stone to something else—not the head of Bounder & Lightning—and I was ready to make that step. I wanted to make my mark in the world on my terms, just as Marcus did.

So anyway, I went through the motions the rest of that Friday night at Fat Bo's and always kept one eye on Sally, who never left the bar or talked with anyone besides Rolf. Pete hooked up with a girl before it was too late and I said good-bye to Rick by eleven.

Saturday afternoon I called Marcus and left a message that I had an unbelievable story to tell him, but he, as usual, didn't call back, even with the teaser I offered.

I tried to get into my classes the following week, but I wasn't inspired. My mind kept going back to Sally. I'm Catholic but not exactly spiritual, yet I kept thinking I had met her for a reason. I was fantasizing about taking her to New York and introducing her around the clubs and being her manager, getting her back on track. My future would be her future, and vice versa. I thought maybe I'd go back to Fat Bo's the following Friday to talk to her again. It turned out I didn't have to wait that long.

My cell phone rang at about ten o'clock the next Thursday night. I rolled over on my bed, where I had dozed off reading about bear markets, and looked at the display on the phone. It just read, "Call," a blocked number, and I wondered who it could be. When I answered, I was shocked to hear Sally's voice.

"What are you doing?" she asked. I could tell right away that she was probably a little wasted.

"I'm studying but not staying awake."

"Such a good boy. Maybe I'd better call back later."

"No! No, Sally," I said, panicked that she'd hang up. "This is as good a time as any."

"Yeah?" She paused and I think I heard ice rattling in a glass. "You feel like coming over?"

"Uh, you mean now?" Shit, it was a booty call!

"Yeah, I mean now." She sounded so sure, I was both afraid to turn her down and afraid to take her up on it.

I realized if I turned her down, I might not get another chance to meet her. "Sure, yeah, I can come over. Can you give me, like, an hour?"

"An hour? Honey, I'm a fifteen-minute drive away. You don't need to get spiffy for me."

"Well, I got to take care of a couple things first." Hell, yes, I was going to take a shower. "Let me get a pencil." I wrote down her address and told her I'd get there as soon as possible.

"You'd better," she commanded, and hung up.

An hour later as I headed up 476, looking for the exit to Route 6 North (thinking she must drive like wildfire because this was taking longer than fifteen minutes), I was nervous as hell, the way I never am around girls my own age. I was rubbing myself in the car to try to get myself up, as kind of a head start.

I finally found the place, a white colonial-type house with a wraparound porch that was set just twenty feet or so from the desolate road. The lightly plowed driveway to the left of the house had barely enough room to hold her Hyundai Elantra, never mind my Toyota Matrix, but somehow I squeezed in.

The air was perfectly still and silent, the moon casting a silvery glow over the glazed snow and ice around the house. I stepped up onto the porch, conscious of the noise I was making. I opened the storm door and knocked on the wooden door with its crackled white paint. "Sally?" No response. I knocked again. There were definitely lights on in the place. Maybe she was lying spread-eagled on the bed just waiting for me to come in and take her, part of her fantasy. I slowly opened the unlocked door. "Sally? It's me, Greg." Who else would it be?

The entryway, with a rather steep, crooked staircase to the right, was dimly lit. The hallway to the left of the stairs led to what looked like a kitchen in the back, its light on, blazing yellow. A doorway to the left revealed some kind of parlor room, completely dark. The room to the right of the stairs was a living room with a standing lamp on. I stepped into it.

There was Sally, lying face down on a well-worn couch, dead asleep, her head sideways facing the back of it. She wore a silk purple robe, but her right leg had escaped its confines and fell over the side of the couch nearly to the floor, exposed up to mid-thigh. My first thought was, *Not a bad leg. A little hefty, but not bad.* My second thought, as I took in the scene, was, *This woman cleans houses?* There were newspapers and magazines on every available surface, some opened, some in stacks. The coffee table, impossible to see under the layers of paper, also had a paper plate with crumbs on it, a nearby plastic bottle of ketchup, and, most significantly, a near-empty bottle of gin with glass beside it, about a quarter full with what was probably just melted ice. The gin had done her in.

Now what? First, I picked up the glass and paper plate and ketchup bottle and returned them to the kitchen. Other than a sink full of dirty dishes, the kitchen wasn't in bad shape. The cabinets and curtains were the color of butter and I imagined this room could wake the dead in the morning. Maybe if I did the dishes, as unsavory a prospect as that was for me, she would be impressed. Growing up, we had always had a cleaning lady. In my own one-bedroom apartment in downtown Scranton, I ordered in a lot. The one thing I can say for Amy: She could cook and didn't mind cleaning either. I sighed and started running the hot water.

When that was finished, I went back to the living room. Sally hadn't moved. I went over to her and crouched down next to her. "Sally, it's me, Greg. Let's get you upstairs to bed."

She moaned and half opened her eyes. "Sorry, baby, long day."

"It's okay." I put one arm under her and tried to pull her up by the arm with my free hand. Although she groaned in protest, she managed to follow my lead and got to a sitting position.

"So strong," she mumbled, eyes still closed, slightly smiling.

"A lot of years of wrestling. Middle Atlantic Conference runner-up last year."

"Mmmmm," she purred as I got her to her feet. Sally was fairly short, a few inches shorter than me, but not a small woman. As we made our way up the stairs, my right arm around her and her left arm snaked around my neck, her robe kept falling open. She was wearing some kind of one-piece black lacy thing under it but her big, soft tits were nearly out of it. She was kind of round all over, but it wasn't a turn-off. Still—and maybe you'll think I'm gay after all—by the time I got her into her bed, even though my dick was raging hard, I just didn't feel right about doing anything with her. First of all, she was just about asleep again as soon as she hit the bed and I didn't want to wreck my chances at anything bigger that might come out of all this for the sake of a one-night stand with someone half-asleep. The second thing, I realize everybody has fantasized about having sex with a hot celebrity, especially one that you had a crush on when you were a teenager, but, let me tell you, once that opportunity actually presents itself, it's not easy to do it. You're not just fucking a regular girl. The stakes are higher. I'm telling you, it's not as easy as you think.

I thought about going home but decided not to. I would stay and greet her in the morning. I could miss my statistics class. Wouldn't she be surprised to see me here?

I found another bedroom down the hall, all made up like it hadn't been used in years, and decided to sleep there. I went to the bathroom and shot my load in a wad of tissue so I'd be able to sleep, went back to the room, stripped down to my briefs, and crawled under the covers.

*   *   *

The next morning the sun bled through the sage-green curtains of the little bedroom and I awoke, forgetting where I was for a moment. There was no clock in the room but the house was silent. I jumped out of bed, quickly threw on my clothes, and walked across the creaking wooden floors, peaking in at the still-sleeping Sally, and went downstairs. As I suspected, the dazzling yellow of the kitchen and the light from the south-facing windows nearly blinded me. The clock above the sink read slightly after nine. I opened drawers and cupboards until I found coffee filters, Maxwell House, a mug, and a spoon.

As the coffee brewed, I decided to try calling Marcus again.

His sleepy voice indicated I'd awakened him. "Yeah?"

"Hey, Marcus, it's Greg."

"Hey, Greg. What time is it? Sorry I didn't call you back last week." He seemed to be rousing himself as if this were an emergency call.

"It's a little after nine," I said and he grunted unappreciatively. "I had to call. You'll never guess where I am."

"No, I won't. Just tell me."

"I am in Sally Testata's kitchen!"

There was a momentary pause as he tried to make sense of the information. "Sally Testata's kitchen? What the fuck—"

"I'm not kidding! She lives outside of Scranton and I met her in a bar last week. So last night she invited me over."

"Are you telling me you slept with Sally Testata last night?"

"No, no. I could have—that's what she wanted—but she got drunk and fell asleep. It was late so I decided to just stay and make sure she was okay. She's still sleeping."

Marcus laughed. "This sounds like a Lifetime movie."

"I know it. It's unbelievable!" Holding the cell phone to my ear with one hand, I poured myself a cup of coffee. "She knew who you were. Wouldn't it be fun if I brought her to New York to meet you?"

"That would be fun. Shit, what happened to her? How did she end up there?"

"She lost her record contract after they pulled 'Bombs Away' off the radio because of 9/11. Then her mother was dying, so she came back to take care of her. She divorced her husband and stayed."

"This is a bad Lifetime movie."

I sipped my coffee. "I think I might be able to talk her into making a comeback."

"You think? It sounds like she still has a few problems; she's probably grasping at straws. How does she look?"

"Well, not bad. Overweight, but in an Anna Nicole Smith kind of way."

"Well, that's not the best reference in the world," Marcus noted, recalling the train wreck of a celebrity that was Anna Nicole Smith. "I wonder how she sounds. The music business isn't easy for anyone, but for an over-the-hill dance artist who hasn't had a hit in years, it will be nearly impossible."

"That's what she says."

"But you think she can manage a comeback?"

"No, that's the thing. *I* will manage the comeback. This will be my business after I graduate."

Marcus started laughing and I wanted to reach through the phone and smack him. "Come on, she's a drunk and older than I am. Which is to say, too old. And what does our dear old mother think about this plan of yours?"

Marcus had always resented that my mother was close to me and that he could never penetrate her iciness. "I really don't care what she thinks," I said. "I am not spending my entire life working for Bounder & Lightning. Besides," I continued confidently, "I have my own money now, I can start my own business."

"I think you're a little starstruck, bro. I'm not sure Sally Testata is the best investment for your hard-earned money." That last bit was definitely a dig at me. Marcus had not been left any trust fund money to help him get a start. He had done everything on his own.

Just then, I heard footsteps coming down the hallway. "Maybe you should talk to her yourself," I said.

Sally stopped in the doorway, amazingly unfazed by the harsh glare of the kitchen. She had on a pair of jeans and an untucked, wrinkled white dress shirt, her fluffy mane pulled back into a ponytail. She gave me a half smile, apparently not surprised to see me here.

"Hey, Sally," I called. "You want to say hello to my brother Marcus? You remember, the deejay?"

"Sure." She strode over, arm outstretched to grab the phone. She put it to her ear and launched right into conversation. "How are things in New York?" Immediately, I was sorry I offered because now I was not hearing his side of the conversation. He was better at schmoozing than I was. Sally let out an over-the-top guffaw. "Oh, really? Can't you find someone besides those goddamn American Idols to promote?" Her smile was suddenly as big as the winter sun as she walked toward a window, leaving me in the background. "These kids have it too easy. They don't climb up the ladder for ten years anymore like I had to." Her voice turned seductive. "Yeah, baby, I can still sing." She laughed again. "Honey, you couldn't *pay* me enough to come back to that fucking city!… On the contrary, there are a lot of people I do *not* want to see!"

That fucking Marcus. It was like two best friends finally found each other after a decade. The conversation went on and on and I started slamming cupboards and drawers, making like I wanted to find bread for toast. "In the fridge," she said, and then turned her attention back to Marcus. I sulked as I noisily clattered a plate and knife onto the table and slammed the knob down on the toaster. At last, she wrapped up the conversation. "If you ever visit your brother in Scranton, come say hello." With that, she said good-bye and snapped the phone shut.

"He didn't want to talk to me again?" I tried not to sound wounded.

"He said he'd call you back later"—sure he would—"but that now that he was up he had a lot of stuff to do." She looked around the room and eventually found a near-empty pack of cigarettes under a newspaper, and withdrew one. "He's a funny guy, your brother."

"Uh-huh." I needed to make a bold move, grab the reins back, show her who was in charge. "Sally, I could be your new manager and help you get back into your game."

She ignored me, blowing smoke toward the ceiling. "We didn't do anything last night, did we?"

"No, not at all." Goddamn, I could feel a hot blush extending to the tips of my ears. "You were pretty well gone by the time I got here."

"It's been a long week. Too many houses to clean. Ski season. Everyone's coming out for the weekends. And I suppose the gin martinis didn't help." She saw me looking around the kitchen. "I know what you're thinking: *This bitch has no business being a housekeeper!* Well, the last thing I want to do when I get home is clean my own house."

"How can that kind of work be satisfying for you?"

She paused to think about her answer. "There's something about being in a quiet place, making things sparkling clean and organized, and then closing the door on it. It's like a little happy ending every day."

"I'm not sure that would be a happy ending to my day," I said. "What about a bigger happy ending, a bigger dream?"

"Been there, done that. The bigger the dream, the bigger the disappointment."

"Sally, this would be a great career for me after I graduate. We could do this."

"I can't be responsible for your career. First of all, what kind of career is that? You're going to make money managing me? This is the kind of business where you have to spend money to make money. Lots of it. Second of all, what about my career? The thought of all that isn't exactly fun for me. It may be a fun little diversion for an ambitious kid with money, but your dream is my nightmare."

"Let me use this trust fund. My grandfather would be so proud that I used the money to start my own business." Maybe so, but surely not *this* business. "I'm expected to go back to Philly and work for my father's company, Bounder & Lightning. I can't do it."

"Bounder & Lightning. That's cute."

"Not really. It would be a life of misery."

"Well, showbiz is not exactly glamour. Far from it." She stubbed out her cigarette in a plastic ashtray.

We heard a car door slam from outside and looked at each other. She started toward the hallway. "Who the hell is this?"

Before she reached the door, it had already creaked open and a loud, gravelly voice barked, "Hello."

"Dad, I keep telling you, you can't keep barging in here unannounced. This is not your house."

"This will always be my house," he stated. I could hear a slight rustling and him stomping the snow from his heavy boots. "Whose car is that in the dooryard?"

"I have company," Sally said, but I could already hear him walking down the hall toward the kitchen.

He walked in and stopped when he saw me sitting at the table. "I see." He chuckled from his throat and smiled as he turned to look at Sally, who had followed him into the room. "This one's a little young, even for you, ain't he?"

Sally rolled her eyes and moved in between us. "Dad, this is Greg Bounder. Greg, this is my father, Charlie. Greg is here to discuss business."

"Business?" Charlie Teskewicz looked like a cranky old politician, except that he wore a red-checkered wool hunting coat and his white hair was pointing in all directions. And he definitely did not have the smoothness of a politician. "Jesus H. Christ, he doesn't look old enough to shovel the sidewalk."

"He has connections to the music business in New York and he thought he'd see if I was interested in pursuing them."

"Is that right?" He eyed me suspiciously, but the leering smile never left his face.

"Yes, sir," I said, rising out of my seat to shake his hand.

Charlie saw the half full coffee pot and helped himself to a mug from the cupboard. "My daughter ain't been in the music business for a long time and has no interest in going back."

"Don't tell me what I do and do not have an interest in," she said sharply. "I'm just hearing him out."

"I'd be interested in hearing him out myself," Charlie said, leaning back against the counter.

"No, Dad, you are not hearing him out. Now, why did you come out here?"

"Can't I visit my goddamned daughter? For Christ's sake, every weekend you plant yourself on that barstool not three blocks from my apartment, but you can't be bothered to come over and say hello."

I sat there, taking little sips of my coffee, trying to figure out how to look at ease during this uncomfortable exchange. "I could come back later," I offered quietly.

"No, no," they both shouted, wanting to keep me there for their own diabolical reasons. Sally fished another cigarette out of the pack. "Now, why are you here, Dad?"

"I need to look around the barn. Ralph thinks we can make a go of the antiques business. I need to see what I got laying around."

"So you've picked a cold day in February to go rummaging around the barn?"

"Spring is coming," Charlie observed, then walked over to the calendar on the wall—photos of barns, come to think of it—and pulled it down, turning over the page to February. "It's Groundhog's Day today. Did you see the news? Punxsatawny Phil didn't see his shadow. We're having an early spring."

"Yeah, I'm sure that's reliable," Sally groused.

"And while I'm here, can you spare the old man a few bucks? Beginning of the month, rent, meds, you name it."

Sally was gazing out the window at the rolling, snow-laden fields that stretched to a horizon of thick pine trees. "Can you imagine," she began, evidently for my benefit, "a man his age coming to borrow money from his daughter who cleans houses for a living?"

"Well, if your mother—God rest her soul—hadn't thrown me aside at a time in life when we're supposed to be settling into retirement, then soaked me for the house, I wouldn't be in this predicament. And you wouldn't have this house, neither."

She whirled around, jabbing her cigarette in the air towards him. "Don't you start bad-mouthing her. She was your doormat for forty years. Unfortunately, it took a national tragedy for her to finally come to her senses."

"Yes, and the same national tragedy for you to lose yours. You couldn't stick it out and wait for things to turn around. Then you had to go and marry that good-for-nothing …" His voice trailed off. "Ah, forget it." He slammed his mug down on the counter, sending coffee sloshing over the sides. He looked at me. "You got your work cut out for you, boy, if you think she's going anywhere at this stage in her life. She can't stay off the booze and cigarettes long enough to croak out a tune."

"Where do you think I picked up those habits?" Sally seethed. She dropped the barely puffed cigarette right on the linoleum and ground it out with her slippered foot. She stormed out of the room and up the stairs, leaving me still sitting at the table and Charlie still leaning on the counter.

He acted as if nothing had happened and began speaking to me. "So what firm do you work with, Mr. Bounder?"

"I'm actually finishing up at the university." He gave me a disapproving grimace. "But I want to get into management, and my brother is in the music industry in New York. He is very familiar with your daughter's work. I think we can make something happen."

"I think you'd better look for greener pastures. That one's already been plowed and forgotten."

I thought my mother was bad, but Charlie was giving old Doris a run for her money. Just then, Sally reappeared in the kitchen, rummaging through a clutch purse. "How much do you need? Will fifty hold you over?"

Humbled, Charlie stepped forward, bringing the volume down a few notches. "That should do it."

She slapped a few bills into his upwardly curled fingers. "There you go. You know your way out."

He nodded and barely whispered a "thank you." Without turning, he said, "Nice to meet you, son" as he left the room and shuffled down the hallway. A moment later, the door closed and Charlie was gone, without another word between them.

I tried another argument. "Maybe you need to get away from him for a while."

She shrugged her shoulders and gazed into the hallway, as if his ghost were still there. "It's complicated. He's the only family I have. When you're older, you'll understand."

I resented being treated like a child, a recurring theme in my life, but I kept my mouth shut. "What was your mother like?" I asked.

That seemed to be the key to unlocking a softer Sally. She poured herself a cup of coffee and sat at the table opposite me. "Pretty amazing," she said. "I don't know how she put up with that man for forty years, but she ended her life on a high note." She lit a cigarette. "You know how 9/11 ended my career?"

"Uh-huh."

"Well, the same tragedy was a wake-up call for my mother. It was for a lot of people." She seemed to drift off in thought as she blew a long white stream of smoke toward the ceiling, but she continued. "Here was this patient, pious Christian woman … Anyway, that day, she called to see how I was doing. Her phone call woke me up from a dead sleep; Antonio and I had been partying hard the night before. I had no idea what the hell was going on a few miles to the south. She was relieved to know I was okay and I told her I had to find out what was going on and that I'd call her back the next day."

"That all seems like normal behavior."

"Wait, it gets better." She reached over, took a fingerful of spilled jelly from my plate, and licked it off as if it were the most normal thing to do. Damn, it was sexy! "The next morning, she calls me back. It seems my father had used the excuse of the tragedy to go out on an all-day bender. She says to me, 'Your father has moved out.' I start swearing, cursing him out, and she stops me by saying, 'No, honey, it's all right. I kicked him out.'" Sally picked up and bit into my bagel, savoring the mouthful. Then she went on. "It's hard to believe, but I think that news was more shocking to me than the towers collapsing! I mean, I never could have imagined my mother having the wherewithal to do that."

"Why did she do it?"

"She said he stumbled in on the twelfth, early in the morning, and she greeted him with, 'I can no longer live with you and I want a divorce. Be out by the end of the day.'" Sally slapped the table and bellowed with laughter. "Apparently, he was so fucking stunned, he didn't put up a fight. Just shuffled upstairs and packed two suitcases and went on his way."

"Wow." I tried imagining either of my parents leaving the other. Wouldn't happen.

"Up to that point, I had always thought my mother was weak. But she changed her whole life in one day."

"Is that when you came home?"

"Oh, no. I offered to—although I didn't really want to—but she said I should only come if I needed to get out of New York, not to come for her sake." She stood up to bring her mug to the sink. A new insight seemed to come to her as she leaned against the sink. "Funny. She really woke up and fixed her life, I spiraled out of control. I lost my contract and held tighter to Antonio and the drugs. Only my mother's cancer saved me. Now she's gone." She rinsed her cup and spoon while I remained silent. Finally, she turned around and offered me a broad smile with just a glimmer of wetness in her eyes. "Now, where were we with our plan?"

I could only offer a grateful smile in return.

CHAPTER THREE

▼

We agreed to meet at Fat Bo's on Saturday night to discuss our plans for Sally's comeback. I got there first and tried to sit in the corner seat, but Rolf was right there and quick to tell me, "That's Sally's seat."

I moved over one spot, then thought better of it. I didn't want Rolf over-hearing our conversation. "Actually, Sally is meeting me here and we'll sit at a table," I told him.

"This is the only place Sally ever sits," Rolf said with a smile.

"Uh-huh," I answered. I took my Heineken and settled at a nearby table. It was still fairly early and, looking around, it didn't look as if much had changed since I'd been there the previous week. Even the clientele hadn't changed. Nor had their clothes. The jukebox was playing mostly rock songs from the seven-ties—Eagles, Kansas, and Aerosmith and the like—with the occasional country tune thrown in. My beer was nearly empty and I was wondering if I'd been stood up when the door swung open and Sally strutted in with a big smile—which, in my limited experience up to that point, was a rare phenomenon. All eyes turned in her direction, and a few guys let out whistles through their widely gapped teeth. She seemed to acknowledge all the admirers as she strode purposefully over to her corner spot at the bar, her black cowboy boots with sil-ver star buckles on the sides pounding out an attention-getting rhythm. Many eyes followed her ass, which was squeezed into a pair of maroon velvet slacks that must have been pulled out of some trunk holding her costumes from the Pillow Talk days. It was one of the coldest nights of the year, and her nipples announced themselves through a tight-fitting bright pink turtleneck shirt. The rhinestone-studded leather jacket she wore over it could not contain her ample breasts. She eased herself onto the stool and then, with all the bad acting of an elder TV spokesmodel, scanned the room before letting her eyes finally rest on me, only a dozen feet away. "Greg, there you are." She patted the stool next to her. "Come on over so we can talk."

"You look great, Sal," Rolf said, placing an Amstel in front of her.

I had to assert myself, now or never. "I thought we'd be better off sitting at a table, where we could have some privacy," I said, unsmiling.

Sally looked from me to Rolf, as if for direction from him. He merely shrugged his shoulders, but his smile looked tentative. "Sure, good idea," she chirped. She picked up her beer and moved towards me. Boy, did Rolf look pissed!

As Sally settled in across from me at the small table, it felt as if a seismic shift had occurred in Fat Bo's. Was it my imagination, or was every redneck in the place giving me the evil eye?

"Sally, I don't think these people like me," I said.

"Oh, they don't," she said casually with a wave of her hand. "I'm like their sister or daughter or fucking fantasy mistress. They don't take kindly to outsiders moving in on their territory."

"I'm not an outsider. I live here."

"Yeah, right. With your leather jacket, Banana Republic clothes, and Air Jordans."

"They don't have to hate me," I whined. "I'm not so bad."

"You're going to have to stand up to a lot more than Scranton's finest if you have any hope of making it in the New York music business." She took a swallow of her beer. "I suggest we get down to business."

I had barely slept the night before, thinking this project could actually happen. I had scrawled ideas into a notebook, pulled out a calendar to map out a plan, researched the current charts in *Billboard* and clubs in New York, and tried to figure out a budget. My enthusiasm could hardly be contained. "I think it has to be a comeback dance song. That's how the public remembers you and we already have Marcus as a big plus to start with."

"Agreed. Who's going to write this song?"

"I'm sure Marcus can put us in touch with some producers and songwriters in New York." Of course, I'd been starting the research but hadn't spoken to Marcus again. I was assuming he'd want to help, he was such a celebrity name-dropper anyway.

"Uh-huh. What about school?"

"Come on, Sally, you sound like my mother." I had already given her some background on Doris Bounder during our long breakfast talk, so Sally knew this was no compliment. "We're close enough to New York that I can still take some classes. Or I can withdraw from spring classes or take incompletes. We need to move on your career now. In time for a big summer rollout."

"*Déjà vu*. That was what happened with 'Bombs Away.' Memorial Day weekend, Gay Pride weekend, summer circuit parties. By the end of July, I was climbing the charts. By September, I was off the charts." She couldn't seem to let go of her bitterness.

"It'll be different this time. No songs that could possibly be about Iraq!" I laughed. The war was still raging and, despite polls showing that most Americans wanted it to end, the sooner the better, it seemed that it would go on forever.

"What about an anthem about women's empowerment?" Sally asked. "We have a woman running for president, a woman Speaker of the House." A few weeks before, Hillary Clinton had announced her run.

Her uplifted tits seemed to be reaching for me halfway across the table. "Yeah, yeah, that's good," I lied. "But don't forget, you have kind of a sex symbol image. We need to capitalize on that."

She ignored me. "The men in this country need to be kicked in the balls. Look at what they're doing to Hillary."

"Uh-huh." I had to get this back on track, and fast. "So something strong, something positive. Something that will have you taking charge as you emerge from your self-imposed exile."

"Yes," she said emphatically. "I need to make a statement if I'm coming back. Otherwise, what's the point?"

Just then, Rolf appeared at the table and placed an upside-down glass on the table. "Tommy wants to buy you a drink." She turned to acknowledge Tommy at the far end of the bar. Tommy—tall, mustached—tipped his cowboy hat in return. "You look great tonight, Sal," Rolf added, again.

"Greg and I are talking business. I needed to show him I still have what it takes."

I started tapping out a beat on the table. I'm no singer, and I certainly hadn't written a song in my whole life, but I tentatively let out the beginning of a tune. "I still have what it takes." Thump, thump, thump.

"Forget the social climbers and fakes," Sally continued.

"I will sing/for my own supper and bling/I still have what it takes," I finished the chorus.

Sally slapped the table. "Write it down! Write it down!" Rolf stood there, ineffectual, in our dust. He turned and walked back to the bar like a wounded dog.

Sally rocked back in her seat, howling with laughter, clapping her hands. "Maybe you *are* good for me, kid!"

"It's a beginning," I said. I was damned proud of our first little collaboration as I scribbled the lyric in my notebook. But the happier we became and the longer we talked, the more the stale air around us grew more ominous, like we were surrounded by a swarm of hornets after we'd stirred up the nest. That's what I perceived, anyway; if Sally had noticed, she didn't seem to care.

After a couple more drinks, Sally said, "Let me go say hello to Tommy. The poor guy's not going to leave me be." She stood up, slipped off the jacket, and hung it on the back of the chair. "Watch this." With that, she sashayed over to Tommy, who had been waiting like an obedient schoolboy. He greeted her with a big grin. His teeth appeared to be intact.

I was aggravated. We had been on a roll and now Sally wanted to turn the night into trolling for a date. As if on cue, Rolf came over to the table. "You need another drink?" he asked with a knowing smile.

"Yes. Yes, I do. Thanks," I answered. As he turned, I caught his attention. "Hey, Rolf. Why does everybody seem to be so upset at me for helping Sally?"

"Because you're not helping Sally," he said.

"And this is?" I asked, indicating the surroundings with a gesture of my hands.

"Yeah, this is," he replied, the smile gone from his face. "Scranton is the only stability she's ever known. You're young and you'll use her to make your fortune and then leave her behind and move on to the next hot prospect. Just like everybody else did in that goddamned city."

"But she's cleaning houses. Surely she can be doing something better."

"She'll find her way. But for the first time in her life, she's slowed down, calm. She needs people around her who love her for who she is. You college kids think there's no happiness unless you're making six figures."

"You act like she can't take care of herself, like she's still a teenager," I said. Maybe women's empowerment *was* the way to go.

"Oh, she can take care of herself," he warned. "You'd better watch out. She may just take care of you." With that, he went back to the bar to get my drink.

Sally seemed to be engaged in a conversation with Tommy, standing close to him, her hips curving to lean against the bar. She had a fresh drink her hand. Apparently, this night was shot. I picked up her jacket from the chair and strode over to the bar, slapping some money on the table. "Never mind the drink, Rolf," I said. "Thanks."

"No problem." His victory smile was back.

I walked over to Sally and handed her the jacket. "Where you going, sugar?" she asked, and then introduced me to Tommy.

"We've had a good night but let's leave it at that for now."

She was nonplussed. "Okay," she said after a moment, leaning in to kiss me on the cheek. "We'll talk tomorrow. Don't call too early." She winked and gave a flirty smile to Tommy. Goddamn him.

Rolf, Tommy, and the whole sorry lot of them seemed to heave a sigh of relief as I made my exit into the cold night air. They didn't know who they were dealing with.

CHAPTER FOUR

▼

I didn't see Sally again for another week but I spoke with her on the phone a few times to firm up our plan to visit Marcus the following weekend. As I expected, Marcus was excited about the visit as well: I was no longer just a kid brother but a kid brother with a diva on his arm.

The complication was that to go to New York, I had to miss a wrestling match, a home game. Rick and I were the most valuable members on the team, so my skipping the match would be a big loss for the team. Yet, with Sally entering my life, all of that seemed of little importance. I'd have to fake the flu or something, but the coach would be pissed.

When I spoke with Sally, I had to play doctor with her over the phone, suggesting she lay off the booze and start to tone up. Man, she cursed me left and right. "I'd like to see the bitches on the pop charts that are half my age keep up with me once I get back on stage," she said.

I had reason for concern: The tabloids and gossip televisions shows seemed to offer a daily dose of one starlet or another falling off the wagon or going to rehab. It was such an epidemic, the publicity was actually harming more than helping those celebrities. As I sped east on Route 80 on our way to New York, the radio deejays were talking about a Lindsay or a Paris or a Britney—I forget which one, they all kind of blended together after a while—facing yet another breakdown involving some kind of drug activity. Even worse, that weekend everyone was talking about the death of Anna Nicole Smith, most likely from a drug overdose.

"I'm nothing like her, I know how to handle it," Sally offered, anticipating my thoughts while shaking a couple of yellow capsules out of a bottle from her purse. "This is my only prescription medication. When you reach my age, you'll understand the need for antidepressants."

"Should you be drinking while on medication?"

"No. That's why I take the pill in the daytime and drink at night. When one wears off, I'm ready for the other."

"Will you be able to keep up with a performing schedule?"

With that, she shrieked and slapped the dashboard in front of her. "Jesus Christ, half of Hollywood and New York is on a lot more shit than this and they keep cranking out the product. I was on a lot more than this in my day. I *needed* it just to keep going! You got a lot to learn, kid."

I veered into the leftmost lane to get past a trailer truck that was cruising along at about seventy miles per hour. "I wish you'd stop calling me 'kid.' Would you like it if I kept calling you 'lady?'"

"I suppose I've been called worse things than a lady." She paused, rummaging through her overstuffed purse for a cigarette pack. "I'll do my best. You've been awfully good to me. I really don't know what the fuck I'm doing in this car and, quite frankly, can't believe I'm even entertaining the notion of doing *anything* in New York. But for now, it's an adventure and I thank you."

"Uh, Sally," I said, slightly panicked. "Could you not smoke in here? I don't want the smell in the car."

"Jesus! Well, then, you'd better stop the car because I'm not going to make it another ninety minutes without a smoke. And don't ask me to give them up."

"I won't," I said, but I was already trying to figure out a way to get her to quit. "We can stop at the next rest stop. It's only a few miles."

"Good enough," she complied. She reached over and stabbed the button to turn off the radio. "Got any CDs?"

At the rest stop, we each took a bathroom break. It was a long wait before she came out of the building, clutching a McDonald's bag.

"Sally, you can't eat that crap."

"Give me a break. I'm hungry. Shit, what do you kids do for fun these days?"

"We go out. We fool around. The usual things."

She lamely pumped her fist in the air. "Whew! Be sure to invite me along next time."

We got into the car and started on our way. She had been polite enough to smoke outside the car but I was realizing the smell of greasy fast food was probably worse. Another hour and we'd be there, thank God.

* * *

The Friday afternoon traffic on the West Side Highway was ridiculous, but Sally never seemed to mind at all. It gave her more time to point out buildings and neighborhoods where things had happened for her: "That area is Harlem, where I met Antonio at an all-night party … That's Riverside Drive, where my manager Eddie Pearl lived … Sound Factory used to be over there. I snorted a line with Keith Richards there … I cut 'Bombs Away' at a studio in Chelsea right over there, off Tenth Avenue." The irresistible pull of New York had her in its grip again, and the ravages of Scranton life seemed to fall right off of her. I parked the car in a garage and we walked the few blocks to Marcus' place.

Marcus lived in a two-bedroom apartment on Washington Street in the West Village. He had apparently inherited it from an old lover who died when Marcus was in his twenties. He'd mentioned that to me on my trip to New York a few years before; it's certainly not something my parents would have told me. I didn't ask for details. Anyway, it was a great place, tucked away in those narrow westernmost streets where you were still close enough to everything but where it was also quiet. Plus, it was big enough that Marcus could throw occasional parties. According to Marcus, people such as Liza Minnelli, Sarah Jessica Parker, and George Michael had graced his rooms. That's when he'd call my mother, when he had someone famous over. And that's about the only time she appreciated him.

A fierce wind cut through us as we quickly strode down Washington Street to Marcus' door. He buzzed us in right away. We entered the quiet, well-maintained building and went to the second floor.

Marcus opened the door wide for us and gave us a beaming smile. "Hey, bro!" He pulled me into a quick hug, all the while looking over my shoulder at Sally. He then extended his hand to hers, and as he took hold of it, he placed his other hand over hers, a gesture of reassurance, I guess. "Such a pleasure to meet you," he said.

"And so nice to meet you," she said. "You do look familiar. I must have seen your photo in *Next* or *HX*."

"Not the back pages, was it?" he joked, and they both laughed conspiratorially. I had no idea what they were talking about.

"Nice digs you got here," Sally observed, scoping the place as we peeled off our winter layers. We stood in a tiny entryway with a side closet where we could hang up our coats, but a doublewide archway gave a view of the large living room area, which Marcus had tastefully decorated with a brown leather sofa and chairs, a plush beige rug, and a few other furnishings. Not a stray item anywhere. The street itself was shaded by the buildings rather close together, but it helped that the living room had a massive double-paned window that was open to what light there was, the sheer panels and brown-print drapes held back on each side.

Inside the living room, to the right, was a kitchen area, long and narrow, with an open bar/shelf separating it from the living room. You had to go to the back of the living room to get to the doorway to a small hallway that led to the bedrooms and bathroom. Marcus gave us the quick tour. The guest bedroom had a queen-sized bed, two dressers and a bookshelf, plus a closet. Although dust-free, it didn't look like it had been touched. It looked more like a museum.

"This is where you two will be staying." Sally and I looked at each other. She had a game smile on her face and I felt the heat rise to my own. Marcus noticed right away. "Oh, I thought you two were sleeping together. If that's too uncomfortable, one of you can have my bedroom and I'll sleep on the couch."

"No, no," we both protested, willing to navigate our own discomfort in order to appear cool or not put Marcus out any further, I'm not sure which. We dropped our bags.

Back in the living room, Marcus played host. "Can I get you anything?"

"Do you have gin?" Sally immediately asked. "I need to relax a bit after that long ride. Your brother would not get off my case the whole way."

Marcus laughed, a little too much. "Sure, no problem." He went to a dark mahogany cabinet to the left of the sofa and pulled out a *Tanqueray* bottle. "I keep it out of sight," he explained. "I use it for parties but I don't touch the stuff myself."

"Christ, between the two of you I feel like I'm living in a monastery," Sally griped.

Marcus screamed with laughter and slapped his leather-clad leg. It was a bit much. His teeth were too white, his hair was too blonde, his hoop earrings too gleaming, his clothes were too perfect, he was Manhattan-thin. "Oh, believe me. I see people partying every night of the week and I offer no judgments. But with the kind of work I do, if I started in with it, I'd be dead inside a year. I did all that in my twenties and I realized, 'Shit, if I keep doing this, I'm going to lose everything.'"

"Well, I don't want to drink alone in front of the holy Catholic brothers of temperance. Come on, have some with me," she coaxed me.

"Okay." I had never tasted gin before then: everything was beer and vodka up to that point.

"On the rocks, three olives. It's like a martini without the useless vermouth." Marcus did as he was told, preparing the glasses on the counter.

I took a decent-sized gulp on my first sip and I shook my head and screwed my face into a grimace to withstand the blow. This brought a cackle out of Sally. "Slow, baby, slow. Take the time to enjoy it."

"I'm deejaying at Splash tonight so why don't you come as my guests? You can dance the night away, but I'll give you an extra set of keys if you want to go elsewhere."

"Sounds good," Sally said. "I don't mind hanging in the booth with you. I don't want to be mobbed on the dance floor." It was as though the good handful of years between her heyday and now had not happened. Did she think she was still a big, recognizable star? I had only recognized her in Fat Bo's because I had *studied* her as a kid. I was not your average man-on-the-street when it came to Sally Testata.

"Sure, no problem," Marcus said. Apparently, Marcus never had a problem.

Over the next couple of hours, we relaxed in the living room while Marcus played a few of the latest dance hits for Sally. She gave the thumbs-down to most of them. Finally, we decided to change our clothes for dinner and the club. It took me about fifteen minutes to take a quick shower, douse myself with Axe, put on clean jeans and a fresh-from-the-dry-cleaners button-down red shirt over a white T-shirt. I waited forever for the other two, jockeying for bathroom time as they primped and perfected themselves. Shit, I'd be spending half of the weekend waiting for them to get out of the bathroom!

At last, they emerged, almost in tandem. Marcus wore black jeans with a fancy black belt interwoven with gold and silver chains, square-toed black boots, and a green print shirt over a brown tank top. Moments later, Sally strutted into the room. She wore spiked boots—I don't know how she figured she was going to walk those cobblestoned streets—black stockings, and she had somehow stuffed herself into a black leather miniskirt. She wisely chose a slimming long blouse with wide, vertical black and white stripes, cinched at the waist with a black sash, and a low-cut black tank top under the blouse, which was unbuttoned about halfway down the front. Her thick curls hung to just below the shoulders. She wore black oval hoops in her ears and a leather string choker around her neck. Her eyes were heavy with mascara. Her lips and nails were a matching scarlet. Sally could stand to shape up a bit, but she still knew how to turn it out when she had to.

"I think you're going to get mobbed on the dance floor," I said, and they both laughed.

"Honey, I have compete with those young bitches and I ain't giving up without a fight."

We took a cab up to this place called Food Bar on Eighth Avenue for dinner. The place couldn't have been more gay. The food was all right, but I could see that it was more of a place for Marcus to be seen. At least half a dozen guys came over to say hello. He'd introduce me as his "little brother" and I'd smile through my gritted teeth, then he'd give a big intro, complete with mini-biography, of Sally Testata. She was glowing with the attention. I wanted to kill them both.

It was a little before ten when Marcus ushered us into Splash, a couple blocks east of overcrowded Eighth Avenue, yet when we walked in, the place was already near capacity. The main floor was the size of a small gymnasium, with two bars, tables along the back wall, and a massive dance floor. And still more of something downstairs. Shit, this was only one club. How many gay guys could there be? The bartenders were incredibly buff and wearing underwear or Speedos. This was supposedly a mainstream gay club. As if I could walk into a mainstream straight club and see bartender babes wearing bikinis. Marcus took us up to the booth and introduced us to the outgoing happy hour deejay, then went back into a back room to retrieve his records. He deejayed there often so he kept a stash of Splash-type music mixes on hand, locked in the back, he explained. "But tonight, I brought something extra," he said, then pulled "Bombs Away" from his inside coat pocket, flashing a flirty smile.

"Oh, Jesus," Sally said, lunging for it. Marcus kept it out of her reach. "I hope these kids know the song."

"Of course they will. It's a classic," Marcus answered. "We'll save it for the right moment, for maximum impact."

Everything was going as planned. Still, I felt so goddamned useless.

Once Marcus started spinning, Sally grabbed my arm and pulled me toward the bar. She ordered us two gin and tonics. After the drinks at home and the frou-frou margaritas at Food Bar, I was already experiencing a healthy, prolonged buzz. Sally stood posing at the corner of the rectangular-shaped back bar and took in the scenery. She unbuttoned the blouse, releasing the heavy breasts from some of their confinement. She was grinning widely all the while, as if she'd come home at last. "I remember playing this club, but those chairs were back there and there was a dance floor where this bar is now," she explained. She sucked that drink down in a matter of minutes and grabbed me by the arm again. "Let's dance."

I left my half-full drink on the bar and headed to the dance floor. Nobody seemed to care that I was dancing with an older woman. In fact, many people moved towards us, to be included in our night. Sally was working her shit, for sure. She let a few guys twirl her around and let a few more grind up against her. Drinks appeared in our hands, delivered by a friendly, shirtless waiter. Sally had a magnetism that drew people to her. I wasn't doing so badly myself. A few older guys seemed to use Sally as a way to gain access to me, and I had to politely move hands from my ass and unlock arms that suddenly appeared around my waist from behind me. At one point I looked at my watch and it was a little after ten; the next time I looked it was after midnight. The night was becoming a fast-moving blur.

Finally, at about one a.m., all of us sweaty on the dance floor and bodies touching each other, I heard my brother's voice boom over the sound system as the opening vamp to 'Bomb Away' started to ramp up. "We have a very special guest in the house tonight. You may remember this song from a few years back. Her name is Sally Testata and starting tonight, she's coming back! Where are you, Sally?" An overhead spotlight swept around the massive room and, as if on cue with the vocal, settled on her right in the middle of all those bodies. An overhead camera was also in on the act, and the big screens that lined the walls lit up with the image of Sally at the same time. The room erupted into screams and whoops. The song pulsed and Sally's voice soared over the electronic beat. When the chorus came, everyone in the place sang, "I'll take no prisoners, bombs away," the last note held out for an eternity, like maybe sixteen bars, like on those old Donna Summer anthems. Suddenly, people were squeezing through bodies to get close to her. "I thought that was you!" and "You look great!" were shouted into her grateful ears.

After that extended mix of the song, Marcus played one of her deep underground hits from the Pillow Talk days, "Are Ya Ready to Howl?" A song about the singer's preference for a certain sexual position, it was way too raunchy to ever hit the airwaves. The Splash crowd seemed to get into it and improvisational doggie-style dancing was the rage on the dance floor.

After two, the crowd was still at capacity. Sally pulled me close and planted a lip-lock on me. "Let's go home," she said. At that point, pretty wasted and physically drained from four hours of almost non-stop dancing—how did Sally do it? I wondered—I wasn't about to argue. We made our way up to the booth and thanked Marcus for a great night, Sally giving him the gay kiss on each cheek.

The frigid February air was a welcome jolt to our overheated bodies. We hailed a cab on Sixth Avenue and went back to Marcus's apartment.

By the time we got inside, I was ready to go. We had been kissing and feeling each other up in the back of the cab. Sally poured us each a gin and we headed to the bedroom. Our clothes came off quickly and Sally pushed me back on the bed as she eased down my 2xist briefs. She uncapped a small bottle in her hand and pushed it toward my face. I reeled from the fuel-like odor. "What the hell is that?"

"I got it from one of the guys at Splash. It's poppers. Take a sniff."

"I don't know, it seems kind of dangerous."

"Please, they sell it in candy stores! Live a little!"

As I tentatively inhaled the stuff, she was already working me over with her mouth. It felt great but after half a minute or so, the poppers took effect. Shit, I thought I was going to pass out! The room was spinning and I thought I would explode. "I'm gonna come," I moaned, and there was no stopping it.

At the last second, she came up for air and worked me with her hand and I shot all over the place, the bedspread, the wall behind me, my own face. Was I still alive? I lay panting on the fully made bed and eventually the room came into focus again.

"I'd say you needed that," Sally said. "Let me get you a towel."

I was speechless as she wiped me clean. At last, she dropped the towel and lay down beside, resting her head on my chest. "That was unbelievable," I said. She simply said "Mmm," in an approving kind of way.

Still at a loss for words, eventually I asked her, "So what did you think about tonight?"

"It was great, wasn't it? It's nice to know they still love me."

"Yeah. You've already got a fan base. It's going to be so fun to watch you come back."

"Mmmm." She didn't sound completely convinced.

"You want that, right?"

"Want it? I don't know what I want anymore. You're only seeing the highs right now. The lows will come, believe me."

"But I'll be there with you. I won't let you down," I reassured her. That's how I felt at that moment.

"As long as you're here now. That's all that matters." She started working me with her hand and tilted her head up to slide her tongue into my mouth. It didn't take long for me to be ready again.

After a few minutes of foreplay, she slid a condom onto my dick. "Come on, are you ready to howl?" she teased. She lay on her side and guided me into her from behind. As soon as I started to pump, her voice went into overdrive. It was like a stream-of-conscious blitz of words, words, words, delivered in ever-greater intensity, designed to turn me on, which it did. I was glad Marcus wasn't home. *Yeah right there right there harder harder oh yeah oh yeah you can do it you can do it come for me come for me now now now!* During all this, she offered me the bottle of poppers over her shoulder. I didn't need them, but I wanted them. The curse was that once I inhaled, I knew my orgasm was soon to follow. I plunged deep inside her and wrapped my tense body around her as I screamed and released once again.

No question, it was the greatest five minutes of my life.

* * *

I opened my eyes. The first thing I saw was a long, J-shaped crack on the ceiling above me. I traced it over and over with my eyes as I got my bearings. I felt surprisingly well, but incredibly hungry. Sally was not in the bed. Just as well; I needed a minute to think.

The night before had been wild. How was I going to tell my mother about this new development in my life? I mean, I could keep the romantic nature of my relationship with Sally from her—*maybe*—but eventually I'd have to tell her about my career plans. I hadn't officially dropped out of school yet and had even attended classes that week, but I certainly wasn't going to get any reading done this weekend. If I was serious about this—and it appeared I was—I had to stand up to my mother. The following weekend was the long President's Day weekend. Maybe I could go down to Philly and try to ease my mother into accepting this idea. Fat chance, but I'd have to make the effort before she found out something was amiss on her own.

I bounded out from under the covers, pulled on a pair of briefs, and wrapped my flannel robe around me. As I stepped into the living room and around the couch, I saw Sally and Marcus sitting at the bar, each cradling a cup of coffee in their hands. Their conversation was so intense, they didn't even hear me walk into the room.

"Good morning," I called good-naturedly.

Sally, whose back was toward me, turned on her stool. "Hey, baby," she said, wiping tears from her cheeks with her hands. What the hell?

"What's going on?" I moved over to Sally and put my hand on her back.

"She was just telling me about her mom," Marcus said.

"I'm okay. I just get worked up. I realized I haven't been to New York since she died." She took a sip of coffee. "I don't know what she'd think of me being here."

"I'm sure she'd be proud of you getting back on your feet and trying again," I offered.

"Oh, God, no. She didn't like anything I was doing here. When I went back to Scranton to stay with her after she got sick, the first thing she said to me was, 'Pumpkin, I'm so sorry this is what brought you home.'"

"What is it about mothers?" I asked. "Why is it they don't like anything we do with our lives?"

"But when you lose them, you start thinking maybe they were right."

I wanted to be sympathetic, but I didn't have time for this second-guessing and guilt from the grave. It would only get in the way, slow things up. I tried a different tack. "But we sure had fun last night, didn't we? People just flocked to you. They remembered you. It was awesome! Don't you think so, Marcus?"

"Oh, yeah, definitely. But Sally needs to do what's best for her, in her own time." Who made him the shrink?

"You need to slow down a little bit, tiger," Sally said. "You'll understand that when you get a little bit older."

"A little bit older, a little bit older!" I mocked. "I'm tired of hearing that. Maybe you guys should try to be a little bit younger," I said, lumping them together the way they seemed to want to be. "It's not like there's all the time in the world."

Sally nodded her head. "That's true. I learned that lesson, too."

There was silence as I rummaged around for a snack and my own cup of coffee. "So here's what's next on the agenda. We need to start meeting some producers, looking at some studios. Maybe look at some apartments."

"Whoa, Greg. Take it easy," Marcus cautioned. "Until this gets off the ground, why don't you two stay here when you need to? In the spring and summer, I'm away a lot of weekends anyway."

"Sounds practical," Sally said. I wasn't sure about combining our business and pleasure under Marcus' roof.

As though reading my mind, Marcus continued. "We can make a lot of plans, do a lot of talking, while under the same roof."

I was acutely aware of his use of *we*. I wanted his help, but I was suspicious that he'd take over and I needed to prove myself. Living with Marcus didn't seem like such a good idea, but I kept my fears to myself for the moment. "Okay, then let's get started. Let's put together a list of contacts. And we need to go out again. We have to start creating a buzz." I was also thinking about the sex that would follow.

"Oh, Jesus. This old girl needs fuel," Sally said. "Marcus, would you mind making me a Bloody Mary?"

* * *

The rest of that weekend became more about Sally getting reacquainted with New York than anything else, despite my plans. We had to have brunch at Union Square Café, we cabbed down to Soho to look in some shops—I bought her a hundred dollar scarf she kept running through her hands, mainly to keep her moving, but she was thrilled and gave me a peck on the cheek—and finally ended up sipping drinks at one of her favorite little hangouts in the West Village, tucked away on one of those streets you can never remember the name of. At least she was happy.

Marcus was with us all the while, and I often felt like more of an observing bystander than a participant. They laughed about music, recalled names from the past that both of them may have known, reminisced about "the good old days" of clubbing in the nineties, cursed near-miss career opportunities. The thing is, for these very reasons, I needed Marcus. For these very reasons, I was beginning to hate Marcus.

On Saturday night, Marcus brought us to Barracuda, a club off Eighth Avenue. It was much smaller, with two long rectangular rooms and a functional small stage in the back. There was no dancing, so we settled ourselves on a sofa and watched the place fill up. Marcus talked with the manager and he assured us that when Sally was ready for a release party, Barracuda would be available to us. It was all very exciting. Of course, I had yet to hear Sally sing a note.

Saturday had not been like Friday. Sally got tired early and wanted to get back to the apartment to sleep. At a loss for conversation, I was all for that plan but when we got there—Marcus had returned with us to change clothes but quickly moved on to a private party he was deejaying that night—it became clear that Sally actually meant *sleep*, nothing more. Sally went to the room a little before midnight and I contented myself with flipping channels on the flat screen TV until the wee hours of the morning. Sleeping next to Sally without getting any action was not my idea of a good time. Maybe I should have never dipped into the well.

We had brunch at a nearby place on Sunday morning, and then we prepared ourselves for the trip back to Scranton and said our good-byes, boosting each other up with pep talks about what was to come. On the drive back, Sally and I recalled details of our first foray into New York, laughing and whooping, but conversation ran dry about halfway through New Jersey and Sally fell asleep, her head against the window, until we reached Scranton. I dropped her off at the farmhouse; she didn't invite me in and she looked tired as she trudged up the three steps to the porch. I made a mental note that this wasn't just about the upcoming song and CD release: I had to get her on that exercise program and off the booze.

CHAPTER FIVE

▼

After my Monday morning class, I met Rick for breakfast at Abe's on Wyoming Avenue. We settled into a corner table and ordered our eggs, bacon, and toasted bagels.

Rick wasted no time speaking his mind. "The coach is pissed at you for missing Saturday's match. He doesn't think you were sick."

"You didn't say anything to him, did you?" Rick was the only person I had told about my plan to go to New York for the weekend.

"Nah, of course not. But I do wonder what you see in this woman. Is she a good lay?"

"Unbelievable," I confided in hushed tones.

Rick toasted his water glass to mine. "Okay. At least you're not going gay on me. I was worried about it, with your brother and the dance clubs and that music and all."

"Come on, man. It's a market. It's how I'm going to make my living."

"If you say so. Are we still on for this weekend?" We had a home match on Saturday and then a handful of us were to go skiing on Sunday. A big snowstorm was forecast for midweek, so it would be good. Still, I was already leaving school behind and dreaming of my New York life.

"I'll be at the match, but I'm not sure about the skiing. I have a lot of work to do. I may be getting an apartment in New York soon."

Rick, probably fueled by steroids, slapped the table. "You're fucking crazy!" All eyes in the place turned toward us and Rick had to calm himself and apologize to the waitress and everyone in the immediate vicinity.

"Rick, my destiny is calling me. I gotta grab this moment and run with it."

"Your destiny: a fucking drunk has-been."

It was my turn to rage. "Shut your mouth about her, Rick!"

A middle-aged woman from behind the counter hurried over. She gave us a frown. "You boys will have to leave if you can't keep it down."

"We'll keep it down," I assured her. "Sorry."

We kept quiet, all right. The food arrived and we hungrily shoveled it in, barely speaking another word to each other.

* * *

I called Sally on Wednesday. It was Valentine's Day and the biggest storm of the year was rolling through. I was horny as hell and hinting for a visit. "How are you doing, Sally?"

"I'm okay. But with this weather, I can't get over to the Poconos to clean houses and it will be a very busy ski weekend coming up, what with the holiday," she said. "I guess I'll be working long days tomorrow and Friday."

"Just remember, all this housecleaning is just short-term now. Before long, that will all be behind you."

"Well, that's all fine and good, but I'd rather not put all my eggs in one basket just yet," she cautioned me.

"Any chance I can see you this Valentine's Day?" I asked, hopeful.

"Baby, you best stay where you are today. These back roads are no place to be during these ice storms." I'd have crossed any tundra or desert for her, but she had continued to keep me at bay since that magical Friday night in New York.

I gingerly tiptoed onto the subject. "Sally, was I all right? You know, Friday night, when we were together?"

She let out a chuckle and I could hear the exhale of cigarette smoke. "Honey, you were fine. You just need to slow down a little. But it was nice to see you so excited."

"Well, I'd like to try again sometime." I was trying to sound confident and sexy but I'm not sure it was translating.

"You betcha. But let's remember what this is all about. It's the music, right? It's my career we're working on, right?"

"Oh, yeah, no doubt!" She was right, and I tried to file away those other feelings. "I was thinking about going to Philly this weekend, telling my mother about my career plans."

"Don't involve me in any of that," Sally stated firmly. "You do whatever you need to do, but I don't want to come between you and your mother. This career project is your decision, I'm just the client."

"I know. But I figure she should know what's going on with me, in case I need to take incompletes or to get her moving on another plan, because I'm not going to Bounder & Lightning in June."

"Okay, get all that squared away. Maybe I'll try to deal with my father over the long weekend as well."

"Sounds good. And Sally," I began, aware I was treading on thin ice, "because you are my client, I want you to think about getting ready for the summer campaign. Laying off the alcohol and cigarettes, getting yourself into an exercise program."

"Yeah, yeah, yeah. I know all about the game. This ain't my first time at the debutante ball. Although it may well be my last."

"Yeah, last because from here it's up, up, up."

"Up, up, up. I'll try to remember that," she said without passion. "Okay, Greg, I gotta go shovel the walk and around the car. First on my exercise program. I'll talk to you soon."

"All right. Bye, Sally." I clicked shut my cell phone and looked over at the coffee table, strewn with textbooks. Maybe I'd try to get something done before the weekend.

CHAPTER SIX

I was raised in Center City, a rectangle of quaint cobblestoned streets in the middle of Philadelphia. There are redbrick colonial houses along the narrow lanes and at night the old-fashioned lampposts cast a shadowy glow along the sidewalks. If you are a visitor, you can get a false sense of security in Center City, one of those rare inner-city neighborhoods where the old-money folks and young professionals and artists live side by side amidst the galleries and cafes, while the dangers surrounding it are always felt by the local inhabitants. Like its little sister city to the north, Philly was at its peak during the industrial revolution, when industry and banking benefited from its easy water and rail access. And like Scranton, it also has a split personality: in Philly's case, it retains some of its early Quaker snobbish morality and yet also has some of the wildest nightlife you are likely to see anywhere.

We lived in one of those historic houses on the corner of an alley off Spruce Street. There in the cradle of America's independence, my parents gave me everything I needed but independence.

As I had told Rick I might, I ended up blowing off the weekend skiing adventure, driving down to Philadelphia after my wrestling match. My mother was pleased to welcome me home that Saturday night. While heating up a plate that Samantha, the housekeeper, had prepared before leaving for the weekend, she rattled off her list of projects since I had last seen her a month before, dropping names of the well to do and up and coming. She was on the board of the Walnut Street Theater and had been involved in some fundraising—she was all for the theater as long as her own kids didn't pursue that profession. Dad had, as usual, already retired to his study and sent his regards through Mother. I was about to eat the last forkful on the plate by the time she finally asked, "So how are you doing, Greg?"

I wasn't quite ready to go into all of that. I looked up from my plate and saw her standing rod-straight against the kitchen sink, one hand leaning flat on the counter. She wore a navy blue pantsuit that complimented her slim figure, a paisley scarf tightly knotted around her throat. Her white hair was swept back into a modern-looking hairdo—a bob, I guess you'd call it—and gray-white pearls accented her ears. Her unlined face, lifted a few times, had an arched, expectant look, and her gray eyes regarded me, waiting, like an amused cat trying to decide if it was time to pounce on the mouse.

"Great," I said.

"You're keeping up with all your schoolwork, then? Don't fall prey to the senior's tendency to phone in the last semester. You'll rue the day and your grade point average will suffer. You can't afford that." Mine was barely above a 3.0.

"So far, so good." Technically, that was true but only because it was too early in the semester to have any way of knowing.

"And what about Amy? Have you heard from her?"

"No," I answered, trying to keep my sarcasm in check. "I didn't think it right to call her after she broke up with me."

"Such a beautiful girl, such good manners. Such a shame."

"I think you need to let it go, Mother."

"I suppose you are right." She paused, strategically. "Is there anyone else?"

"No." I answered too quickly. I knew it as soon as it was out of my mouth.

She smiled, her eyes turning to slits, ready for the attack. "Ah, you are lying. I am not surprised. My Greg Bounder is not one to remain unattached for long." She stepped over and tousled my hair.

I opted not to answer her. "Do we have any ice cream?"

"Yes, of course. Butter pecan." She moved to the refrigerator and opened the freezer to get it. "So, you can't tell me anything about her?" She winked at me as she dropped a perfect round dollop from the scoop to the bowl.

"There's really nothing to tell."

"Okay. You'll tell me when the time is right. Just keep in mind, you are finishing up your undergraduate studies. It's no time to be fooling around and no time to latch onto a freshman girl. Your future is almost here."

The thought of a settled future at twenty-one was a bit too much to handle. Now was the time I should be fooling around, enjoying myself before the long plunge into a fifty-year retirement plan. "Yes, well, I plan to use this weekend to study and do some research toward that end," I replied confidently.

"Wonderful. Do you need to get into the office? Your father can bring you over."

"No, no. I don't think it's time for that. I mean, I have other projects to research."

"Very good. I'll stay out of your way." Fat chance. "I would like you to go to church tomorrow. So many people would love to see you."

St. Mary's. The phoniest place on Earth. It was exactly as my mother said: a place to be seen. Worship and spiritually came in a distant second. "I'd love to," I lied with a straight face.

She walked over and squeezed my shoulder affectionately. "I do believe you are growing up, my son. Well," she sighed, "it's been a long week and I must do some correspondence before going to bed. Say hello to your father before he goes up. I will see you in the morning." She kissed the top of my head and strode out of the room.

After finishing my ice cream, I walked through the dining room and living room to the study to greet Dad. As it turned out, he had already gone to bed. It was not unusual for me to go through an entire weekend without speaking to him.

* * *

When the house seemed safely quiet, I tiptoed outside. I wanted to check out some of the dance clubs. The fact is, most dance clubs are, by definition, pretty much gay. Or, I should say, dance music like Sally's would most often be heard in the gay dance clubs, not the straight ones. But for my first stop, I decided to go to Spin, a big straight club in South Philly, and managed to get in before the long lines formed behind the velvet rope. I'm the rare straight guy who can actually dance to disco-type music, so I could have gotten laid if I'd wanted to—straight women love a guy that can dance because they are so hard to find—but I was seriously into my research purposes that night. Besides, I couldn't do that to Sally. I wrote down the names of several songs and tried to notice which ones were the crowd favorites, but I didn't manage to get the attention of the deejay on his perch above the crowd. After that, I headed back to Center City and went to Key West, a gay club that covered three floors, dancing on the third. I talked to the deejay, a guy named Ron. He was straight but he said he loved playing the gay clubs because when the gays would bring in their fag hag friends, he could have his pick of the best ones at the end of the night. And a lot of the girls were like putty in his hands when he played their requests. What a life!

I spent a lot of time hanging out with Ron, telling him my plans and about Sally—he remembered her too—and I thought he would be a good connection in Philly when I wanted to expand into that market. Needless to say, I didn't get home until after the clubs closed at two a.m.

The next morning, my mother rapped on the door three times. "It's after nine; you'd better get up and get ready."

"I'd really rather sleep in. Give my regards to everyone."

"Lisa Meade will be there," she said in a singsongy voice. I had gone to high school with her and my mother had always liked her. It seemed she was already onto Plan B with the matchmaking.

"Tell her I said hello," I called out, my head still on the pillow.

"Suit yourself," my mother snapped, and I heard her heels clicking down the hallway as she bellowed, "One day you'll do right by me, Gregory Alan Bounder! One day!"

It was nice to get up and make myself a bagel and coffee without her overbearing presence. I could almost live in Philly, if not for that presence.

When they returned after church, my mother ignored me and went straight to the kitchen to begin preparation for the afternoon dinner. Father eased himself into his wingback chair and turned the TV to some golf tournament.

"How are things at Bounder & Lightning?" I asked him.

"Oh, not bad. We're trying to work on more energy-efficient products, because the cost of fuel keeps going up, and that affects our business as well."

My father, at eighty, actually liked the business and still went into the office every day. I couldn't imagine. I couldn't even continue the conversation. "Sounds good."

He put his feet up on the ottoman. "I don't think Tiger Woods is going to win this one."

There was nothing to say. The passivity was killing me. "Dad, would it be terrible if I decided not to go to Bounder & Lightning right after school?"

He hardly perked up. "What did you have in mind?"

"I'm not sure, but I'd like to try doing my own thing for a while."

"That's a natural thing for a boy your age."

"So you're okay with it?"

"Oh, yes. Just don't tell your mother until you have to. Otherwise, I have to hear it for months on end." He hadn't taken his eyes off the television, nor had he cracked a smile. I had great affection for this stranger, his squarish head with wispy white hairs moving to and fro, his stolid expression showing a fight to continue rather than to change. He might last another twenty years without ever showing an emotion.

That was all for that topic. We continued to watch golf, wordlessly, until Mother announced that dinner was ready. We moved into the dining room, where she had an impressive display of steaming dishes set in the middle of the long table. Our placemats were arranged around one end of it. We filled our plates with ham and scalloped potatoes and vegetables and seated ourselves.

After standing at my father's side and kindly asking if he had everything he needed, my mother started right in with me. "So, did you have a good time last night? I noticed your car was parked in a different place, so I guess you went out?" Nothing escaped her.

"Yes, but I was also doing research," I answered smugly.

"Research? On a Saturday night? The city is still very dangerous at night."

"I know that."

"What kind of research?" she pressed on.

It was now or never. "Night clubs, that sort of thing."

She remained speechless for a moment, but I could see the storm clouds gathering in her graying face, the eyes darting about the room searching for a landing. At last they landed on me. I was intently looking at my plate, but I could feel the heat of those eyes. "I don't even want to think about why you'd be researching night clubs."

"Then don't." At the head of the table, my father remained expressionless, shoveling in the potatoes.

"Is that why you went to see your brother last weekend? He'd better not be cooking up some scheme …"

"It's not him. It's all my idea; he's just helping out."

She turned to look out the kitchen window and let out a big, dramatic sigh. "I can not have another son pursuing a ludicrous career."

I remained calm. "Marcus has done very well for himself. He has a great place in the Village and travels all over the world."

"So that's what you want after all this education? To be a *deejay?*" She said the word with disgust, as though she were holding a snake.

"No, Mother, I'm not going to be a deejay. I'm putting my marketing skills to good use. I'm going to be a personal manager."

"For whom, pray tell?"

"I met a singer—"

"A singer! A *singer?*" she bellowed, no longer able to maintain her composure. I may as well have said I met a hooker. I caught a glance of my father, who had at last lifted his eyes to mine. He said nothing, but gave me a sober stare as if to say, *What did I tell you?*

"It's not just any singer, it's someone who's already had a career."

"Had! Had! Had a career! Where is she now? Where did you meet her?" My father stood up and moved to the living room with his plate. Mother ignored him.

"I met her in Scranton, where she lives now."

"Oh, for God's sake! After all we've given you …"

"Give me a chance to do something on my own. I think I can talk my adviser into giving me credit for an internship."

"You are three months from graduation and this is the lark you want to pursue." She stood up with her plate—I don't think she'd eaten more than two bites—and headed for the kitchen. As she reached the doorway, she whirled around with a gasp. "You are in love with her!"

"No, I'm not—"

"You are! You are! You've never been able to hide anything from me and you still can't! What's her name? How old is she?" God in heaven, the questions would never cease from that point on.

"Her name is Sally. That's all you need to know right now."

She glared at me. "That's all I need to know right now? Is that what you said to me?"

"Yes, Mother. I'm twenty-one now; I can do what I like."

"You wouldn't be so cocky if you didn't have your grandfather's money in your account. Try working your way up without the head start from your family, like your grandfather—who foolishly left you that trust fund—did, and see how that feels."

"Dad doesn't care if I go to Bounder & Lightning." I was trying to win the argument, but letting that out of the bag probably wasn't the smartest move.

Her voice became a harsh stage whisper. "Don't you dare bring your father into this. The only reason he's been going into the office all these years is so he could wait for the day when you'd be out of school and he could proudly hand over the reins to his son."

"No," I said, walking past her into the kitchen and slamming my plate down into the sink. "I think he's been going into the office all these years to get away from you." I didn't dare look at her after that outburst, but out of the corner of my eye, as I passed, I could see that she stood ramrod-straight, hands still holding her plate. I headed straight up to my room to gather my things. The weekend was over, but it may have been the necessary pain to get me to the next level.

A few minutes passed and I had almost finished packing my bag when my mother at last reacted. I heard glass breaking down in the kitchen and then her roar followed. "I'm not finished with you, Gregory Bounder! You will not disregard me so easily! See where that tramp gets you and don't come crawling back to me!"

"I will walk back with my head held high, with more money than you ever had!" I shouted through the walls.

There was nothing left to do at that point but prove myself. No use hanging around the house in Philly, enduring more threats from my mother on the warpath. I took a piece of stationery from the desk and wrote, "I love you, Mother, but I need to do this for myself. I hope you understand." I left it on the pillow. I managed to sneak out the back without her seeing me. A terrible end, but what else could I do? The tires screeched as I turned onto Spruce and sped out of that burdensome city. Back to Scranton and my new life.

CHAPTER SEVEN

▼

I left a message for Sally as soon as I got back to Scranton on Sunday night. I still hadn't heard from her on Monday morning, but I resisted all temptation to call her again.

I did get a call from Marcus on Monday. As soon as I picked up the phone, he started in with, "Why the hell did you tell Ma that I was helping you out?"

"I thought you were."

"But she thinks I'm behind this whole crazy comeback scene!"

"Crazy comeback scheme!" I roared. "You sure didn't mind kissing Sally's ass when we were up there and offering us your apartment to live in."

"Yeah, well, that's off the table at this point. After all the years trying to make peace with her, I can't have her blaming me for how you turn out now."

"What do you care what she thinks? Since when did that matter to you?"

"It doesn't matter to me. But *you* matter to her. I can live with my own decisions and make it on my own—and have—but I can't take responsibility for you."

"Who asked you to? It will be a relief not to have you take over the project like you seemed to want to."

"Greg, don't be ridiculous. I was being a good host. I have no interest in taking over Sally's career. If there is one."

"Thanks for your vote of confidence."

"I call it as I see it," he said smugly. "The fact is, Sally has a lot of problems. Too many. Ma is probably right: You're better off saving your money and working at Bounder & Lightning, at least until you have a better plan for what you really want to do with your life."

That did it. "Oh, go fuck yourself!" I hit the red STOP button and snapped my cell phone shut, which didn't have quite the dramatic effect of slamming a receiver down on its base, but such is life.

I was now motivated to succeed in a way I hadn't been before the Philadelphia weekend. I cracked open a notebook.

Marketing is different from sales; sales comes later. Marketing is making your customers aware of your product, and you have to do your homework to make it effective. The first thing I did was construct a situational analysis, which is basically a bunch of questions to help me figure out where I am and where I need to be. Questions like this: What is my five-year plan? Who is my market? What is the unmet need in the marketplace? Where is my customer base—keeping in mind the 80/20 rule, that 80 % of my sales would come from 20 % of my customer base? How would I test the market? How would I get distribution? What kind of company did I want to create—a sole proprietorship, a C corporation, or an S corporation? Should I incorporate in Pennsylvania or New York? The first would be less of a tax burden, the latter is where I wanted to end up. Who would be my sales force? How much could I do on my own? What was my skills list?

From there, I was able to start outlining a business plan. It's true that I would be bankrolling the project in the beginning—thus, the business plan wasn't needed to gain investors—but I kept in mind Professor Dash's mantra: "If it isn't written down, it isn't going to happen." Concrete plans make concrete results. Also, the more work I could do now, the more money I would save later. Eventually, I'd have to bring in a business attorney. If I used him to polish up my work, it would be far less costly than having him create a business plan from scratch. A good business plan should be about fifteen pages long, and cover all the bases: a description of the company, the market, product development, management and ownership, personnel, and funds required. The last two are the ones that started to overwhelm me. A lawyer, a publicist, a producer, musicians, licensing fees, studio time, manufacture, distribution, keeping Sally fed and fit—these covered the bare minimum and I saw a sizeable chunk coming out of my considerable trust fund. Just as doubt was starting to creep into my consciousness, the phone rang. It was Marcus.

"I'm going to pretend you did not tell me to go fuck myself this morning," he said calmly. I looked at the kitchen clock; hours had passed. "But I do have some good news. I have copies of *HX* in my hot little hands and in the 'Seen Around Town' section is a photo of Sally and you dancing at Splash." *HX* was a glossy gay magazine, a weekly. Leave it to Marcus to change his tune if there was publicity involved. He was nothing if not an opportunist. I let my irritation pass.

"Shit, that's fantastic!" I cried, not realizing that *HX* had a shelf life of, well, one week. "What about *Next*?" The other gay party rag.

"No, nothing. But you can be sure they won't want to be left out of the loop next time around."

"What does it say?"

"Well, it's just a blurb. It says, 'Revelers at Splash were treated to a surprise appearance on Friday night by former club diva and one-hit-wonder Sally Testata, accompanied by her handsome boy toy. Apparently, Sally has a comeback project in the works. We can't wait.'"

"Boy toy! I'll show them the brains behind this operation!" I crowed.

"Anyway, I'll send you a copy. Your first brush of fame."

"Yeah, but without a name. I won't be nameless for much longer."

"Good attitude. So what's next for you?"

"I'm writing a business plan as we speak. You know, marketing, projections, budgets."

"Well, I can see you *are* serious about this."

That was the curse of being the little brother, the youngest son—nobody ever takes you seriously. "Hell, yes, I'm serious. We need to move quickly to ramp up for a summer release." The fact was, I did need Marcus, so I had to perform a delicate dance with him. "Would you mind scouting around to see if you can come up with a good producer, and maybe find the songwriters who wrote 'Bombs Away.' Maybe they want a comeback too."

"Well, one of them, Chester Sweethouse, is still around, showing up at deejay booths with new demos he tries to foist on us. He definitely needs a comeback. The other guy, I think he's scoring films out in Hollywood, doing quite well."

"Okay. Feel out Chester next time you see him, see if he's up for it."

"Oh, he'll be up for it. Anything to get himself a line of copy." It seemed everyone in New York was out for a line of copy.

"Great. Okay, I need to get back to work." What a nice feeling it was, to be telling Marcus that *I* was too busy to talk, for a change.

I did some online research of *Billboard Magazine*, the pop music authority, and got a chart history of "Bombs Away" in the summer of 2001. It went like this:

Week Ending	Club Airplay	Dance Radio	Hot 100 Singles
July 14	41		
July 21	27		
July 28	20		
August 4	14	37	
August 11	9	25	
August 18	5	15	
August 25	3	9	(video released)
September 1	2	6	94
September 8	1	3	82
September 15	1	2	67
September 22	1	43	98
September 29	3		
October 6	9		
October 13	16		
October 20	30		
October 27	32		
November 3	45		

Billboard compiles data ending on a Tuesday, which is then published in the Saturday charts. So you can see that Sally was literally on top of the world on Tuesday, September 11 and by the next week pretty much off the charts—except in the clubs; gays have never been particularly PC about their music and often, the more controversial the better. The Hot 100 (combining airplay from all music formats plus sales figures) is the all-important mainstream pop singles chart and there is no doubt "Bombs Away" would have been a major hit had 9/11 not happened, just as Sally had told me. This year, I wanted the same summer ramp-up and rollout, but with a different result. The world had changed a lot in the years since 2001. The war on terrorism was raging and as controversial as ever. I wouldn't go near it with a music project.

The year 2007 was also when it became clear that the music industry was changing forever. It was no longer about the artist or the CD—sales of them were plunging every month—but it was about the song, which could be downloaded on iTunes for ninety-nine cents. This was good news if we came up with a killer song; not so good news for trying to develop an artist who would last longer than the life of the song, let alone years or decades. I had to be careful with my approach in marketing Sally as well as the song.

The day went on and I kept refilling my coffee mug. When I finally looked up at the clock again, it was after ten and I had crafted several pages of rough draft on my laptop. I would be able to present it to my adviser for some kind of internship credit, I thought. I'd never felt so proud.

* * *

My first expense on the project was getting a gym membership for Sally at a Crunch in downtown Scranton. I, of course, used the gym at school but Sally wouldn't be able to use it, and I wanted to train her. So I took advantage of the midwinter sale and got a two-for-one six-month membership for both of us.

On Tuesday night, I waited by the receptionist desk at the gym for our seven o'clock appointment. I was getting pissed and ready to leave—she not had answered calls from my cell—when she breezed in at 7:30. She saw the look on my face. "Relax, Greg. Did you forget I clean houses all day? But I'm still here."

Yes, she was. She had obviously purchased some new threads for this venture—at a Target or K-mart by the looks of them. Her thick hair was tied back in a ponytail, which slipped through the back of a Phillies baseball cap. She had on her game face and I was happy to see her.

"Okay, go put your coat and stuff in the locker room, and I'll meet you down there in the stretch area."

"Can I have a cigarette first?" She saw the stunned look on my face. "Just kidding, just kidding. Jesus, lighten up. I'll be right back."

She got through the stretches okay, although she wasn't exactly limber. She even surprised me with her aggressiveness on the weightlifting machines. "What, you think I've never done this before?" It was the aerobics part of the program that gave her the problems, as I suspected. She kept looking at the monitor on the treadmill in front of her. "Only a mile?" she gasped. I covered up the monitor with a towel.

"Only twenty-five more and you'll have a marathon," I told her.

"You have to … start me off … slow," she panted as her feet pounded the track. She wasn't even going that fast; it was more like a trot, to be honest.

"Take some water, keep running." She scowled, but didn't stop until the machine beeped and started to slow at the programmed twenty-minute mark. She had covered a little over two miles. The entire workout was seventy-five minutes.

"You're going to be sore tomorrow," I told her.

"You're going to be sore tonight." She flashed me an evil grin.

I felt my face flush and I glanced around to see if anyone overheard her. "Yeah? I can come over?" I begged in hushed tones.

"No. You're going to be sore from whacking off. You torture me, I torture you," Sally laughed, wiping her glistening face with the towel. She almost skipped to the locker room, yelling over her shoulder, "See you by the desk in ten minutes!"

CHAPTER EIGHT

▼

For the rest of the winter, everything went as planned. Every day there were calls and e-mails back and forth to people in New York, trying to set up studio time, getting lyric drafts from Chester Sweethouse—who was eager to be on board for Sally's comeback—and quizzing potential publicists. In the meantime, Sally managed to keep her workouts going three times a week and she even found a local voice teacher—just to warm her up for a New York coach, she said. She was toning up, body and voice.

For me, the timing was perfect. The wrestling season was over at the end of March—and none too soon, probably, because my winning ways of the previous season had become a dismal fifty-fifty or so in my final season, disappointing my coach and teammates—and that month would see me through my midterms as well. At a time when I should have been having the last hurrah, partying every weekend with my U of S friends, I was gearing up for my move to New York. I was barely keeping up with my studies and my friends and I were drifting away from each other. At the very least, Professor Dash had okayed my project as an internship—he had been impressed with my eagerness and my business plan.

As for Sally and me, the dating part of our relationship was kind of cat-and-mouse and I'm not sure who was the cat and who was the mouse. I'd chase after her but couldn't always catch her, and then when I least expected it, she'd turn and pounce on me. It could be frustrating but it was good. I think the electricity between us—yeah, Scranton the electric city thing—kept things exciting, not only for the sex but for the project at hand. She let me speed up the project, but in return got me to slow down on the lovemaking. "Slow down, tiger," she'd tell me. "If you give it all away in the first five minutes, there's nothing left to look forward to." One time, she had me lay naked on the bed and then she put a sheet over me and made love to me with the sheet between us. She wouldn't let me remove the sheet for at least an hour. Drove me crazy!

During all that time, up until mid-March, she said she never went back to Fat Bo's. She wanted to "make an entrance" next time she went so that her old friends could see that she was serious.

So here was the plan: Marcus had found us a two-bedroom sublet in midtown that would run from April through August—perfect timing to get our project off the ground and running. There was no way I was going to live with Marcus. On the other hand, I had wanted a one-bedroom apartment, but Sally said no way to that request: Her exact words were, "It's bad enough I can't have my own apartment. We need to concentrate on the work, not each other." Not exactly a boost to my ego as a potential boyfriend, but I thought she was right. It was one of those old walk-up, railroad apartments near Tenth Avenue, but even so it was twenty-five hundred bucks a month—plus I'd keep my Scranton apartment, another eight hundred dollars a month. I convinced Sally to put in her notice with her agency and quit the housecleaning at the end of March. She did so, but told her boss it was a "leave of absence," just in case she had to come back. We would be spending most of our time in New York starting in April and we even had some studio time booked that first week. The idea was to start with three songs for an EP—which stands for Extended Play, a mini-CD—with one of them being pushed as the major single.

March was a long month and, as it turned out, the coldest month of that winter. By the end of it, though, all the pieces were in place and we were ready to make our entrance in Manhattan. First, though, we'd start a little smaller, and make our entrance at Fat Bo's.

It was the last Friday of March. I had invited Rick and Pete to stop by because they had been there at the beginning and had been skeptical. In Fat Bo's, where it all began, our climb to the top would begin.

Sally had wanted a real send-off, so she called Fat Bo herself and he and Rolf promised a party atmosphere. When I found out about that, I went one better: I sent a press release to the *Scranton Times-Tribune*, complete with a bio and copies of old print clippings as well as the page from February's *HX*.

When we arrived at Fat Bo's a little after eight o'clock, yellow crepe paper streamers were looped across the big room every which way and bouquets of yellow balloons bobbed at the corners of the bars, and a single daffodil in a miniature vase sat at each table. Any stranger walking in would think Fat Bo's was welcoming home the troops, but in fact it was only that yellow was Sally's favorite color. A big "Best of Luck" banner draped from one end of the bar to the other.

Sally had decked herself out in a fluorescent yellow blouse and a single silver necklace with a heart-shaped locket. Her hair, newly blonded, was piled high atop her head, and simple quarter-sized silver hoops dangled from her ears. All in all, a pretty conservative outfit from the waist up. However, it wouldn't be Sally without some kind of sex appeal. She wore shimmering black silk slacks and black high heels. She wasn't exactly showing leg, but the effect was definitely startling. Her improved, slimmer figure was evident for all to see. When we entered, the room erupted into applause and calls of "Go, Sally!" Sally covered her mouth in surprise and then fearlessly worked the crowd from one end of the bar to the other, embracing all her friends, mostly men. I was ignored and stood back while she did her thing. There were only a few people in the room, mostly around the pool tables, who looked over with puzzled expressions, not sure who she was.

Rick and Pete came over and we all shook hands. "I got to hand it to you," Rick said, "I really didn't think you were going anywhere with this. And she cleans up pretty well."

"So she's unbelievable in the sack, huh?" Pete ribbed me.

I shot Rick an angry look. I had purposely been laying low with my friends at U of S about my relationship with Sally. The truth is, there was some shame involved and I think the secretive element added to the excitement between us. I wanted people to think it was all up-and-up business on my part.

"Why don't you go back to your nineteen year olds," I said, winking at Pete. "You can't believe how it is to be with a woman who knows what she's doing."

"If you say so. Anyway, you better invite us to New York for the big parties," Rick said.

"Sure enough," I said. "What do you guys want to drink?"

I went to the bar to get beers. Rolf nodded at me without smiling. "I hope you know what you're doing," he said by way of greeting.

"You have nothing to worry about, Rolf. Everything is carefully planned. Nothing is going to stop her this time around."

"Uh-huh." He handed me the Heinekens. "Her stopping is not what I'm worried about."

Just then, Sally appeared at my side. "What do I need to do to get you two to be friends? No gloomy face tonight, Rolf. You're the head of the party tonight."

"Anything for you, Sal. You're ready to go for it again, are you? I just want you to be sure."

"Do I look it?" Sally did a twirl.

The front door opened and everyone turned as Charlie Teskewicz shouted, "Where's my girl?"

"Oh, shit, he's drunk already," Sally said, rolling her eyes. "I'm over here, Dad!" She had begrudgingly decided to let her father have access to the farmhouse while we were in New York, which would be most of the coming months, save for a few quick trips back to Scranton.

Charlie had on the same coat and hat that I had seen in the farmhouse kitchen. He shuffled over to us. Inspecting her, he said, "Well, old girl, maybe you have a hit left in you."

"That's the nicest thing you've said to me in years." Sally said, embracing him.

"And you," Charlie warned, pointing his finger in my face. "You'd better not be leading her on a wild goose chase."

"Oh, no, we have the financing and the plan is all ready to roll."

"Well, that's what they always say. It's a hell of a business, a hell of a business." Charlie regarded Rolf. "For Christ's sake, Rolf, when are you gonna get out of here? What's it been, twenty years behind that bar?"

"Something like that," Rolf answered with a half smile. "I can think of worse places to be. Like New York."

Charlie cackled. "Yes, goddamn it. You're right about that."

The place was filling up. Many of the pool tables had been moved aside and covered with plywood and tablecloths to create a buffet kind of atmosphere. Extra chairs and small tables had been brought in to give it a kind of cabaret feel, I guess. For someone who cleaned houses all week and showed up at Fat Bo's once or twice a week to drink, I couldn't believe how many friends Sally seemed to have. She read the look of surprise on my face. "You think I've been a hermit since I moved back to Scranton, don't you? I know how to make friends." She grazed my cheek with her newly manicured hand and sashayed over to a few middle-aged guys who had come in. Most of her friends seemed to be guys, and they weren't shy about patting her ass or giving her a big kiss when they greeted her, either. I gritted my teeth with each greeting and contemplated getting tested for STDs.

The night went on and Sally continued to surprise me and probably everyone else there as well. She'd sip a gin and tonic and when it was gone, she'd order a bottled water. She never got drunk like I had been afraid she would, instead remaining upbeat and talkative.

The big surprise came at about eleven, when Miguel the barback wheeled out a karaoke machine for the occasion. Everyone started chanting "Sal-ly! Sal-ly! Sal-ly!"

After much coaxing, Sally finally walked over to the mike. "I want to thank you all for this wonderful party," she began. "So many great friends here, who have known me since way back when. And you all believed in me every step of the way, even when I didn't believe in myself. I can hardly believe it, but I'm giving this singing career one last shot. Speaking of which, give me a shot of Jameson's, Rolf!" Everyone laughed and cheered as the shot was delivered and she downed it and then went on. "I want to thank my manager, who I met right here at Fat Bo's. Greg Bounder!" There was polite applause as I waved to the crowd.

"I think she manages you," Pete cracked from beside me.

"I hardly know what to sing for all of you," Sally continued. "I guess I have to do one for Rolf, who has known me for—shit—twenty-five years!" She whispered some instructions to Miguel, who was in charge of the tracks. "This is a song that takes us back to those times, Rolf."

The music started up and a cheesy, slow supermarket-type musical intro calmed the boisterous crowd. Finally, she began. "The first time ever I saw your face …" Ah, it was that song Rolf had mentioned before. I hardly knew the song—maybe had heard it once or twice in my life—and it was about as far from "Bombs Away" as you could get. It occurred to me that I was hearing her sing live for the first time—the first time ever I heard her voice, I might have sung. Her voice seemed a bit lower than I remembered from the recordings. Honestly, it wasn't a great voice, no Christina Aguilera or Kelly Clarkson. In fact, she seemed almost to be speaking the song, but she was getting into it. Out of the corner of my eye, I saw Rick and Pete flash each other a look that may have said, "What the hell has he gotten himself into?"

Despite my slight panic, however, when she finished the song, the place went wild—screaming, stomping, you name it. She seemed to have a loyal following. In Scranton. Well, the studio could do magic, I reminded myself.

For her second selection—she needed further coaxing from the crowd—Sally chose an old blues/rock tune from the 80s, "Black Velvet." This one seemed a little more suited to her voice and style—it captured her strong-woman persona. Again, she left the crowd hollering for more.

"Well, dude, maybe you've got a hit on your hands," Rick said sarcastically.

"Fuck you, man. You'll see what she can do."

"I'd rather see it than hear it," Rick said, and both he and Pete laughed like locker room frat boys.

"Well, you never know," I said, controlling my anger. "Recording is just a start. We'll go to TV, movies. The sky is the limit." I looked over at Sally, graciously accepting a drink from Tommy. The first thing I had to do was get her out of here, and that was coming none too soon.

I walked over to Sally, who had not been at my side all night. "Sally, that was great. Are you about ready to go? We have a long weekend ahead of us." We would be moving to New York the next day. We weren't taking a whole lot of stuff—mostly clothes—but still, we had to settle in and be rested for the studio the following week.

"Are you fucking kidding me? It's not even eleven o'clock. We'd be just getting ready to go out if we lived in New York."

"We have a big week ahead. You need to be rested."

"Okay," she whined like a teenager. "Just one more drink." She took Tommy's arm in hers. "Tommy, you'll have to come visit us in New York." I cringed at the thought.

"You betcha, babycakes," he said, bending and kissing her on the lips. "I'm not gonna let you get completely swallowed up in the city."

"This time, I'm gonna be doing the swallowing. And I'm not going down twice!" Sally vowed. I was proud of how she pulled herself together in the last two months. If she kept up that attitude, we'd stand a fighting chance.

CHAPTER NINE

▼

Our New York apartment was in the west forties in what was known as Hell's Kitchen. However, the neighborhood was definitely coming up from what it was, according to Sally, who'd had an apartment in the same neighborhood years before. The neighborhood may have been coming up, but the apartment was still firmly planted in the hell of Hell's Kitchen, I thought. The guy who had lived there previously kept it neat, with a clean area rug and an entertainment center and full-length bookcases, but all of that couldn't hide the fact that it was four small rooms, back to front, with a sloping floor, a kitchenette with aging appliances, and bathroom tile that needed regrouting. It had one kitchen closet and two small closets, which hardly seemed adequate to hold my clothes, let alone Sally's wardrobe. Luckily, we'd still be in Scranton for much of the time as I finished school and Sally went back to check on the house. A cockroach scurried behind the sink as I turned on the light. This is what twenty-five hundred a month got you—and what Marcus told me was a bargain.

After we settled in, Sally took me on a walking tour of the neighborhood and we ended up at Rudy's Jukebox Bar for hot dogs and beer—kind of a miniature Fat Bo's, now that I think about it. It was supposedly famous for those "in the know." Sally prided herself on being "in the know" even after all those years away.

We didn't have long to rest. On Monday, we had our first rehearsal session with Chester Sweethouse and his latest tracks at a studio in the East Village. Chester Sweethouse was a big man in every way: big voice, big laugh, big appetites, big belly. Bigger than life, as they say. He was also black, which gave him a certain kind of authority that you might not notice if he were a big, pasty white guy managing a supermarket, for instance. You couldn't ignore Chester; I know I couldn't. Sally and Chester embraced like old friends and he introduced us to the engineer, ML, a younger black man who looked more like a basketball player. All of us were on time and ready to go.

Chester had us listen to a song he wrote especially for Sally's comeback, something called "Every Day is a New Day." The sentiment and orchestration was every bit as over the top as you might think, like something Celine Dion might sing to open her Vegas act. Sally wasn't thrilled with it either.

"Let's hear some other stuff, Chester. No offense, but it sounds a little like seventies disco," Sally said.

"Don't start with me, Sally," Chester warned. "I can't take direction from one more singer who thinks she knows everything. Or a college kid," he finished, regarding me with a scowl.

"Look, these college kids are the ones we have to sell to," Sally said. She was absolutely right. "What about the lyric we sent you? Were you able to come up with anything for that?" She meant the song we had started at Fat Bo's on a lark back in February. We had managed to finish the lyric, believe it or not, to "I Still Have What it Takes."

"Yeah, I looked at it but it didn't really inspire me," Chester said. Fuck him and his wounded ego.

"I think it has hit potential," Sally said, unfazed.

"And look at Sally, how good she looks. We still need to capitalize on her sexiness," I offered. She gave me the finger.

"ML, play 'Grind' for them," Chester said. Within a minute, a deep house mix came up and a low, soulful voice oozed over the rhythms through the monitors: *Some want to fill their hearts/Some look for their missing parts/Some want to save their souls/ Others want to be made whole/But I've got something else in mind/I just want to grind/grind/grind/grind.* And so on. I laughed out loud. It was pretty brilliant.

"Why are you playing us schlock when you have something like that? That's perfect for Sally!"

Sally shot me a look of contempt. "Is that what I'm really all about? A meat-grinding machine?"

"Of course not," I said, stroking her back. "Don't take it personally. It's just what will sell."

"How can I not take it personally? That's my whole fucking image being put out there, and the package is going to have to fit the song." She was right, in a way. I was already picturing her in something like what Olivia Newton-John wore at the end of *Grease*.

"But the fact is, you can still project that image, but with strength and maturity. Don't let Chester give that to some twenty-year-old pop tart," I said, momentarily forgetting that I was just over twenty myself.

Chester was delighted that I liked the song. "Of course, that's a rough mix. I'll need to rework some things with ML, make it a little more radio-friendly and not so late-night-after-hours-club. On a dance song, you want a couple of mixes."

Sally gave me a pleading look. "Come on, I can't do that song. I'd rather do the schlocky one."

"But I think that will be a hit, Sally. Then we can have the freedom to do whatever we want after that."

"You mean whatever *I* want," she said sharply, suddenly in a bargaining mood. "Well, if I do it, I don't want that to be the only message. If we're doing an EP of three songs, I want to show other sides of myself on the other two songs."

"Perhaps I can do something with 'I Still Have What it Takes,'" Chester said, his mood brightening at the thought of a co-credit and more money coming his way.

"And for the third song, I want to cover a ballad. Something classic that shows I can interpret a song," Sally said.

My smile remained frozen on my face. I didn't think that was the right direction, but what could I do? I couldn't have her walking out on my investment; I had to make some concession to her happiness. "Okay, deal," I said. "For now, let's work with the basic track on 'Grind' and see if we can nail down a vocal."

As the afternoon wore on, the old pro that was Sally did her part. She must have sung that thing a few dozen times. Chester kept cheerleading and doing a grind in front of her while she sang, and with that Sally was able to gain a sense of humor doing the song. ML remained quietly amused in his booth, adding this and that to the mix, experimenting with new sounds. It didn't take long for me to want to grind with Sally myself, so convincing was the performance.

At last, I called an end to the session. Since we were only rehearsing one song, it seemed silly to keep paying expensive studio time when ML could cut her a scratch demo to practice with at home. "Chester, you work on a mix for 'I Still Have What it Takes' and Sally and I will go through some music to try to come up with the cover song," I advised.

"I'll write you out a contract," Chester said. "I want half songwriting credit if I'm doing the melody and the mix."

"But we gave you a melody," I argued.

"It ain't down on paper. What, you think I'm a magician? I have to arrange that in some way. I'll take a music credit rather than charge you an hourly fee to do that."

"Let's have our lawyers iron that out."

"Are you crazy? You involve the lawyers at this point, they'll be the only ones making any money. Shit!"

"He's right about that," Sally said. "I lost more money fighting my contract release than I would have lost had I just walked away."

"Send me your contract and I'll look at it," I told Chester.

"Let's not get too bogged down. The important thing is getting product out there. If it sells, then we can haggle. Then there's something to haggle about."

We left, agreeing that we'd talk soon about a recording session. There was so much to do, but things seemed to be moving along. I could feel that dream turning to reality and Sally was as ready as I was.

CHAPTER TEN

▼

I was back in Scranton for a quick couple of days that week, to turn in a paper and grab a few more things from my apartment. The following weekend would be Easter and the beginning of a weeklong spring break for me. It was perfect timing for our plans. We got a good deal on a rehearsal studio for the Saturday before Easter, a long weekend when many of the local New Yorkers were out of town. Sally had stayed in New York that week. She'd wanted to get reacquainted with her town, she said. I was reluctant to leave her alone. It was weird: I was fresh out of college and she'd had a whole career and life in New York, but I felt protective of her.

On Good Friday, Marcus had the early part of the evening off and the three of us decided to go out to a piano bar called Nostalgia in the West Village. We didn't want to stay out too late because of the studio session the next day, but it was a chance to relax and a chance for Sally to maybe sing a song or two, to try out her chops on more standard fare for that crucial third song on the EP. Sally told me she'd spent Wednesday at the Lincoln Center Library looking through stacks of old music.

Marcus told us Nostalgia was a historic place that had been there for decades. It certainly looked that way. It was a hole in the wall on one of those tiny back streets that only the locals and the most adventurous tourists ever find. You walked into these old black double doors and down a few steps to a small room with an L-shaped bar and a few round black tables with chairs crowded around them. The ceiling sagged, a couple of the dim light bulbs that circled the bar were out, and there were a few worn holes in the dark tile floor. It was early when we arrived, maybe seven, so there were only a handful of people seated at the bar, but apparently the place was jam-packed late at night. Even at that hour, there was a jolly, balding piano player named Bill working the small crowd from behind a well-tuned upright. A microphone was affixed in front of him and another standing mike was next to the piano, rimmed by a single cheap spotlight, for use by the singing staff or a guest vocalist. The piano player was good—I mean, *really* good—which made me realize that if he was working this shift, someone even better came in to work the big crowds. Shit, there was a lot of talent in New York.

We casually approached the bar. The three of us made a total of about ten in the place, so introductions were made all around. Most seemed to be regulars, older gay guys, but I remember the bartender, Jody, a blond guy with a beak-like nose and a nasal voice who had a sarcastic joke about everything. He wasn't that old, maybe his thirties, but he had a beer gut that looked kind of odd with his skinny arms and legs. Then there was Sierra, an older black woman who planted herself at the corner of the bar closest to the wall—come to think of it, like Sally's seat at Fat Bo's; it must have been the diva seat—sipping her Makers and ginger. We learned that she had been in about a half dozen Broadway shows and she also worked at Nostalgia on the late shift and was kind of a local legend. It seemed working behind the bar wasn't enough for her and she liked to come in during slow happy hours to prime herself with liquor and relax and tell her admirers stories of her triumphs and dramas so many years before. She dropped first names constantly throughout her tales—Liza, Nina, Chaka, Luther, Rosie—that left no doubt as to who she was talking about. After one such story, the three of us took our drinks and went to one of the small tables.

"With those connections, I wonder why she's working here," I said.

"I tried to tell you: A lot of endings aren't happy," Sally answered. "She's like the Broadway version of me."

"No, you're going to make it," I said, perhaps a bit too eagerly.

"And Sierra probably has another comeback or two in her as well," Marcus said, probably trying to make me feel better. Looking at Sierra, I had my doubts.

"I can't believe I lived here all these years and never knew about this place," Sally said.

"Different circles," Marcus offered.

We chatted aimlessly for a while, listening to the songs and playful sniping back and forth at the bar. After about an hour, Sierra rose from her seat and announced that she needed to have dinner and that she'd be back in about an hour to start her shift behind the bar. Only after Sierra left did Sally graciously approach Bill with her music.

She had chosen a rare old song that neither Marcus nor I knew, but after she showed it to Bill, he apologized to her by saying, "That's one of Sierra's songs." Apparently a big no-no around there.

"To hell with Sierra," Jody blurted out in his lame-trumpet voice. He then sharply pointed his finger into each face around the bar. "Any of you queens tell Sierra I said that and you'll never get a free drink in here again!" Everybody laughed, then turned to Sally and urged her to sing the song.

Sally smiled and took up the challenge as Bill began the intro. It was a slow, brooding ballad and as she began singing her eyes were glistening. *Everything must change/Nothing stays the same/The young become the old/And mysteries do unfold . . .*

Again, it wasn't a perfect vocal that sold the song, but the heartfelt delivery from someone who had lived a life and had nothing left to lose. When she finished, the small crowd stomped and hollered for more.

Marcus whispered to me. "That's your ticket. She should be playing the Algonquin, not this dance club stuff."

I resented his interference but let it pass for the moment. "Well, we can put a song like that on the EP to see what kind of reaction it gets, but we need to play to her base first. Besides, we have a killer dance track that is going to burn up the charts!"

Sally followed up with "Black Velvet," which also went over well. I had to wonder, though, if these old queens were any kind of market. Did they still buy CDs or download songs? Besides that, when Bill had introduced her to the audience as Sally Testata, nobody seemed aware of her previous fame. Sally returned to the table, satisfied with her performance. "I'm starting to feel good about it again, like in the old days, before everything got fucked up," she said.

"It's not going to get fucked up this time," I assured her. Finishing my drink, I said, "Well, let's get out of here. It's been a good night, but we have a long day tomorrow."

"Oh, let's have one more," Sally said, appreciative of her new fans, all drunks.

I put my foot down. "No, not tonight. There will be plenty of time for that later. We need to make a good recording and move into the future."

She playfully nudged Marcus while speaking to me. "Honey, you're the only one here with a future. I've already had several. But cheers," she said, lifting her glass, "to one more future! And one more drink!" She strode over to the bar and ordered another one and then continued on to the bathroom.

"She's a real character," Marcus commented. "You will have your hands full with her."

"I can handle her," I said, although I had my doubts.

"It looks like she just handled you."

"Trust me, she'll get into the studio tomorrow and be good as new."

"Uh-huh," he said self-righteously. He was becoming a real prick. "Well, I have to get back and get ready for my gig at Stereo," he said, standing. "Say good-bye to Sally for me." He dropped a ten on the table. God forbid he should buy me a drink.

Sally seemed disappointed he'd left when she came back from the bath-room, but stayed standing at the bar talking to her new friends. I casually walked over to stand next to her.

A silver-haired guy who had been talking to Sally squeezed my ass. "Nice."

"Hey, hey, hey," I raised my voice, pushing his hand away. "I'm straight."

"Sorry, I didn't mean any offense," he said. "You still have a nice ass."

Sally snaked her arm around my waist. "Yes, he does. But hands off, boys, he's mine." They whooped it up, evidently impressed that she had landed me. I so wanted to get out of there. I wished I could have taken her at her word, too, but she had been withholding herself from me lately, pretty much since we'd arrived in New York. I wondered what was up with that.

"Well, then prove it to me," I said without humor. "Let's go."

She pulled a cherry out of the nearby condiment tray and, holding the stem, lowered it into her mouth, biting off the fruit between her front teeth. "I don't have to prove myself to anybody," she growled, staring me down. The guys cheered her again.

"Sally, we need to go. We're in the recording studio tomorrow," I explained to her new friends, who seemed reluctant to let her go. That, of course, opened up a whole new round of interest and questions, wasting more time.

A half hour later, I managed to get her out of there after a long good-bye with her kissing everyone in the room. We grabbed a cab over on Hudson Street and headed uptown.

"I didn't come back to New York to go to bed at ten o'clock every night," she told me.

"You can do what you want when you've established your career. Right now, you're on my time and my dime," I said. As soon as I'd spoken, I had the frightening realization that I sounded like my mother. "I'm sorry—" I began.

Sally held up her hand to silence me. "No problem, I hear you."

We rode in silence the rest of the way. Back in the apartment, I didn't dare ask her to join me in bed and she didn't offer. She made herself a quick snack, said goodnight, and retreated to her room, slamming the door just a little too loudly for my comfort.

CHAPTER ELEVEN

▼

It turned out that Sally got up even before I did. I thought she was still in her room as I was fixing coffee for myself, but she came in the front door, wearing a track suit, her hair pulled back. "I walked up to the marina and back," she chirped. On the upper west side, it was easily three or four miles round trip.

"Great," I said. It seemed she had forgotten about the night before, so I didn't want to say anything that might reopen a wound. "I'm looking forward to today."

"Me, too. I'll go shower and get ready." She went back to her room to start her morning routine and I breathed a sigh of relief.

We had a lockout rate on the studio starting at noon, which basically means a lump sum rate for the whole day rather than an hourly charge. That was good in the sense that I didn't have to be looking at my watch all day long counting both the hours and how many dollars were slipping through my fingers. It wasn't so good in the sense that we had the entire day to record two songs, the basic tracks of which had already been recorded, so there was no sense of urgency at getting the task done. Chester Sweethouse took his sweet time getting there, arriving around one o'clock. In the meantime, ML had been setting up mikes and cables and testing sound levels and chatting with Sally. I was the executive producer of this whole affair, but you'd think I was the tag-along nephew for all the respect and attention I was given.

Chester came in with his usual high-spiritedness, cheerleading from the start and giving a warm welcome to everyone except me. He casually handed me a one-page document, the songwriter/producer contract.

"What's this? You're charging me eight hundred dollars for use of the tracks? But you're making money as a producer and getting songwriter royalties on the song," I protested.

"Yes, but I spent a lot of time and money on those tracks. I have to protect my property. You have access to the tracks and could do whatever you want with them."

"So what you're telling me is you've created your own licensing fee beyond the legal licensing fee?"

Chester rolled his eyes. "This is standard practice. We're all independent contractors, freelancers. We're not Warner Brothers, in case you hadn't noticed."

"He's right," Sally piped up. "If we were part of a major label, they'd be deducting for God knows what. That's what I found out when I tried to sue for being dropped from my label. Their lawyers were able to prove that everybody from Clive Davis to the janitor lost money because of me."

"Everyone except the lawyers," Chester corrected.

"But you want a fee for use of the track as well as a music-writing credit for 'I Still Have What it Takes.'"

"And a producer's fee for the work I do today and with the mixing. Now you're catching on," Chester said, unruffled. "You are free to go elsewhere and find a better deal, if you think you can."

I think I could have found a better deal. Chester alone was costing me two thousand dollars for the day with that added fee, plus whatever royalties he would collect later. And yet, he had me. There we were, already in the studio and time was ticking by. If I abandoned everything on principle then, I'd lose all the studio money and have to start over with everything. The time and money spent rebooking everything and finding a new team would be too much at this point.

"Okay, okay," I said, throwing up my hands. "Time is wasting. Let's get this done." I scribbled my signature on his lousy contract.

"Now you're talking," Chester said. "We need to get this product out."

"I'm not a fucking product," Sally snapped.

ML was on the other side of a large glass window, seated in front of a massive soundboard with knobs and graphics and whatnot. He seemed amused by all of our bickering. Gary, a guy in his forties with wavy, shoulder-length hair that he kept pushing out of his face, was brought in to man the synthesizer, in case we wanted to add new sounds. He was all business and didn't seem to want to socialize with any of us. Fine with me. Basically, it was just the five of us, although two female backup singers would come in later that night to lay down some vocal tracks.

I thought things were going well for the first couple of hours as Sally began her vocals for "Grind," but then she kept doubting herself and wanting take after take. Then Chester wanted to add more instrumental to the track, like strings and horns. It was beginning to sound like a fucking orchestra.

"I don't know, Chester," I said. "I think we need to pare it down, not beef it up."

ML unexpectedly allied himself with me. "Kind of like a deep tribal groove," he suggested.

"Oh, yeah, I like it deep," Sally said and she and ML exchanged looks and a laugh.

Chester laughed along. "Sal, you have to sing that line into the song, as a riff: *I like it deep, yeah, I like it deep,*" he demonstrated.

"This will never get on the radio," Sally said.

"Well, we can clean it up for the radio version," I said.

"Been down that road before," Sally reminded us.

So then ML took out the strings, then the horns, then the piano, then added bongos and a heavier bass line. It ended up being practically the same track we started with, but it seemed to do the trick. In her little booth, Sally was writhing around to the music as she sang, eyes closed, and for a minute I thought she was going to give head to the microphone dangling in front of her lips.

It was well after six by the time we all felt satisfied with "Grind," cheering ourselves for making a hit record. Then Chester wanted to order in food. The studio was windowless, so there was a weird feeling that time had stood still. I suggested pizza, but they all looked at me like I was crazy. Ultimately, we ordered from some upscale diner and Chester got the most expensive seafood entrée he could find. By the time the meal was delivered and eaten—a total of a hundred and fifty bucks, with tip—another two hours had passed where little was done. It was time to start on "I Still Have What it Takes" and we hadn't even heard Chester's new track yet.

The track wasn't bad, but again Chester had overproduced it to a lush, strings-filled seventies disco feel, not at all what I wanted. We played around with it some more and eventually came up with something we liked. Sally, now complaining of being tired, was ready to start singing her vocal track at about ten o'clock. The song was more vocally challenging and Chester, for all his faults, pushed and coaxed her every step of the way with unflagging energy. Sally produced.

The two backup singers, a blonde with a nose ring and a busty black girl, had been waiting for quite some time and they complained that now that it was after midnight, they were onto a second day and wanted more pay. Then ML, in a more humble way, looked at me with a puppy dog look and said, "You know, that's true. It's another day. The union would pay us another day." I just wanted to get out of there, eventually, with two hit songs, so I relented and my fee for personnel literally doubled overnight. I felt all I was there for was to write checks while they had fun with their toys.

Finally, we were ready to wrap it up at about four a.m. Chester said he was starving and suggested we hit an all-night diner, and he magnanimously invited the backup girls as well. At my expense, of course—another hundred and fifty, with tip. Man, that guy could pack it away. Sally seemed to be coming off her diet, too, loading up with a burger and fries. She sat next to ML on one side while Chester and I sat on the other and the backup girls sat on the ends. Only Gary didn't join us but he asked if he could order something to go—why the hell not? We congratulated ourselves on a job well done.

It was still dark when we left the diner. Chester and ML took separate cabs going downtown. Sally and I started walking up Second Avenue. We were about to walk west to Third to catch an uptown cab when Sally noticed a few people crossing in front of us to walk up some steps. She let her gaze follow them, then looked up. "Oh, my God, it's a church," she said, delighted. "It's Easter, Greg! There's a sunrise service!"

For the life of me, I couldn't understand why it was giving her such a thrill, especially since we'd been up and working hard for twenty hours or so. "So it is," I said, getting ready to cross the street.

"Let's go to the service," she said, grabbing my hand.

I looked at the name of the church. "It's not a Catholic church."

"So what. God doesn't care. This is a sign that my mother is watching over me."

Sally was nothing if not unpredictable. Reluctantly, I followed her up the steps into the sanctuary. A middle-aged woman greeted us warmly as she handed us a program. The space was pretty big, with a wide center aisle and two aisles down each side. We chose to sit on the left side. It wasn't very crowded, maybe thirty people or so, but they seemed to be alert and overly friendly.

Throughout the service, I was more interested in watching Sally out of the corner of my eye, seeing yet another side of her character. She enthusiastically sang along on the hymns and closed her eyes tightly during the prayers. A male soloist sang a Christian pop number of some kind, with words to the effect of rising again and not being kept on the ground. To me, it was more lame than anything Chester ever wrote—even my mother would turn her nose up at such Protestant sentimentality—but there was Sally, tears running down her cheeks, the same woman who was moaning to "Grind" only hours before.

A red-haired woman in a plain green dress walked to the podium, offered an earnest smile that showed the deep character lines on her face, and began her homily.

"'Mary, why are you weeping?' the angels asked the woman sitting at the tomb. It's a question we might ask each other today: Why are you weeping?" She let her eyes scan the small crowd to see each one of us. "And we can find many of our own answers: I am weeping for a war that seems to have no purpose and no end … I am weeping for an Earth that is decaying because of our thoughtless actions … I am weeping for the corruption of government that makes us feel cynical and without hope … I am weeping for a celebrity culture that offers no spiritual values for our children to admire." She paused again for effect, and then spoke just above a whisper. "Or I can weep for my own failings: my addictions, my inability to stand up for what is right, my unwillingness to help those around me who have less, my incapacity to recognize help and hope when it is offered. Because, you see, Mary was so caught up in her own grief that she didn't recognize Jesus himself when He appeared and asked, 'Mary, why are you weeping? Who are you looking for?' Who are *you* looking for today? Will you recognize God when He speaks to you? Thankfully, Mary did eventually recognize God and when He said to her, 'Don't cling to me, but go and tell the others,' she didn't hesitate. She found new hope and a new purpose in life, and she became Jesus's first ambassador."

The message went on a bit longer, but I lost the words as I became distracted by Sally's near sobbing beside me. I awkwardly put my hand on her hunched shoulders. Sally as political protester was one thing, but Sally as Christian martyr was quite another. I wasn't quite sure how this transformation was going to fit into the big picture.

As we left the church, receiving blessings and kind thanks from the parishioners, Sally thanked me for agreeing to go to the service with her. "And one more thing," she mentioned casually as we settled into the back of a cab, "I don't think I can go along with releasing 'Grind.'"

CHAPTER TWELVE

"You *what?*" I screamed. I'm sure the last thing the cab driver wanted to hear at the end of his midnight shift on Easter morning was a heated argument from the back seat, but after a long, costly day in the studio—between all the rental fees and personnel costs, about four thousand dollars—and dealing with the whims of Chester Sweethouse, staying up all night, and then being dragged to a church service, Sally's sudden devil-may-care comment brought me to the breaking point.

"I'm not comfortable with it. That's why the session took so long. I just don't want that to be my image."

"Weren't you accusing me of being from a monastery a while back?" I reminded her. "Now, after an Easter service, you want to play a nun?"

"That has nothing to do with it. I have no problem with my sexuality or my spirituality. If they don't go together for you, that's your own Catholic guilt. I just don't want to be marketed as a sex object. Or *product*, as Chester says. Been there, done that." She was serenely looking out over the gently rippling waters of the Hudson River as we sped up the West Side Highway. "God has another plan for me."

"Perhaps you could have said something about it long before we got into the studio and spent all that time and money," I said, scowling.

"I did, in so many words. You didn't listen."

I let a moment pass while I considered my next move. "We have an agreement and I am the executive producer and owner of the record label. We are releasing 'Grind' and that's all there is to it."

"Fine. Release it. But I'll be damned if I'm going to be performing it live in front of a bunch of sweaty, shouting men."

"Trust me, those sweaty, shouting men are not going to want you. They'll be wanting each other. Don't you know who your market is?"

"Yes, I know who my market is. I'm sure 'Grind' is going to be such a wonderful message for those Ecstasy-popping club kids."

"You never struck me as someone who felt the need to deliver a message." We had reached our building and Sally slid out of the car as I paid the fare.

"Well, maybe I'm changing." She strode purposefully toward the front door, forcing me to run to catch up.

"Let's establish a hit, first, then we'll move in whatever direction you want to go." I felt myself caving in order to keep this project going.

We were huffing and puffing by the time we reached our apartment on the fourth floor. "I can hardly wait to see what you come up with for the video," she said sarcastically.

"Yeah, I need to put some thought into that." I realized that would be a touchy project as well.

After all the drama of the preceding twenty-four hours, I was physically exhausted but mentally still keyed up. I figured sex would relax me enough to be able to sleep. I reached over to help Sally pull off her top.

"Whoa, boy!" She pushed my arms away. "Are you insane? I'm in no condition for all of that right now."

"I just need to relax, Sally. You don't have to do much, I'll do most of the work."

"Well, as flattering as that offer is," she said drily, "I think I'll pass. You can do your business in the bathroom, using whatever *products* you need." She had to emphasize the word, get in her dig one more time.

"Sally, you know you are not a product to me. You are a real person, full of life, sexy and smart. If you weren't exciting to me in every way, there is no way I'd have gone to all this trouble. I believe in you. I believe in me. I believe in us."

"That's wonderful, Greg," she said, touching my face. "But it may take more than belief and even hard work. And if it doesn't work out, then what?"

"But it will. It *will*." I couldn't seem to conceive of failure.

Sally said nothing, but reached down and began stroking me through my jeans. She didn't need to say anything; that's just what I needed.

* * *

After we woke up late that afternoon, we leisurely took our showers and then went out for a stroll around the neighborhood. Eventually, we had dinner at the Film Center Café. It was a rare evening when it was just the two of us, and I forced myself to not talk about business, for once. Unfortunately, I found it hard to make conversation about anything else.

Sally broke the silence as dinner was served. "I don't know why my mother is so important to me now. She becomes more important as time goes by."

I thought of my fiasco with my mother back in February. I hadn't spoken with her since then. "Uh-huh," was all I could manage to say.

"She let my father dictate how her life was going to be, like many Christian women of that era. Or this, I suppose. But I think she had her proudest and most Christian moment when she finally showed my father the door at sixty years of age. She told me she had a sudden realization that when Jesus said, 'Love others as you love yourself,' that he meant that you can only fully love others *if* you love yourself. And she hadn't loved herself by staying with an abusive man." She stabbed a cherry tomato with her fork. "See, most people get it wrong: They love others in the same way that they love themselves, which is to say they don't love properly! Because who loves themselves? Nobody!"

"Yeah," I said out of politeness.

"You'll understand someday. After you've had a few failures, you'll start beating yourself up and then it's a long journey back to loving yourself."

Sally was turning into more than I bargained for—one minute like a sex-crazed stripper, the next a New Age Christian. I preferred the former. "I think you'll learn to love yourself more when you're back in your game," I reasoned. "Living in Scranton and cleaning houses couldn't have been doing much for your confidence."

"And yet there was peace and a chance to reexamine myself, take stock."

"What did you discover?"

"Not a damn thing. I don't think I was there yet. Then you came into my life like a tornado." She smiled and lifted her glass to toast. "And baby, I'm not sure if it was God or the devil who sent you."

"I'd prefer to think of it as good fortune, without the religion."

We spent the rest of the meal engaged in small talk and commenting on some of the music videos that were being shown on the hanging TV monitors. I seemed to have her back in my corner by the end of dinner, but I had a feeling it would be a daily battle.

As we were walking by the bar on our way out, a man turned on his bar stool and reached out to touch Sally on the arm. "Well, I'll be damned!" he said, surprised, a big grin on his face.

Sally turned to him. "Well, well, well. If it isn't Eddie Pearl, the beginning and end of my music career." She leaned in to give him an air kiss on each cheek, then introduced us. "Eddie, this is my new manager, Greg Bounder. Greg, Eddie Pearl."

"Well, I can't believe it, girl. I never thought I'd see you again."

"I think you tried to make sure of that," Sally said. It was a slap, but delivered with a good-natured smile, as if to let bygones be bygones.

"You know, Sal, that was the hardest decision of my life. But let me buy you both a drink, as a peace offering." He pulled us into his fold. There was one empty seat next to him and I stood between them. Eddie Pearl was a short, wiry man with curly gray hair and an expensive, glossy silver button-down shirt open too far, halfway down his sunken, hairy chest. A miniature gold Grammy award emblem hung from a chain around his neck. He wore designer jeans that no self-respecting straight guy should wear, and black, pointed boots. He had those fake, gleaming white teeth that look ridiculous on a man his age and he never stopped smiling. In short, he was everything you'd think a sleazy manager would look like.

"So, new manager, eh?" Eddie continued, giving me the once-over. "You look like an up-and-comer, Greg."

"I guess you could say that," I said.

"He has big plans for me; I can hardly believe it myself," Sally said, all of a sudden eager to show off to Eddie. "We just spent all day in the recording studio yesterday."

"No kidding! What kind of songs are you doing?"

I felt I had to take charge. "We're going to keep it under wraps for a little while, but let's just say we have a new dance song that's going to make 'Bombs Away' Sally's second-biggest hit."

Eddie threw back his head and laughed, one of those rat-a-tat laughs that sounds like a machine gun, very annoying. "Sally, it looks like you found yourself a young firecracker."

"That I did," Sally said, then motioned for us to raise our glasses in another toast. "To new beginnings." After a sip, she continued. "And what about you, Eddie? Is that Grammy the closest you've gotten to the real thing?"

Eddie, undaunted by Sally's continued bitchiness toward him, answered, "You're goddamned right it is. My big star, Olive Martini, won a Grammy for best dance recording last year and bought this for me. Real gold." He caressed the emblem in his fingers.

"Olive Martini?" Sally scoffed. "You've got to be kidding me."

"I guess you're not keeping up with the latest music news. Olive Martini has been a sensation in the clubs. She's a drag queen, but this one doesn't lip-synch, she can really sing. And writes, too. Her first hit, 'With a Twist,' went number one and got her the Grammy. It was actually a witty song about a gal who swings both ways."

"Did it cross over? I'm not familiar with the song," I said.

"Greg, you want to play in the big leagues, you got to know what's out there," the prick said, patronizingly. "No, there was no crossover. Very rare for a dance song to hit the pop charts any more. But nowadays music is just part of the package, a tease to something bigger. Kids today download songs, they don't buy CDs. With Olive, we didn't even record a CD to sell, just promo copies for the club and a downloadable single. Right now, we're trying to figure out a follow-up, but in the meantime Olive has recognition and that's getting her endorsement deals and appearances on VH1 and club appearances across the country." Eddie talked fast. He was the kind of guy who had an answer for everything.

"Sounds like you're doing well," Sally said.

"Never better. I got a girl, Josie Hernandez, who's breaking into soaps. She's gonna be huge, huge!" Eddie paused to stuff his mouth with peanuts. Still chewing, he said, "But it wasn't like coming up with you, Sal. Those were the hungry years for both of us. We had some memories, didn't we?"

Sally allowed herself to smile, her eyes taking on a far-off glow as she stared at the bottles on the shelf behind the bar. "God, yes. Remember when you finally got a distribution deal for Pillow Talk and you were so happy you rented the stretch limo and about a dozen of us rode around Manhattan all night blasting our music through the sunroof? That was about the most fun I've ever had." They both laughed and sipped their drinks. "Sometimes the anticipation ends up being more fun than the real thing, right?"

"Yeah. You know, I don't let myself think big and expect much anymore. Then when something happens, you can actually enjoy it. Like, who knew a fucking drag queen named Olive Martini would be my return ticket to the top? You know," Eddie went on, turning unusually serious, "When our deal fell through and your career went south after 'Bombs Away,' you weren't the only one who suffered, Sal. You were my big act at that time. Besides you, I was basically booking jugglers and clowns for private parties."

"Then why did you let her go?" I asked, feeling superior.

"Sally wasn't a juggler or clown. She had a track record and then a hit record. The cost of keeping her and investing in her for another go seemed prohibitive." He put on the game-show-host smile again. "But, hey, it looks like it all worked out for the best, right?"

"Yes it did," I said. "I can't thank you enough for letting her go."

"Yeah, well, you can thank the schmuck," Sally said, laughing a little bitterly. "I'm gonna hold a grudge until I'm back on top again."

"That shouldn't be too long," Eddie said. "You look damn good, Sally."

We finished our drinks and Eddie handed each of us his business card. "I want to know what happens, Sal," he said.

"Oh, you'll know," I promised him, "And it won't be because she has to call and tell you."

Eddie pointed his finger at me like a gun and winked at Sally. "Hold onto this one. He may be the one to take you around the world."

"The world is my oyster, isn't that what they say?" Sally winked back, gingerly lifting one of the mucousy appetizers from a tray on the bar and easing it into her open mouth. "But you should read the news, Eddie. Oysters are now considered dangerous."

CHAPTER THIRTEEN

▼

I had decided to call my company ScranNY Multimedia Enterprises. ScranNY was short for Scranton-New York, the direction both Sally and I were taking. I came up with this really cool logo that had a mountain, representing the mountains surrounding Scranton, that then seamlessly became a New York skyline, with miniature skyscrapers that kind of looked like the Chrysler Building and the Empire State Building. The word "ScranNY" ran under the scene and "Multimedia Enterprises" in smaller letters under "ScranNY." Getting a professional logo designed so that it can appear on all your products was not cheap, by the way. A cool grand, to be exact. "You're branding an image," the designer assured me as I wrote out the check.

I had further decided to incorporate as an S Corporation in New York at the urging of my accountant because I would have more flexibility in being able to roll over losses from year to year. It's not that I expected any losses, but he showed me how quickly my expenses were mounting up—as I wrote him a check for filing and accounting fees, nine hundred fifty bucks. The tax burden in New York would be greater, but I could also write off the New York apartment as an office, the travel back and forth, and probably even a bunch of meals. As my business grew, I was obviously expecting to find a bigger pool of talent out of New York. I mean, really—did I want to keep scouting bars in Scranton for talent?

The idea to go with Multimedia Enterprises was because I didn't want to limit myself to just music, or even to just Sally. It was a name that could serve as an umbrella for many business ventures. Sally was the tip of the iceberg, as far as I was concerned.

That week after Easter, as I said, was a vacation week for me, so I was able to stay in New York and continue business. I called promoters and distributors and sent a teaser press release to some of the smaller nightlife rags to alert them that Sally Testata was coming back. I checked out pricing on various manufacturers and looked at Web sites where I might be able to sell downloads of our songs. I called a pianist that Marcus recommended for the third track of the EP. Sally and I decided to go with "Everything Must Change" for that track. The message of the lyric seemed to fit her and, for Sally, signaled to the listening public that even she must change—don't get used to the same old sex symbol/dance diva. That message was important to her. We would do just a piano/vocal track, which would showcase her vocal expressiveness without all the bombast of the dance tracks. For me, it was the throwaway track to appease her.

At one point during the week, my mother had left a message on my cell phone: "Hello, Greg. It's your mother. I have spoken to Marcus and he tells me how hard you are working with this Sally person, and that it is counting as an internship for school as well. Your father thinks it may be a good experience for you and I am inclined to agree with him. I am willing to put our February disagreement behind us. Please call when you get a chance. I would welcome the opportunity to meet Sally if you should want to bring her to Philadelphia. Good-bye, now." Right! Can you imagine my mother and Sally in the same room? This message was my mother in her kind and gentle mode but I wasn't fooled; it only meant that she wanted something else—first and foremost to be all into my business. I wasn't about to call her right back but I was trying to figure out how I could get the latest angle in the ongoing drama with my mother to my advantage. It would require the strategy of a four-star general.

Anyway, while I was working my ass off that week, Sally was getting reacquainted with her city. Every night it was, "I'm going to meet So-and-So for a drink," and that it was important for her old crowd to know she was back. I couldn't really stop her as she was using her own money for those outings. I hadn't realized she was so eager to be back in touch with her New York friends—I didn't know she'd had any. In Scranton, she claimed to have never missed them. Towards the end of the week I had to yell at her for coming home drunk and stumbling up the four flights. "This can't be what this is all about," is how I began my tirade, and it ended with her crying and promising never to do it again, and then falling dead asleep until halfway through the next day.

I had to go back to Scranton the next week to at least show up at a class or two but Sally seemed to have no desire to go back with me. Of course I worried about her the whole week and called her nightly. She rarely returned my calls—which made me nuts—but when she did, she was as chipper as ever.

We managed to record the third song in a smaller studio near the end of April and, to my relief, the session only took a couple of hours. Sally laid down the track without much effort and it was damn good. Chester had offered to come in to coach and produce the session—for a fee, of course—

but I declined. I figured I could tell a good vocal when I heard it and thereby get my own first producing credit—for a mere five hundred bucks, as it turned out.

So, the recording part was finished by the end of April. I would send it to another specialist to do the mastering—a day's work which would cost about another grand—then it would be ready for downloading and pressing hard copies. But before that, I had to set up the promotional arm of the operation so we could hit the ground running. I needed a promoter to get the song to clubs and radio; as manager, I would handle the publicity until I felt it absolutely necessary to hire a publicist, and I would book Sally for gigs. Marcus could certainly help with that in the dance clubs.

For promotion, I turned to Gus Vanderwall. He had a great reputation in the business and I knew he was not going to come cheap. I knew, though, that however good the product was, if you couldn't market it and sell it, it was as good as dead. I'd have to spend more on publicity and promotion than on the actual making of the recording itself.

I met Gus at his office in midtown, on a high floor of one of those nondescript skyscrapers. As soon as I sat on the leather sofa and as he took a seat opposite me across an expansive glass coffee table, he began talking and it was obvious he had done his homework.

"Sally Testata is going to be a tough sell. She'll have a cult following but kids your age don't know who she is. And she's closer to Madonna's generation and she's going to be competing with the teenagers." This brought on a lecture. "Jesus, they tart 'em up and shove them out there at fifteen nowadays. Most of them are closer to porn stars than actual singers. In my day, it didn't matter what you looked like. Fat like Mama Cass or skinny like Karen Carpenter, it didn't matter. They could sing and sell records. Now my daughter's a teenager and she wants to sing. Everybody wants to sing, for Christ's sake." He pulled out his wallet and showed me a photo of his daughter. She was very pretty, with long blonde hair.

"Very nice," I told him.

"Oh, yeah, she's got the look. I just wish I could get her to go into business. A good-looking singer, a dime a dozen. But an attractive girl who can sell you something, now that's money in the bank."

"Don't you think singers are trying to sell you something?"

"Yeah, sex, sex, and more sex. I'm in the business of selling it. You can see why I don't want my daughter in it." Gus reached into a cabinet next to his chair and pulled out a smooth wooden box. He opened it to reveal a row of fancy cigars. "Have a cigar. These came right from Cuba," he said, holding the box in front of me.

"Oh, no, thank you," I said as he lit one up for himself.

"So," Gus began, "Sally Testata was quite the looker in her day. Has she still got it?"

"Yeah, she still has it. I think she can compete." The truth is, I thought she could still stand to lose ten or fifteen pounds, mostly in the hips.

"What are you doing for publicity photos, for the CD cover?"

Damn! In all the planning, I had completely forgotten about the photos! How could I do anything without photos, an image to project? "We just had a photo session," I lied. "We tried a number of things. They haven't come back yet."

"Uh-huh. I like the songs." I had sent him a copy of the songs in advance of our meeting. "If 'Grind' is the one you're pushing, you definitely have to do something provocative for a cover. Shit, if she's really looking hot, maybe you can push her to some of the men's magazines to hype up some publicity that will also pay the two of you."

I laughed uncomfortably. "I don't think Sally would really go for that."

"You're probably right. Easier to talk a twenty-year-old into that than someone twice that age. Still, the song ain't Julie Andrews." *Who the hell is Julie Andrews?* I wondered. Gus leaned back and exhaled a plume of smoke toward the ceiling and looked out the window behind me at the East River and Queens beyond. He was about fifty years old, but he took care of himself: The blond hair was slicked back and perfectly parted on one side; his nails looked manicured; his skin had the orange glow of one who travels to Arizona just to play golf. In his suit, he looked more like a CEO than someone in the music business. In his way, he stood out from those who were younger and more hip looking, and everyone still listened to what he had to say. I sat in silence, watching him consider. Finally, he announced, "I think this can work. 'Grind' is a bit risqué for mainstream radio, even these days, but I think that she's older and doing it can actually make her stand apart. Like she can be the elder sex symbol. I mean, young guys would still want her, right?" He winked at me as he sucked on the cigar and I felt a hot flush of blood rush to my face.

"Yes, sir, for sure."

"Call me Gus." He put down the cigar. "So, you are okay with my fee?"

"Yes, of course." I was so aware of his fee—twelve thousand a month, with a three-month minimum guarantee—but also aware that he could make a hit out of "Mary Had a Little Lamb" if he wanted to.

"Great. I'll have my secretary give you our standard contract when you leave. Now, as soon as you have that shrink-wrapped CD in your hot little hands, you get that right over to me. I'll need about five hundred copies to start. Let me know about two weeks in advance of the shipment, and I'll start on the phone calls."

We spent another few minutes in chitchat and then I left. I was in deep at that point; there was no turning back. My heart was pounding with adrenaline as I walked west across Midtown. I was going faster than the lumbering buses. I was a real New Yorker and part of the music business. Could it get any better than that?

CHAPTER FOURTEEN

▼

To my surprise, Sally was pretty excited about doing a photo shoot. She was even more excited about getting a new wardrobe for the shoot, insisting that her outfits from the nineties would not be right for the new look. I had to agree with her on that.

Spring finally broke through in late April. What better time to go on a whirlwind tour of Fifth Avenue boutiques? I'm talking the high end stuff. I justified the expense by reasoning that the clothes could be used for live shows as well as television interviews. Sally had a good eye for fashion but her choices didn't quite mesh with what I had in mind for the "Grind" video or jacket photo for the EP.

Nine thousand eight hundred and seventy-five bucks later, we happily hailed a cab with our bags and headed back to the apartment. For "Grind" we agreed on a short, flimsy black dress by a designer named Marc Jacobs. It showed a lot of leg but was not too tight, so had something of a slimming effect. I decided for the cover photo I'd have her crouching, leaning up against a mirror, and looking provocatively into the camera. With one hand, she'd reach down and hold the cloth of the short skirt over her privates.

I'd scheduled the photo shoot—a photographer who was "one of the best," Marcus assured me, at nine hundred dollars per session—for the first week in May and had already sent the mastered recording off for pressing. I'd start with a run of ten thousand—I'd found a manufacturer in Florida who could do the whole package including a four-page color insert for just under fifteen thousand dollars—figuring most of the sales would be in digital downloads anyway. I had even found an independent distributor that handled international sales as well. They were willing to give my label a shot because Sally had some kind of name in the business and whatever she lacked, Gus Vanderwall's name made up for it.

Sally didn't even give me a hard time at the shoot and we came up with a lot of good poses. I think she cooperated because I'd spent so much on the clothes.

All in all, things were going well, without a lot of major drama. Of course we'd have to move very quickly. I got the quick pressing of five hundred copies of "Grind" to Gus so he could begin his onslaught. I also gave several to Marcus for him to push on his deejay friends. We could start some club airplay immediately, really, as long as the song was available for download sales.

The other thing was, we wanted to have a release party for the song the weekend before Memorial Day—the same time I was scheduled to graduate. I believed I actually would graduate, although not with honors. My grades that final semester would not be impressive—Bs and Cs—but my advisor was impressed with the documentation I was showing him on the internship. Who cared about grades at that point? My career was in launch mode.

In the meantime, I was working the press angle. I'd get the photos—which also included a couple classy headshots—just in time to send out to the rags to advertise the song release party. Plus, Gus would be working his high-octane connections. In fact, Gus wanted a bigger venue than Barracuda, but I thought we should start small but with a packed house. "It's your money," was all he said as he hung up the phone.

Speaking of money, early May was a good time for me to take stock of exactly what I was spending and what I had left. Let's see: I was paying two rents, four gym memberships (Sally's one in Scranton a complete waste, as she hadn't been back), all basic living expenses for both of us, the recording and mastering, Chester's fee, Gus's ongoing fee, manufacturing costs, press package costs, minimal—so far—attorney and accountant fees, the photo session and reproductions, a voice coach, advertising—a bare minimum at that point—moving expenses, car payments—and parking!—and whatever expenses would be associated with gigs coming up. Plus, I was advancing Sally two hundred dollars a week as an allowance for her own needs. And let's not forget meals and taxi cabs, a uniquely Manhattan lifestyle choice that sucks the cash right out of your wallet. All told, it added up to about ninety thousand bucks, nearly a fifth of my inheritance—and the product hadn't even been released yet. I'll admit, it was a little bit scary, but everything was full steam ahead. The ship had set sail and there was no stopping it. I only hoped it wouldn't be The Titanic.

I had called my mother at a time when I knew she wouldn't be home to leave her a message telling her not to bother coming to graduation, that I would not be there. My friends at U of S, like Rick and Pete, were pissed that I was blowing off graduation and the weekend of partying to follow. They certainly never understood the whole Sally thing. But while my friends were pissed, it was nothing compared to the volcanic reaction from my mother. I was treated to another message from her, and the short-lived kind and gentle demeanor of the previous message was no longer there: "Greg. How could you do this to us after we paid for your schooling? This expensive whim of yours couldn't wait another week? Well, that does it. I am coming to New York and we are going to talk this out. If you insist on skipping graduation, I will come to you."

I didn't know how I could avoid it. She didn't know where I lived, but she knew where Marcus lived and he, of course, would be a big part of the festivities at Barracuda and beyond that weekend. I'd have to ask Marcus to tell her not to come. It would be a disaster for all concerned.

I wasted no time calling Marcus. "Hey, Marcus, it's Greg. Do you know that Mother plans on coming up to New York the weekend of the release party?"

"Yeah, I know, she's already called me."

"What did you tell her?"

"What could I tell her? I told her I didn't think it was a great idea, that you had a very important weekend, but I can't keep her from doing what she wants to do. She didn't even ask to stay with me; she's staying at the Marriott."

"Oh my God. Don't tell me she's dragging Dad up here, too?"

"Oh, no, she wouldn't do that. This is her mission and she doesn't want any distractions."

"We've got to stop her."

"You've got to stop her. I've had a long life of bad relations with her. You've always been her favorite, her great straight hope. You have some capital to fight with, I don't."

"Then you've got nothing to lose."

"Come on, Greg. Be a man and deal with it. You're building a little empire, here, don't let your mother do you in."

I think the bastard wanted her to come. He was so smooth and perfect on the surface, but he wanted to see me sweat it out with the family like he had. I never completely believed his nice guy act. He hadn't gotten where he was by playing nice.

I hung up the phone. I had too much to worry about with the party itself. If my mother showed up, I'd just have to do my best to avoid her. I couldn't let her sabotage my big moment.

I called Gus and he immediately picked up the phone. "Hey, Gus, just wanted to check on how things are going on your end."

"We're covered. The song has been sent to major deejays and clubs on the east coast—Montreal, Boston, Philly, DC, Miami. We're following up with calls and now I'm hitting radio too. That will be a harder sell, but the product is good, if a bit on the raunchy side."

"Great! I also got us into Splash for the Sunday afternoon Tea Dance after the Friday night party at Barracuda."

"A one-two punch. Good going, kid. You need to start booking up summer stuff. Shouldn't be too hard since she's just making appearances, doing a few songs. Not like a concert. What about Gay Pride?"

"Locked up. Too late to get her own float this year, but I may get her a special guest spot on the Barracuda float with a couple of other artists." That was Eddie Pearl's idea, and one of the other artists was Olive Martini. I hated that he was weaseling his way into favor with Sally, but I welcomed the chance for Sally to wipe the floor with that skinny, no-talent drag queen.

"Terrific," Gus said. "We're making a go of this." In the background I heard someone speaking to him. "Listen, kid, I gotta go. I'll let you know as things start to move."

My heart was going a thousand beats a minute. I couldn't believe everything that was happening, and so fast. It was what I imagined a drug high was like but without the side effects.

Just then, Sally came in. I could tell by her frown and slow movements that she was in another one of her funks. "Where have you been, baby?" I asked.

"Oh, just over at the Chelsea Grill, having a cocktail and watching the people go by. They've opened the sidewalk café, you know."

"Cool." It was a Friday afternoon in early May, two weeks before the big party at Barracuda. I left the desk to give her a hug. "Is something wrong?"

She shrugged her shoulders. "I'm scared, Greg. I know this is all exciting for you, but I've done this before. It's scary for me."

"But look at the team you have now. Me, Marcus, Gus Vanderwall. It's going to be done right this time."

"Do you think I can spend all summer selling 'Grind' in live performances?"

"Of course you can. You're a pro, you never lose that experience."

She reached into the refrigerator and pulled out a container of macaroni salad. "I think I'd feel better if I had a coach."

"You mean, besides the voice coach?" Did the expenses ever stop?

"Yeah, you know, like a choreographer or something. So that I'm not just standing there on the stage singing that song."

"I don't know anyone like that. Who could we get?"

She plunged a fork into the plastic container and fed herself a heap of the salad. "Antonio."

"Antonio? Your ex-husband Antonio?"

"Don't be upset. He's a very successful choreographer now. He's clean, no more drugs."

The last I'd heard about Antonio was that she had finally left him to take care of her mother because *he* was a bad influence on *her*. "I thought you hadn't been in touch with him."

"Oh, please. It doesn't take much effort to research someone nowadays." She continued to eat with abandon. "I'm comfortable with him and we could pull this together very quickly."

"Yeah, I can imagine how comfortable you are with him," I said. "Maybe he's not even available."

"Maybe not. But it might be worth a try."

"I don't feel good about this, Sally."

"Don't be jealous. It won't be that kind of relationship. That's over." She capped the container and returned it to the fridge. "Besides," she said, smiling, "Don't you want the best possible product to market your song?"

"I think a choreographer is a good idea, but I don't think Antonio is a good idea."

"It's just for two weeks." She tugged at my arm, begging like a schoolgirl.

"All right, I'll call him. But I want to talk to him, do the negotiations."

"Okay!" she cried, giving me a kiss on the cheek.

After a quick Internet search—he had his own Web site and a My Space page—we were able to get a number for Antonio Grant in LA and I left a brief, businesslike message. He called me back a few hours later. His voice was smooth and friendly. "Hello, Mr. Bounder. This is Antonio Grant."

"Hello, uh, Mr. Grant. You can call me Greg. Thanks for returning my call. As I told you, I am managing a singer and we have a major launch party for a new song in a couple of weeks and I was wondering if you might want to work with her."

"I'm tied up with a television project until the end of next week, so not sure if that gives me time to work with your singer. Who is it? Anyone I might know?"

"Oh, yes. Sally Testata."

There was silence on the line and then he broke into a hearty laugh. "No shit! And she wanted you to call *me*?"

"Actually, yes. She said because of your past relationship, she could work with you very quickly and easily."

"It may be more of a challenge than she thinks," he said, still chuckling. I kind of liked the guy.

"Well, that's what I tried to tell her."

"My fee is not cheap. I've worked with the best, in TV and music. Janet, Pink, Ricky, you know, top names."

"I understand. But I think some exciting staging will help boost Sally's confidence and get the audience excited."

"No doubt about it." Antonio then quoted me a fee—four thousand dollars per week in addition to flight and hotel. Plus the cost of rehearsal space, of course. He assured me he would work with her for hours and hours for a week leading up to the show. How could I say no if it would strengthen the show and at the same time make Sally happy?

This added expense would bring my total to the hundred grand mark. As they say, you have to spend money to make money.

CHAPTER FIFTEEN

▼

Antonio Grant was not at all what I had imagined. First off, Sally never told me he was black, so that was the first surprise. Second, when she had told me about his drug problems, I imagined a strung out, skinny loser, and that's not what Antonio was. He was well dressed and masculine, and yet he could have passed as a model, clean-shaven, with a broad smile and lively, friendly brown eyes. He was built like a gym regular. I guessed he was in his mid thirties. In some ways, I had been hoping for the strung out, skinny loser.

Antonio had come up to the apartment after checking in at the Edison Hotel in Times Square. Upon entering, he looked at Sally across the room and threw his arms open, saying, "Hey, look at *you*!"

"Look at *you*!" Sally laughed, and ran into his arms for an extended bear hug.

"And I'm Greg," I said from the sidelines.

"Of course," he said, gripping my hand tightly. He had to have realized we lived together in that dump, but it didn't seem to faze him. That was a good sign.

"Antonio, I know everything ended rather abruptly back in 2002, but the circumstances were just—" Sally began.

Antonio put his hand up to stop her. "No explanation needed. We were both in a bad place and you needed to take care of your mother. Getting away from each other may have been the jolt we both needed to wake up," he graciously explained. "The important thing is, it looks like we both cleaned up pretty well."

"Thank you. I don't think I could have done it without Greg," she offered. Finally, I was getting credit for something besides writing checks.

"Yeah, how did this all come about? Honestly, I didn't think you'd be back," Antonio said.

"Me neither," said Sally.

From there, Sally and I went back and forth, relating the whole incredible adventure up to that point. "And so now we need you to make 'Grind' a stage event, to really capture people's attention," I said.

"The trick will be to make it artistic and provocative at the same time," Antonio said. I had e-mailed him the song file in advance of his arrival.

"And, of course, we'd love to use the moves in the video as well," I said.

"Ah, you didn't tell me about that," Antonio said without missing a beat. "My agent will want to negotiate a substantially higher fee, of course."

"Of course." In terms of money, nothing surprised me anymore.

Antonio then told us of his life since 2002, including an extensive stay in rehab and then starting his own business as a choreographer, using his experience as a backup dancer for several singers as an entry to gaining new clients. My feeling was that if Antonio could come back in such a big way, so could Sally.

* * *

They started immediately the next morning at a midtown rehearsal studio. I put together some press packets that morning but my anxiety got the best of me and I decided to go up and check out the rehearsal.

I quietly opened the door and sat down on a bench. Antonio didn't stop what he was doing, but Sally flashed me a scowl in the mirror.

"So, five, six, seven, eight … squat, and up … hip right, hip left," Antonio instructed while demonstrating the moves, Sally behind him trying to follow along, but missing a step or two.

"Aw, what's the matter? You just had it!" Antonio said good-naturedly.

"I lost my concentration," Sally apologized. "I can't do it while Greg is watching."

Antonio turned to me with a smile and a shrug of his shoulders. "You heard the boss," he said to me.

"Actually, I'm the boss," I asserted. "Just wanted to check that rehearsals are going well and that my money is being well spent."

"The best money you ever spent," Antonio said.

"It's always about money for Greg," Sally commented.

"That's a producer's job, Sally," I said. "And I ought to be able to check and see what my singer is doing."

"Like making sure we're not fucking in the closet," she deadpanned. Antonio howled, bending over and slapping his leg as I turned a hot shade of red.

"You know what? I just wanted to check in. As you know, I have to go to Scranton this week for finals and to hand in some papers. Keep up the good work." With that, I stormed out of the room, slamming the door behind me.

"Greg!" Sally called, running after me. I turned to her, hands on my hips, and waited for her to speak. "I'm going to miss you, but don't worry about us. Antonio is all work and I know we have work to do." She gave me a hug and I went on my way.

The truth is, I wasn't worried about Antonio; I just didn't think they'd sleep together. I was more worried about Sally's urges, both chemical and physical, and the motives of that slimy Eddie Pearl.

* * *

All that spring, I had been returning to Scranton almost once a week to maintain the bare minimum presence as a student in my classes. That was enough to keep myself updated on assignments and keep me afloat with the professors.

While in Scranton that week, I stopped in at the Copper Penny, one of Scranton's only dance clubs, with my press packet in tow. I wanted to see about getting Sally booked in there as kind of a homecoming appearance. The manager, a guy not much older than I was, was eager to book a show. It was a rare event for the Copper Penny to have any kind of special guest. I wanted the appearance to be in September, when the downtown college students were back and when, I assumed, "Grind" would have already made a national impact. What better way to return to Scranton?

After my stats final, I hit the gym with Rick. "I'm probably going back to Pittsburgh just for the summer until I figure things out," he said as he raised and lowered himself on the Gravitron.

"Your parents are great; it won't be so bad," I said.

"I got to save some money before I get my own place."

"I understand. New York is killing me on that score."

He finished his set and moved aside so I could work in with him. "I have no desire to live in a place like New York. I mean, what you pay for a fucking shoebox . . . not to mention the noise ... all the bums and fruitcakes. I don't know how you can stand it."

"When you're making it big, though, there's no place like it."

"Yeah, but the shit you gotta go through to make it big. I couldn't do it."

He had a point. "I'll give it a couple of years, see what happens. I'd rather starve than go to Bounder & Lightning." I finished my reps. "Hey, after the workout, drop off at my apartment. I'll play you Sally's new song."

"Okay," Rick said. "But you're never gonna get me to like that faggot music."

Chapter Sixteen

The following week, I returned to New York, eager to get ready for our big day. Gus had called with the good news that the song had already been getting some enthusiastic airplay in some of the clubs on the east coast. My ads about the Barracuda and Splash parties had appeared in that week's *HX* and *Next*. The management at Barracuda wasn't happy about sharing Sally with Splash on the same weekend, but I assured them that they were first and would get the press coverage. The only big cloud on the horizon was that Marcus told me that our mother was still planning to arrive in New York that Friday to check out the Barracuda party. The woman could not possibly have been in a gay bar in her life and this was her big coming out party. Great! I decided not to tell Sally about that—the last thing she needed was to become nervous about performing in front of my mother.

To my delight, working with Antonio seemed to do the trick. Sally seemed to be brimming with confidence and ready for her opening night performance. "We're going to celebrate tonight," I told her as she primped her outfit for the show that Friday afternoon. "I'm so proud of you, Sally. You've done so much in the last few months."

"It is really pretty unbelievable. What surprises me is that I haven't really missed Scranton," she said. "It feels good to be back."

A couple hours after that, we were ready to head downtown. She wanted a shot of Jameson, but I had forbid any liquor in the house as part of my reform policy. The temptation would have been too great for her. However, once we arrived at Barracuda, I allowed her one shot, just to steady her nerves.

There was already a sizeable crowd at the club. I'm not sure if they were all for Sally, but my hope was that they would convert once she started performing. As I've said, Barracuda was not a large club. It was basically two rectangular rooms, the front room with a long bar on one side, a few round tables in the middle to stand around, and a wooden banquette with full-length mirrors on the other side. Then you'd go through a narrow passageway and enter the back room. There was one pool table, a deejay booth off to the right, and several couches and easy chairs spread throughout the room. At the back was a raised stage, small but functional, and, most importantly, it could be seen from anywhere in the room. The back room could probably hold a hundred to a hundred and fifty people seated and standing, tops.

We quickly greeted Marcus in the deejay booth and then I went backstage with Sally so she could get ready. Antonio joined us so he could give her some last-minute coaching. The show was still an hour away.

I headed back out into the room. Chester Sweethouse was there, making the rounds like a politician. Eddie Pearl was sitting on the pool table with a female companion. I was getting tired of his many surprise appearances. Gus was over by the deejay booth in deep conversation with Marcus. Even ML, the engineer, stood quietly in the opposite corner sipping a Bud Lite.

And then there was my mother, Doris Bounder, seated rigidly in one of the cushioned chairs, eyes staring straight ahead at the empty stage. Some flamboyant guy next to her said something to her, probably about her outfit, and that seemed to soften her. She smiled and answered him while finger-ing her scarf, mostly likely what he had asked about. If she had seen me, she didn't register it. Just as well. I planned to avoid her until after the show, at which point I'd have to at least thank her for coming. At the very least, she was going to see a success of some kind, by the looks of the crowd.

Just before show time, the manager came up to me and asked if I'd like to do the introduction. "You're young, like most of the guys in here, and you're hot, so you'll grab their attention."

This was not what I had bargained for, being a spokesperson or emcee. "I don't know," I hesitated.

Just then, Marcus announced from the booth, "Please welcome to the stage Greg Bounder."

That bastard! They had planned this and didn't give a shit whether I con-sented or not. I pushed my way through the crowd and as I walked onstage, I heard several catcalls and whoops.

"Good evening, guys ... and ladies. Yeah, I see a few ladies out there," I fumbled.

"Show us your ass!" some guy yelled from the crowd, and others cheered him on.

"Thank you, I guess." I felt so uncomfortable. "Listen up, I'm here to bring you a former star and a future star. It was my great privilege to redis-cover her in the valley of Scranton, Pennsylvania, and now she is about to take the world by storm again!" Loud cheers went up. "She's going to sing for you her biggest hit, then a couple of new songs." I looked to the wings to make sure she was there, and Sally gave me a thumbs-up. "Please welcome back to the stage Sally Testata!" More whoops and cheers followed and then Sally came out in her little black cocktail dress, gave me a quick hug, and waved to the crowd.

"Hello, New York! The first song I'm going to do for you was a hit back in 2001, but after 9/11 it was thought to be too controversial to play," she told them. "But these days, I think our current administration might like it as a theme song!" The crowd screamed its approval and Sally launched into "Bombs Away."

Antonio joined me off to one side of the room, probably about ten yards from my mother on the other side but, thankfully, there were many people between us. Sally did well with the old song and had the crowd singing along with her on the chorus. She then sang "I Still Have What it Takes," after telling everybody that she was proud to have co-written it with me. It, too, got an energetic response, which led me to believe it might get some airplay as well.

"Finally, I'd like to close with a song, which is the reason you're all here tonight. It was written by Chester Sweethouse—say hi to Chester, everybody!" From the back, Chester gladly turned to all sides of the room and waved like royalty. "I want to see you all getting down with me on this one," she said as the deep funk of "Grind" began.

As she started the song, I caught a quick glimpse of my mother, slack-jawed. I couldn't tell if she'd already had a stroke or was about to receive dental care. For this performance, we had Sally doing the eight-minute club track, not the shorter radio mix, so this gave her more room for theatrics. The dancing on this was clearly up a notch, thanks to Antonio, and the crowd was roaring its approval.

After the main part of the song was over, the groove continued and Sally was in her element. She fell to her hands and knees, doggie style, and sang, "Do me from behind/Let's grind." She had completely made up the lyric! Then she turned over on her back and thrust her hips up into the air, the short skirt falling back to reveal her black g-string panties as she sang, "I want to be sixty-nined/Let's grind." These words, too, were completely made up! This was the same woman who hadn't wanted to perform the song because it was degrading? And as for the dance, this is what Antonio had in mind as artistic?

As if reading my mind, Antonio said into my ear, "This is all improvised. I didn't tell her to do this."

I was horrified, and yet the crowd was screaming so heartily, Sally had to push her vocals to be heard above them! Gus came up behind me. "We'll have to re-record the club mix to incorporate Sally's new lyrics," he said. Like seeing a car wreck, I had to slide a glance over to my mother to catch her reaction. She was not there, but looking back I caught the back of her head as she angrily pushed her way through the crowd to leave. Just as well.

Gus continued. "This could be the sensation of the summer. I didn't know she was willing to go this far. She's pushing the envelope."

Sally was on her feet again to close out the song. She got a rousing standing ovation. She threw kisses to the crowd and went backstage. We hadn't planned an encore. "Everything Must Change" didn't seem right and the old Pillow Talk stuff was crap compared to what she'd just done, so that was out. Given the response, I now bounded up on the stage. "Wasn't she great?" The crowd bellowed again. "You have overwhelmed us. What I want you to do is request 'Grind' whenever you go out dancing, and tell all your friends to come join us at Splash for Tea Dance on Sunday at four o'clock!"

I ran backstage and hugged and kissed Sally, who was ecstatic. "It's going to happen, isn't it?" she cried, almost in tears.

"I told you it would!"

She quickly changed her clothes and she ran ahead of me out into the crowd, accepting hugs and congratulations from everyone. I watched her make her way back, clearly enjoying having her public moment. Oddly, she worked her way to the far corner, not toward Chester or Eddie in the middle, or toward Gus or Marcus at the booth, but toward ML. Well, maybe she was going to start with the least important to give thanks and work her way leftward. But no! ML greeted her with a shot glass for each of them. They downed the shot and then he leaned down to kiss her! A long, lingering, tongue-trading kiss, and his hand was on her ass! I stood in shock, probably with an expression similar to my mother's a few minutes before. How could I have missed this? How long had this been going on?

I felt lost, confused, on the verge of crying or hollering, I'm not sure which. I had barely had a glimmer of success and now it felt as if it was evaporating like a puff of smoke.

Antonio made his way over to me and whispered in my ear, "Once you go black, there's no going back."

He was smiling but I was not. "Uh-huh."

"Wait," he said, getting a full look at me. "You didn't know about this?" I remained speechless.

"No," I said softly. My quick temper came up, which resulted in an accusatory tone: "Did you?"

Smooth Antonio chuckled. "Yeah, she says they've been seeing each other since the recording session."

"Why is she telling you and not me?" I cried.

"Probably she was afraid of this very reaction," he said. "Look, you've got to swallow this, put this behind you right now. You're on the verge of something, you don't want this exploding right now. Put on your professional hat."

"You're right," I said. "It's just that, well, I wasn't expecting this and ..." My thoughts were swimming as I tried to find the right thing to say.

Antonio grabbed me by the shoulders and looked into my eyes. "Sally is her own person, and completely unpredictable. You're going to make a lot of money here, and you'll have your pick of all the girls in New York."

"Yeah, you're right," I repeated robotically. "I just need a few minutes to digest this."

"I'll buy you a drink," he offered.

Why couldn't everything go the way it was supposed to?

* * *

A few hours later, I was at a crowded loft party above the busy corner of Ninth Avenue and Fourteenth Street. A friend of Marcus's had decided to have the post-release party. The atmosphere was festive but I was still in a funk.

Marcus, who had to stay a bit late at the club to work the transition to the next deejay, had not yet arrived. Sally arrived before I did. I scanned the room, looking for her. I didn't see her, but ML was leaning up against a counter talking to some guy. The crowd was typical of Manhattan's dance club scene: about seventy-five percent gay men, a few fag hags, and various industry types. Eddie Pearl was among them and he brought along his "star," Olive Martini, who, you can imagine, was dressed head to toe in green garb and sipping a martini. She seemed to be sucking up all the energy in the room, not happy unless everyone within earshot was listening to her.

I first approached ML. "ML, have you seen Sally?" My tone was of a worried mother.

"Chill, man," he said. "She's around, greeting her fans."

"So how long have you and Sally been seeing each other?"

ML turned to his buddy and said, "Excuse us for a sec. I gotta talk to this guy." Turning to me, he said, "A few weeks. Is there a problem?" ML never raised his voice above a low monotone, which made him seem slightly menacing to me.

"Well, only that she and I were dating."

"Whoa," he said, putting his hand up. "She never told me that. Homey don't play sloppy seconds."

"Yeah, well maybe you'd better talk to her." I walked away and felt only slightly bad that, in truth, Sally and I hadn't had sex since that Easter morning hand job—the day after she met ML at the studio.

On a roll, I made my way over to Eddie Pearl. "Eddie, have you seen Sally?"

"Oh, she's around somewhere," he said. "You've met Olive Martini?"

"Not officially," I said, offering my hand for a quick handshake. "I need to find Sally."

"Let her enjoy herself," Pearl said. "Trust me, the more you try to control her, the more she'll rebel."

"Thanks for the advice, Eddie," I said. "And now let me give you some advice. I'll tend to my client, you tend to yours."

"Ooohhh," Olive intoned. "This ain't sounding too pretty."

"And what do you mean by that?" Eddie said, turning to face me head-on.

"I mean, now is not the time for you to be sticking your nose into her affairs and giving her advice. She has a contract with me."

"I'm well aware of that, son," he said. "But sometimes old friends come in handy in this business."

"Yeah, suddenly after a half dozen years, you're ready to be her friend again. Only if there's something in it for you, I'm sure." I gulped down a glass of champagne that was offered and turned to leave. "Better watch your back, Olive."

I smiled as I walked away, hearing him growl, "You son of a bitch."

I went down a hallway, peeking into rooms looking for Sally. Somebody told me she was in the bathroom and the line in the hallway suggested she'd been there a while. I pounded on the door. "Sally, are you all right?"

"Yeah, yeah, yeah, don't worry about it. I'm on my way." The door opened and she flashed me an anxious smile. "See? All done."

I saw, all right. I saw moisture and a slight tinge of powder under a nostril. I grabbed her arm and pulled her into a nearby bedroom. There were a few people on the bed smoking a joint; there was no privacy to be had. "What are you doing? You cannot be doing that stuff, not now, not ever!"

"It's a special occasion," she said. "Besides, you want me to lose weight. This will help."

"Sally, we are at the start of something big, and you are set on derailing it already."

A drowsy-eyed guy with slicked-back hair looked up from the bed. "Hey, it's Sally. Hey, Sally! You were great, tonight, just great. You wanna toke?"

"Wonderful," she purred, and plopped herself on the bed. They all introduced each other as she took a hit. "That's Greg, my manager," she told them, pointing to me. "He's really a great guy and has done so much for me, but he's a little too high-strung. He needs to relax a bit." She held up the joint. "You want some, honey?"

"No, I don't want any," I said. "You're obviously hell-bent on having your fun tonight, but don't forget we have a lot of shows coming up, interviews, appearances."

"You don't have to tell me. None of this is new to me. It's new to you, however, so relax and enjoy it." The other three on the bed, two guys and a girl, were listening but there was no telling what they'd remember the next day.

"ML is obviously not the greatest influence," I said.

"Who invited my mother to this party?" the slick guy asked, and the others, including Sally, doubled over with laughter.

"Look, I didn't know how to tell you about ML," Sally resumed after she'd composed herself. "But he's very responsible, a good guy."

"Where does that leave us?" A soap opera was playing out in the most unlikely of places.

"What do you mean, where does that leave us? It leaves us as manager and singer, right where you wanted us."

"You go, girl," the other guy said.

"Shut the fuck up," I barked at him.

"*You* shut the fuck up!" the girl said. She had dark, straight hair that hung in her face, multiple piercings in her ears, and a pierced nose. One of those East Village losers.

Sally got up and tried to diffuse the tension. "Look, Greg, if this isn't your scene, why don't you go home and rest? You worked hard and we all did well. We have another gig on Sunday. I'll be ready."

"Maybe that's not such a bad idea. But promise me you are going to take it easy and not come home too late."

"Promise." She gave me a kiss—on the cheek—and walked me out into the large loft area and then turned around and went back the bedroom. I saw Marcus standing at a window on the opposite side of the room talking to a much younger guy. However, I had barely focused on them when my eyes caught another sight in another far corner: my mother! Holding a glass of red wine and talking to two adoring twinks who couldn't have been much older than I was! Apparently, hanging around gays was fine as long as they weren't her kids.

I pushed my way over to Marcus. He looked up and started to introduce me to his friend. "Hey, Greg. This is—"

"Marcus, how the hell did she get here? You brought her here?"

"Calm down! Look," he explained. "She was waiting for me outside on the sidewalk. We talked and she was kind of upset. I suggested she come to the party to see for herself that your night was a big success and that people were very friendly."

"Here? Do you see what's going on around here?" I swept my arm with a wide gesture. "There are drugs going on in those back rooms. And look! Olive Martini and all these, these ..."

"These *what?*" Marcus asked with gritted teeth. "Get a hold of yourself. She's not going to go back there. And she seems to be having a good time."

"You did this to sabotage me! You want her to hate me like she hates you!"

"You know what, Greg? When you grow up, you can go fuck yourself," he said in a steely voice. "Come on." He took his young friend by the arm and they walked to another part of the room.

Just as I was trying to figure out what to do next, my mother walked over, sporting a cat-got-the-canary smile with her arms open for an embrace. She pulled me into her thin, yoga-toned arms. "Darling, why do you look so upset? You seem to have done very well tonight." She was performing another one of her acts, waiting for the right time to thrust the dagger in again.

"You left before it was over—how would you know?"

"Well, I admit it wasn't to my taste, but the crowd was on her side." She took a sip of wine. "By the way, where is, uh, Sally?"

"Is that why you're here, Mother? To meet Sally?"

"Well, it would be nice. You seem to be banking your fortune on her."

"And why were you talking to those guys?"

She let out a laugh, like a tinkling bell. Merry fucking Christmas to me, it seemed to say. "I'm at a party, dear. Shouldn't I be talking to people?" She lowered her voice to a whisper. "Do you mean that they're gay? You forget that I'm on the board of the Walnut Street Theater. I'm around the gays all the time."

"But it's not okay for your son to be gay."

"Every mother eventually wants to be a grandmother. Besides, your brother flaunts the lifestyle, throws it in everyone's face. He embarrassed us terribly when he came out."

"Wasn't that, like, twenty years ago?"

"Yes, but he never apologized for it." Jesus, that woman could hold a grudge! "However, as you can see, I'm not a complete tyrant. As tonight demonstrates, Marcus and I are capable of some very wonderful moments together."

"Well, good for you. Enjoy yourself. I'm going home. I have a lot of work to do this weekend."

"I know you've been working very hard," she conceded. "And I'm willing to come up here to show my support"—she had to be fucking kidding me—"but I must remind you that you are on your own. This kind of business does not do much for the family name. And I fear that Sally is going to be nothing but trouble."

As if on cue, Sally breezed into the room from the hallway, glassy-eyed and with a big grin pasted on her face. She saw me and started toward us. Jesus Christ!

When she reached us, before she could say anything, I made introductions. "Sally, this is my mother, Doris Bounder. Mother, this is Sally Testata." Thank god the coke was no longer evident under her nose.

"Oh, my gosh, what a pleasure to meet you!" Sally gushed, a little too theatrically, holding out her hand, which my mother daintily shook.

"And you as well," she said with a wolfish smile.

"Greg has done *so* much for me! He convinced me I could come back and be a star and he wouldn't take no for an answer. Does he get that iron will from you?"

"Perhaps so," Doris answered.

"Perhaps so," Sally repeated and then giggled, gently mocking my mother's manners. "Your mother is so refined!"

"Thank you," my mother said, not amused. "Sally, wherever did you learn to dance like that?"

High or not, a moment of sobriety flashed in Sally's eyes. She knew exactly what my mother was trying to do. "Mostly from my ex-boyfriend, Antonio, that handsome man over there." She pointed to Antonio, who seemed to be holding court with a bunch of admiring young dancer types. "But the part near the end, I completely made that up on my own," she said defiantly.

"I see. Well, it certainly was memorable."

"Yes, well, I want to be remembered this time around," Sally replied without missing a beat.

"That is certainly one way to be remembered."

The smile disappeared from Sally's face. "Greg, I think your mother needs to relax a bit. Shall I find her something to loosen her up?"

I had to put a stop to this. "Sally, why don't you go talk to ML or something? I'll see you back at the apartment."

"Good enough," she said. "Nice meeting you, Madame Bounder." She turned abruptly and went to ML.

"You *live* with her?" Leave it to my mother to not miss a thing.

"It's a two bedroom. It's a way to save money. I still have the apartment in Scranton and the car."

"I guess you'll be learning about budgeting very soon," she observed. She slugged down the last of her wine. "Look, I won't torture you any further. I've seen all that I need to see here. I'll go back to my hotel and leave in the morning."

She was probably expecting me to beg her to stay, but no way. "Okay. Thank you for coming to support me," I managed to say with a straight face.

She said her good-byes to Marcus and her new little friends, and I walked her to the curb to catch a cab. I decided that I, too, had seen enough and grabbed the next cab back to the apartment.

* * *

Later that night, I bolted upright in bed as I realized that I hadn't heard Sally come in. It was after five and light was already coming into the windows. What was worse was that I could not get a hold of her. Her cell phone—or rather, *mine*, another one of my expenses—rang and allowed me to leave messages, but she never called back. Despite our blowup the night before, I called Marcus. "She's not home yet," I blurted into the phone when he answered.

Marcus sighed as he roused himself. "Greg, she's a big girl. She's over forty and she's lived here before. And she has a boyfriend. I'm sure she's with him."

"Why wouldn't she call me to tell me?"

"I don't know. I don't know her that well. But I'm sure she's fine. Get some sleep." He hung up the phone. Nobody was taking me seriously, after all I'd done.

The next morning, I flipped through channels with the remote and paced back and forth through the small apartment, awaiting word from Sally. I couldn't concentrate on anything. At last, I called Chester.

"Chester, it's Greg Bounder. I need ML's number. I need to get a hold of Sally."

"I am not at liberty to give out his personal number," Chester informed me, like the fucking queen that he was.

"This is important!" I shrieked.

"I shall deliver the message," he said serenely. "You should really calm down, Greg. We're going to make a lot of money this year. In fact," he went on, "I've started writing a follow-up song to 'Grind.'"

"I can't talk about this right now," I told him.

Ignoring me, he went on. "It's called 'Wet.' It goes like this: *I'm gonna make you sweat/You're gonna make me wet*," he sang. "That's just the hook."

"Chester, it sounds just like 'Grind.'"

"You don't know what you're talking about," he said, his voice rising. "I'll deliver your message. And you'll need to do a better job of controlling your client, or we'll all end up in the poorhouse," he warned, and hung up the phone.

Within minutes, however, Sally opened the door and strolled in. "Where have you been?"

She held up her hand. "I have a headache. I'm not getting into this now."

"I'm not surprised, with all that shit you were taking. Were you with ML?"

"Of course. Where do you think I was?"

"I don't know. How many boyfriends are there?"

"Oh, dozens and dozens!" she hollered. "Christ, Greg, I wasn't aware you were in this for marriage."

"Maybe not, but I don't deserve to be completely dissed!"

"Look, this is going to be easier in the long run. You can concentrate on the career and we don't have to have the messy relationship interfering."

"Easier? Easier?" I repeated for emphasis. "Your boyfriend didn't know we had a relationship!"

"We didn't have a relationship after I met him. Thanks for giving him that idea. We ended up hashing that out all night long!"

"I am a champion, All-State wrestler. I could whoop his ass if I wanted to."

"Charming," Sally commented. "Why don't you wait until you can get some publicity out of the fight?"

"So are you moving in with him?"

"No, we're not ready for that."

"So I'm supposed to sleep in the same apartment with you and have an erection every night?"

"Yes, that way it will feel like a marriage to you," she said with a laugh. "But seriously," she went on, noting that I didn't share her humor. "Before long, I can get my own place. I have confidence that we're all going to do well with this recording. You were right all along."

"Then how come I don't feel so happy about it?"

"Nobody does. That's the dirty little secret about showbiz that nobody tells you. You work your ass off and if you're lucky enough to hit it big, you end up no happier than anyone else. The happiness is in the anticipation."

"You seem to have all the answers, Sally. At this point, I just need you to show up and do your job. Go take your damn nap. I'm out of here."

"Where are you going?"

"What difference does it make? Just be there at Splash tomorrow." I grabbed my jacket and slammed the door behind me. Looking at my watch, I realized that if I drove fast enough, I could be in Scranton in time for the three o'clock graduation ceremony.

CHAPTER SEVENTEEN

▼

It would have killed my mother to learn that I did, in fact, attend my graduation. I arrived late, somewhere in the middle of the commencement address but before diplomas were handed out. Rick and Pete and a few other friends just laughed and shook their heads as I made my way into my seat.

It was good to get away from the whole Sally mess in New York, even for just twenty-four hours. I ended up going to a house party that night and hanging out with a few friends and flirting with some girls. It was fun telling them, "I manage a singer in New York," that I had already started a career. Honestly, though, I was already getting the feeling I didn't belong, and while I may have thought I was a big deal from New York, they didn't. Pete basically blew me off with a slap on the back and a, "Hey, I hear you're doing great," before disappearing into another room. Had I missed the present by always focusing on the future?

I decided to leave the party early after getting phony promises from friends that they'd come to New York before they got too settled into their new jobs and locations. I had an urge to visit Fat Bo's, where it all started.

When I walked in, right away I noticed that things hadn't changed much. Even the people looked the same, except the flannel shirts had been replaced by T-shirts and tank tops, with pale, droopy arms coming out of them. I went over to Sally's corner. A gray-haired guy was sitting there, his head bobbing as he tried to keep from falling asleep. It was just before ten o'clock.

Rolf came over. "Hey, what's up?" he said, without a smile and without surprise.

"I'm great," I said, perhaps overselling. "I'll take a Heineken."

He opened the bottle and placed it in front of me. "Are you still with Sally?"

"Of course. I just came back for graduation today."

"Uh-huh. How's she doing? We haven't heard from her."

"She's doing well. We just released her first song and it looks like it will be a hit."

"Really?" He didn't look happy about it. "What's it called?"

"Um, 'Grind.' It's called 'Grind.'"

"'Grind'? It sounds like something you do to meat."

"It's a little edgy," I offered. What else could I say?

"She's okay, though? Her father's a little worried about her. He doesn't say much, but you can tell."

"I've tried to get her to come back and visit, but she's really taking all of this very seriously. She's going to make it big this time."

"Well, I hope she doesn't forget where she came from."

"Oh, she won't. In fact, we're coming back in September to appear at Copper Penny's. It will be a big homecoming, so come out with all your friends."

"Cool. But we'd like to see her before then, just for a visit. Not just a career appearance."

"I'll definitely let her know. I'll have her call. Does she have your number?"

Rolf glared at me and then growled, "Yeah. She has my number."

I felt my brief welcome was coming to an end. I downed the last of my beer. "Okay. Well, I just wanted to stop in and say hello while I was here. I'll tell her you said hello."

"You do that."

I stepped out onto the sidewalk, breathing in the refreshing spring air of Scranton. I walked east for a bit, and stood at the corner of Main and Lackawanna, which offered a great view of downtown from the top of the hill there. The big orange "Electric City" sign was almost dead center in the valley, surrounded by lesser twinkling lights, headlights of light traffic on the streets, and, gloriously, stars in the sky above it all. My lease was up at the end of the summer, but I wouldn't be back much before then, perhaps only to pack and move my stuff. This chapter of my life was coming to an end. In a way, I would miss this old town, and yet, I'd never really felt a part of it. I was always looking ahead to the next thing. Now I was at the next thing, New York, and there wasn't really any moving beyond that. Who would I keep in touch with from U of S, I wondered? Where would we all be next year, five years, ten years down the road?

I needed to get laid. I couldn't rely on Sally for that anymore. Marcus and Antonio were right; I had to let her go emotionally and concentrate on the good thing I had going with our burgeoning careers.

I decided to go to the Copper Penny while I was in town. I could maybe meet the manager whom I had spoken with the week before and check out the scene, the girls. It was downtown on Linden Street. I backtracked to Fat Bo's to get my car.

The Copper Penny was Scranton's only real nightclub for young people but it was seldom full, even on the weekends. That night, however, it was quite packed, given that it was graduation night at U of S. It wasn't quite as big as Splash, but it did have three floors of activity. The first floor was a basic dance club, with mainstream hit music, the second floor pumped out music with a more urban, funk beat, and the third floor was more of just a meeting place with a lot of sofas and chairs, and, in the nice weather, a door leading out to a roof deck with potted plants and such. It was an old building from Scranton's heyday as a touring theater capital of the northeast. All three floors had a raised stage area. I wasn't a frequent visitor, but I can't remember the last time the Copper Penny actually had a live performance. Sally Testata would be an event.

The manager wasn't in that night but I introduced myself to the two dee-jays, telling them who I was and what my plan was, and, of course, hand-ing them a CD—you should always have your product with you, you never know. The biggest surprise was that right away I saw a girl I wanted to meet. She was dancing by herself on the second floor. She was pretty uninhibited—nothing like what Sally had exhibited the night before in Barracuda, but she moved well. She had nice legs and wore a denim skirt and black T-shirt, and had short black hair with gold hoops dangling from her ears.

When I introduced myself, she gave me a big, dimpled smile. Her name was Belinda and she had been in town for her sister's graduation. When she told me her sister's name, I thankfully didn't recognize it. Belinda had gradu-ated the year before from Oklahoma State and was now living in LA trying to make it as an actress.

"Wow, how is it going? I manage a singer in New York," I told her.

"And you just graduated today? I like a guy with ambition," she said.

I offered to buy her a drink, and she followed me upstairs so we could talk in the relative quiet of the third floor. Belinda told me her story, which I supposed was no different from any other young woman's journey to LA, but from my perspective it was exciting. She worked the front desk at a hotel by night and tried to make the rounds of auditions by day. So far, she had done some extra work in TV and movies, but no big breaks. Belinda remained optimistic, though. "You have to be persistent, do a little bit for your career every day, and I believe it will happen."

"Yeah, me, too."

We had a good, easy chemistry and after another drink, I invited her back to my place. She agreed to go and was refreshingly direct, none of that coy shit that girls are so good at. Belinda knew what she was doing in bed, too, and the sex lasted quite a while, the two of us eagerly trying to please each other. We finally passed out in the wee hours of the morning.

A clatter woke me from a dead sleep. I opened my eyes to see Belinda coming in from the hallway, all dressed and slipping into her shoes.

"Sorry," she said. "I knocked the glass into the sink. But it didn't break!"

I looked over at the digital clock, which read eleven thirty-five. Shit! Sally was performing at Splash at four o'clock and the drive was at least two and a half hours back to the city.

"Oh, Jesus!" I pushed myself into a sitting position and rubbed the sleepiness out of my face. "I got to get back to the city for a show!"

"And I need to get back to the hotel before my family wonders where I am. I have my own room, but still." She pressed a button on her cell phone. "Yup, I have messages."

"Shit," I said. "What are you going to say?"

"That I met a manager and tried to sleep my way to the top."

"Sounds good." I stood up and gave her a kiss. "Did you take a shower?"

"No, I can take one at the hotel. You know, all my stuff is there." She grabbed her purse and started heading for the door. "I had a really great time."

Damn it, I had driven her here. "Where are you staying? Let me give you a ride." I scanned the floor for various pieces of discarded clothing from the night before.

"The Radisson. It's not far, it's really not a problem."

I pulled on my jeans and fumbled in my pockets as I followed her to the driveway. "Shit, let me get my wallet so I can at least pay for your cab," I said, heading back toward the house.

"Don't worry, I got it. Hurry up, don't miss your gig," she said with a smile. "Stay in touch, Mr. Manager."

"I will." I kissed her again. "I gave you my card, right?"

"Got it. I'll send you an e-mail with my info."

"Sounds good. Listen, just walk down to that corner by the bus station. You shouldn't have any trouble getting a cab."

With that, she blew me a kiss and was on her way. I ran back inside and jumped in the shower. I left a message for Sally in New York, although I figured she probably had stayed at ML's the night before. I was praying she'd been more responsible than I had been, and would get to Splash on time.

By twelve thirty, I was dressed and out the door. I drove down the hill to the Mobil station and filled the tank. The attendant came around and I pulled out my wallet and—what the fuck? I had no cash! No credit cards! No debit card! I felt a wave of heat rise through me as I realized the bitch had cleaned me out.

"I'm so sorry," I said to the attendant. "I live right up there. It appears I had my cash and credit cards stolen last night. I think I can go right up there and find some money for you."

The attendant looked no older than a teenager. "Ray!" he hollered and an older guy ambled out of the station and over to the car. "This guy says he lives up there but he lost his cash and credit cards. What do we do?"

"Let me take down his license number," Ray said, and went to the back of the car. I could see in the rearview mirror a middle-aged woman scowling with impatience, waiting to get into my spot.

I showed Ray my actual license and gave him my name. "I just graduated, honest. I'll be right back with some money."

I hightailed it out of the lot and sped back up to my place. I began ransacking my own bedroom, just to make sure there was not another explanation for this, all the while cursing Belinda up and down. I didn't even know her fucking last name. I called the Radisson and told some story about how I had something of Belinda's that she'd left at a graduation party, but that I didn't know her last name. The clerk came back at me with, "I'm sorry, sir, but I need more information than that. Our records don't show any first-name Belinda registered here." Of course not. What was I expecting?

How did she get away with this? I wondered. I hadn't remembered leaving her side for more than a minute, although she was up and alert before I was; I guess that's all it took. Fortunately, I kept a stash of small change and bills in an industrial-sized jar in the bottom of the hutch in the dining room. She certainly couldn't have walked away with that. I pulled it out and fished out a wad of ones and then picked out a few dollars worth of quarters for various tolls. All together, I counted almost forty dollars, which would barely cover the gas and the tolls. So much for food; there certainly wasn't much in the apartment, but I opened the refrigerator to see what I could scrounge up for my growing hunger. The juice was good but the milk had expired. I drank the OJ from the carton until it was empty.

I decided to call Rick to see if he could lend me fifty bucks. "Dude," I droned into the phone, leaving a message, "It's Greg. I went home with this chick last night and she cleaned me out. I need you to lend me a few bucks to get back to New York. I have a gig this afternoon. Call me back ASAP." I snapped the phone shut. I couldn't wait around all day for him to get back to me. I'd have to make do. At least I had my New York checkbooks back in the city and could get cash the next day. Still, I'd have to cancel all my other cards. I swept my hand through my desk drawer, scooping up bank and credit card statements, and shoved them into my backpack. I'd have to call all the companies that evening to cancel the cards. What shit luck I had!

I jumped back into the car and went down the hill, paid my gasoline bill, and was on my way. Because it was a warm spring weekend, I ran into a lot of traffic the closer I got to New York, and I cursed and honked and weaved the best I could. On top of that, try finding parking in Chelsea on a Sunday afternoon. Not easy.

I had left a message with the manager of Splash that I had had traffic problems and that I'd be late, but it was nearly five when I got into the club. The place was packed and I pushed my way to the back to the deejay booth. I asked if Sally had performed and he laughed and said, "Oh, yeah, she performed, all right." I dreaded to think what that meant.

Eventually, I found Chris, the manager. "Has she left already?" I asked him.

"Yeah, she got out of here pretty quickly. Left with some older guy, not sure who it was."

Curiosity was killing me. "Well, did everything go okay? Looks like a great crowd."

Chris smiled. "Yes and no. Yes, great crowd. They loved her and she put on a show that won't soon be forgotten."

"Then what's the *no*?" I asked.

"Well, Sally is a bit of a free spirit, maybe a little too much," he said, then went on to explain. "See, she came out and did 'Bombs Away' and everything was great. She was wearing a short black cocktail dress and looked fine. The crowd went wild, then she said she wanted to slip into something more comfortable and briefly went backstage as the music for 'I Still Got What it Takes' was revving up. A minute goes by and she still doesn't appear and it's obvious she should be out there singing. So we're all looking around, I'm up with the deejay asking him if we should start the track over again. Just then, as it gets to the chorus part, she comes storming out and across the catwalk, in the same outfit, except"—he paused for dramatic effect—"minus the panties!"

"Jesus Christ!"

"The place went wild! She had started right in with the chorus, *I still have what it takes/Forget the social climbers and fakes*, and then she yelled out, 'This is all real, baby!' in the middle of the song. As you can see, there was nothing left to the imagination."

I turned to look at the stage and runway, which was set up over the central bar area, so viewers had a full upward view of whoever was performing. "Jesus Christ," was all I could mutter.

"Well, the crowd was loving it, it was so … audacious! But I have to tell you, even in New York there's a law against full nudity in bars. Our male strippers can't do that."

"So what did you do?"

"What could I do? I figured I'd let her finish the song, but there was no way I was going to let her do 'Grind' like that. So while the crowd was applauding, I got to her with two security guys and we pulled her off the stage. I told her she had to put the panties back on for the last number, that she was breaking the law. Of course, while I'm trying to do the right thing, the crowd was booing us like crazy."

"Then what happened?"

"She just said, 'Fine,' and went backstage to put on the panties. I had a security guard stay on the edge of the stage in case she pulled another stunt. So," he continued, "we start up the music for 'Grind' and she comes out on the stage to wild applause, of course. 'You know, my manager told me the guys wanted a sex symbol, but when you give them the real thing, the men are bigger pussies than we are!' Of course, the crowd ate that up; she had them in the palm of her hand."

"Did she keep her clothes on?"

"Technically, yes. But that didn't stop her from grabbing a bottle during the writhing on the floor part of the song and starting to do something suggestive with it. We had to put a stop to it."

"Jesus Christ." I hadn't invoked the Lord's name so much since Christmas mass.

"Well, she was a hit, I'll give her that." He asked the bartender for an envelope from the register and he handed it to me. It was a check for the performance.

"Would you invite her back?"

"Oh, sure. But let's see how this plays out as the summer goes on. This is going to go down as one of those legendary performances. It will probably help her career in some ways."

"Thanks, Chris." I told him I'd be in touch, then headed out to the still sunny street. I drove back to Midtown and parked in the lot where I had purchased a monthly spot. I labored up the four flights of stairs, praying Sally would be there.

The blinds and curtains were drawn in her room and Sally was covered up in a fetal position on the bed, facing the wall. I tried to make noise as I threw my keys on the glass coffee table and rushed into the bathroom and pissed without closing the door. She didn't stir.

"Sally? You okay?"

She muttered a low, "Mmmm," without moving.

"When did you get home?"

"Half an hour ago." She remained motionless.

"I heard you put on quite a show." Sally ignored me. "Look, I'm sorry I was late. I went back to Scranton for my graduation yesterday and then had some car problems this morning."

"I managed."

"That's what I heard. I got there as fast as I could but you had already left. I spoke to Chris."

She didn't take the bait. "How are things in Scranton?"

"Great. You know, I stopped in to see Rolf."

"That must have been fun for you to rub my success in his face." She still hadn't turned around.

"That's not what it was about," I said, but maybe it was. "He says hello, he'd like to hear from you."

At last, Sally turned around. "I'm doing everything you wanted me to do, and then some. Don't go getting sentimental on me."

"Yeah, well," I began, as though tiptoeing through a minefield, "as far as that goes, I'm not asking you to take off your clothes, Sally."

"That was a bonus."

"How did that feel?"

"How do you think it felt? It felt degrading."

"Then why did you do it?"

"Because I have to live up to—or down to—that degrading song. You want a pro, I can be a pro. You want a sex symbol, I can be a sex symbol."

"But exposing your twat on a live stage?"

"Look, I did what I felt was right in the moment. The crowd loved it. Don't expect me to always know what your rules are."

"Okay, let's put that behind us." After a pause, I went on. "Who did you leave the club with? Chris said he saw you with an older guy."

"Jesus, am I your daughter or your client?"

"You are my client, but I need to make sure my client is being protected."

"It was Eddie, just taking me out for a drink and getting me into a cab."

"Why is he coming to all your gigs? Doesn't he have enough to do with Martini Twist?"

"Olive Martini," she corrected. "Eddie and I have been friends for a long time; it goes beyond him being my former manager."

"Really? How many times did he call to keep in touch when you were living in Scranton all those years?"

I got her on that one. "Nobody called when I was living in Scranton," she stormed, throwing the sheet aside and stomping towards the bathroom. "It was a self-imposed exile." She suddenly turned to face me as she reached the bathroom door. "And where the hell were you? My second gig, and you're not there?"

"I got held up in Scranton, overslept, and then had car trouble."

"Overslept? Probably 'cause you were screwing some college chippie all night long. And to think, you get on my case. Well, honey, I was bringing home the bacon while you played school."

"I'm sorry, Sally. But just because I missed the gig, doesn't mean you should be having drinks with Eddie Pearl."

"Please, I can handle Eddie Pearl."

"It's just that now you're back, everyone wants a piece of you."

"Including you!" Sally slammed the door.

Summer would soon be fully upon us, but I already felt the blazing heat, mere steps into my journey on the way to making it big.

CHAPTER EIGHTEEN

▼

Later that week, Gus called with the incredible news that "Grind" was already getting heavy play in the New York dance clubs and that other East Coast cities would soon be following suit. Helping along the publicity was all the mentions in the gay rags—*HX, Next, The Blade, Gay City News*—about Sally's debut weekend at Barracuda and Splash. While her singing and dancing were praised, the real story, of course, was her nude antics at Splash, reported by the tabloid gossipers with breathless hysteria.

"Comeback-diva-with-a-vengeance Sally Testata whipped up the testosterone of even her gay male fans at Splash last Sunday with a pantiless performance of a new song called 'I Still Have What it Takes' before launching into her raunchier song, 'Grind,' which is being pushed as her new single. Of course, by then the panties were back on, due to New York's strict code on nudity in bars that are not designated as strip clubs. We say, 'Let her rip, Sally!' There's nothing better than pussy power to make a strong statement!"

After that, calls were coming in from all over the place, from Provincetown to Miami. Club managers explained to me that their states didn't have such enforcement against nudity or they didn't care—they'd take a chance for the publicity. I tried to explain that Sally was a legitimate performer, that I couldn't book her with the guarantee that she'd slip off her undies. It was clear that was their main interest.

In the meantime, we had a previously booked gig at the Ice Palace on Fire Island to kick off Memorial Day weekend. I convinced Sally to take the train rather than a limo out to Sayville for the ferry ride to the island. I needed to cut expenses where I could. The boat was packed with weekend revelers and Sally, with her big round sunglasses and wide-brimmed straw hat, wasn't recognized by anybody on board. As the boat pulled out of the marina and out onto the open water, the feel of the salty breeze and the sun on my face and the sight of Long Island getting smaller behind us—as if my worries, too, were shrinking—was quite remarkable. I hadn't felt so good since this whole adventure began.

The truth is, Sally's appearance at the Ice Palace wasn't until Sunday night and we were given a free room at the nearby Cherry Grove Hotel for that one night, but seeing as the schedule was about to heat up like the summer sun and as a reward for the good start "Grind" had gotten off to, I persuaded Sally to come out for the whole weekend. So basically, the fee Sally's appearance was earning was paying for our little extended vacation. For my own selfish reasons, I wanted to get her away from ML and see if I could rekindle the spark we'd had. Looking around, I appeared to be the only straight guy on the island—an ideal vacation spot! Of course, outside of Sally, I'm not sure how many straight women there were either; Cherry Grove could have passed for the Isle of Lesbos.

We had adjacent rooms, rather tiny but neat, on the backside of the hotel—thank God, away from the noisy pool. The way Sally had been lately, I didn't want to force her to sleep with me in the same bed, nor did I want a case of blue balls if we shared a bed and she decided not to put out. As soon as we unloaded our stuff, Sally announced that she needed a drink. It wasn't even sundown.

There were no cars on Fire Island, just boardwalk and sand, and it's only about a half mile wide from bay to Atlantic Ocean, so it really was an escape. However, I soon realized, as I joined Sally for a cocktail, that there wasn't much to do besides sunbathe and drink. And have sex. In the time it took for me to have one beer and Sally to suck down two frozen fruity concoctions, at least three guys came over to talk to me. I think they took Sally to be my fag hag friend and, with a sly smile, she didn't correct them. She liked seeing me weasel out of the come-ons, usually with a variation of, "I'm straight, I'm Sally's manager and you'll have to come by to see her on Sunday night." I could turn them down and promote at the same time.

"What would you do if you didn't have me here to be your excuse?" Sally wondered aloud as another guy wandered off.

"First of all, I wouldn't be here at all. We're here for business."

"Really? Three nights for a one-night gig? We could have come out and back on Sunday, rented a private boat or helicopter."

"How rich do you think I am? Do you have any idea how much money has been spent so far?" I decided not to dwell on the business, given the surroundings. "Besides, I wanted to give us a little vacation time. We deserve it."

"Separate rooms?" She kept that Mona Lisa smile as she sipped from her goblet through a straw.

"I didn't want to presume anything. I know you're with ML."

"I appreciate it," she said unconvincingly. She gestured to the people surrounding the pool just outside the bar area. "Aren't you a little curious? So many hot guys."

"No, I'm not curious," I said.

"Here's your weekend to try something, no strings attached, see how it fits."

"No thanks." I decided to play along. "What about you? Thinking about any girl-on-girl action this weekend?"

"Absolutely. Why not?"

"Can I join in?"

"Have you ever done that before? A threesome?"

I couldn't lie. "No, I never have. I'm not as …" I paused for the right word, "as *experienced* as you are."

"I sometimes forget that you are barely legal. Well, maybe this would be a good weekend to experiment. Maybe you and me and another guy."

"No fucking way."

"A gay guy once told me that a man gives a better blow job, because they know how it feels to be on the receiving end, they know what feels good. And they also aren't afraid of it, aren't afraid to take it all in."

"Glad to hear it." I ordered a second beer. I wasn't sure where Sally was going with all of this, but it suddenly felt like a long weekend was brewing. "Where can we eat around here?"

"I don't know. We'll have to explore. So much has changed since the last time I was here. Well," she corrected herself, "rather, new places but same scene, if you know what I mean. We'll have to taxi over to the Pines at some point, just for fun. You'll have to see the houses."

"Sounds like a plan." We finished our drinks in more or less silence—she wasn't getting anywhere trying to get me on a bisexual adventure—and went off to a place that overlooked the bay, ordering clams and fries and watching the sun go down. It was pretty spectacular, I have to say. After that, I suggested a walk on the beach—in my mind, something romantic—and she politely went along, but she seemed restless, always looking around at what was happening with everyone else.

After that there wasn't much else to do other than go to the bars and dance clubs. I wanted to go into the two dance clubs and give the deejays a copy of "Grind" and promote Sally's appearance, but I would have been breaking my own self-imposed rule: This was to be a time of relaxation, not business. Sally was holding me to the rule. Fuck it, I'd sneak off and give them the CDs later.

Naturally, Sally wanted to go to a bar. There was a small piano bar on the bay side called Cherry's that was to her liking. At one point, she even got up to sing, doing an old country song called "Crazy" and then something called "Hit the Road, Jack." I had to admit, singing that kind of music kind of relaxed her and seemed to fit with the tough broad image she had. But would it sell? After that, a lot of people around her age came over to talk with her and buy her drinks, which she readily accepted. They didn't seem to know or care who she was but I told everyone to come to the Ice Palace on Sunday to find out. The people swarming around Sally were cool and everything, but I suddenly felt so young that I briefly wondered what I was doing there, on a gay island hanging out with people twice my age. At least the Ice Palace had guys my own age, but all they wanted were drugs and sex—unfortunately for me, same-sex sex.

After midnight, I was getting restless myself. I wanted to go back to the room and have sex, but the prospects around Fire Island were pretty dim for me, outside of Sally. And Sally didn't seem to be in any hurry to go anywhere. I yawned in a big way to get her attention.

"Honey, why don't you go back to your room and get some sleep? I'm a big girl; I can take care of myself." She wanted to get rid of me.

"You're not coming?"

"No, I want to hang out, listen to some music."

"Are you sure?"

"Yeah, I'm sure."

"Sally, you're giving up the chance to go home with him?" one of the guys sitting with us asked her.

"You have to keep them wanting more," Sally advised. "These young studs think that everyone just can't wait to get in the sack with them, especially if we're older."

"He's right," the guy said.

"Well, perhaps an older woman has more to offer than an older guy," Sally said, and her new fans applauded her with, "You go, girl!" and like-minded expressions.

With that, I excused myself and said goodnight to all, reminding Sally that she could feel free to knock on my door. I was pathetic.

The pool area outside the hotel was still pretty crowded and music was still blasting from the nearby Ice Palace. I was getting the once-over from a few guys as I passed and it made me realize how uncomfortable women felt when men did the same thing to them. Sex was hanging in the air and yet there was nothing for me. Still, I decided to stop at the bar for a nightcap to relax me, and to hear what kind of music the deejay was playing and see what the dancers liked.

I was only there a few minutes when this tanned, blond guy came over and introduced himself as Toby. I shook his hand and he sat down next to me. "Did I see you with Sally Testata earlier?" he asked.

"Yeah. You know who she is?"

"Uh-huh. I was at Splash last Sunday."

"I missed the performance, but I heard about it," I said. "I'm her manager."

"Really?" He looked to be in his late twenties and I assumed his reaction meant he thought I was too young for the job. "How did you get that job?"

I told him the whole unlikely tale, which had him laughing and asking more questions. Toby was pretty cool, even aware of sports, and we got into a discussion about the baseball season. Another drink appeared in front of me, which he had bought me without my realizing it. What the hell, we were having good conversation.

A while later, Toby put his hand on my knee and suggested continuing the party in his room. I politely declined, letting him know that I was definitely straight.

"That's all right. I can make you feel good and it will be our little secret." Shit, I wondered if Sally had sent him! Two more drinks appeared.

"Look, I'm flattered, but it's really not my scene. In fact, I should be going."

"I'm sorry; don't worry about it. But stay and finish your drink."

"Okay." It took a minute to get the conversation back on track, but soon I was able to forget about his come-on. I mean, if I'd seen a hot straight girl next to me, I'd be working her, too. However, it didn't take long for the hand to land on my leg again, and lightly rub it.

I was getting drunk. "Toby, really," I said, moving his hand away with mine, which he then grasped in his own.

"Okay, sorry." He tried another tack. "Hey, I have some grass. You want to smoke some grass? Just to end the night on a little high, I won't try anything."

I didn't think it was a good idea, and so we started talking again and before I knew it, the place was emptying out and the bartenders were announcing last call. "I guess it's time to go," I said, standing.

"Yeah," he agreed.

As I walked, or staggered, back to my room, I noticed Toby was right behind me. "What's going on?"

"You look a little out of it, so I just want to make sure you get back okay," he said.

I opened the door to my room—forgetting to notice if Sally was back in hers—and Toby barged right in behind me. I fell back on the bed and closed my eyes. "Toby, you should probably go."

"Let's have a little toke." I opened my eyes and he was standing in front of me lighting a joint. He took a long drag from it and offered it to me. I got up on one elbow and took a hit. It was good, but my eyes were drooping, I was losing it. I lay back again.

"Yeah, just relax, Greg."

You won't believe it, but I didn't even hear him unzipping my shorts. The next thing I knew, he was working me over with his mouth! "Hey, hey, hey!" I whispered urgently, bolting up to a sitting position. The quick movement was probably not the smartest thing I've ever done. "Ah, your teeth!" I screamed.

"Sorry. You shouldn't have moved." He stroked the half-hard thing. "It felt good, right?"

"Come on, man. You can't do this," I begged.

"That's what I say. Come on, man!" Then he resumed his work. I lay back again and closed my eyes, pretending it was Sally or someone else, anyone else—any female. Before too long—understand, I hadn't had any sex in weeks—I was moaning and ready to shoot. He pulled away and started moaning himself and then came all over my stomach just as I was coming, too. It was disgusting, but I figured I had to be polite and let him because he'd been doing all the work. He wanted to lie there on top of me and probably go to sleep, but I wouldn't have it. "Toby, you've got to go. Wipe me off, please. You've got to wipe me off!" There was no way I was touching anything.

"Don't worry about it, dude. Relax." He had a slight edge to his voice, but he got a towel and did as I'd asked him and was out the door with a dismissive, "Take care."

The next morning I woke up starving and wanted to find bacon and eggs somewhere. I tiptoed next door to Sally's room—it was after eleven—and saw that the blinds were closed and her door was locked. She probably wouldn't be up for hours. I went back to my room and threw on a fresh pair of shorts and a T-shirt and headed out to see what I could find. It was clear that most of the island was still asleep, but I found a diner that was already doing a bustling business. As I sat to order, there across the room sat Toby with a couple of guys. He gave me a sly smile and wave and then started talking to his friends. I guess I was going to be outed after being the recipient of a blow job. Fire Island had to be the smallest fucking island in the universe.

By early afternoon, there was still no stirring from Sally's room, so I decided to knock on the door. Nothing. I knocked louder and heard a moan from inside.

"Sally, are you okay?" I asked.

"Yeah, I'm okay." She didn't sound okay.

"Sally, let me in."

I waited for a minute and at last I heard her padding to the door. She turned the knob to unlock the door, then went straight back to the bed as I entered.

"Hangover?" I asked.

"Uh-huh."

"Are you hungry?"

"No. I just need rest. I'll probably be in bed most of the day." She managed a smile as she hugged her pillow. Maybe this vacation on Fire Island wasn't such a good idea. "And how was your night?"

"Not much happened," I said.

"I heard something happening," she teased, "from outside your door."

"Fuck you, Sally. I was really drunk, and this guy took advantage of it. It was very quick and meant nothing."

"Okay, tiger. I guess I'll have to keep my eye on you. Or your mother will be blaming me for that, too."

"I am not gay! And leave my mother out of it!" My mother was a frightening thought at that moment.

"Good idea."

"So you're not getting up?"

"No. I'll be fine and check in with you later. See what your friend is up to," she laughed, and rolled over to face the wall.

I ignored her remark. She had more than a hangover, I thought. She had found a way to get some drugs, not hard to do in that little paradise. So much for getting Sally away from the pressures of the city. This was like Greenwich Village on a sandbar.

"Fine," I said. "But Sally, you are still my client as well as my friend. You can't party like this or you're going to ruin your life, never mind your career."

"I just got caught up in the moment. I'll be all right."

"Okay. I'll check in with you again around dinnertime. You need to eat something. Don't forget, you do have a performance tomorrow."

"I'm not forgetting. I'll see you later." With that, she pulled the sheet over her head, shutting me out completely. I turned wordlessly and left the room, locking it on my way out.

I took a blanket and towel and headed out to the beach with my iPod and a crime novel. Relaxing was not a normal state of mind for me, and the afternoon dragged on. I had met a lot of people in New York, but I had no new friends. I had immersed myself in a business that offered me no side benefits.

By the time I returned to the hotel, Sally was up and gone. I could see through the open slits of the blinds that her room was empty. There were only so many places she could be. I walked over to the bar, then down the boardwalk to the other bar-restaurants, but still no sign of her. Maybe she was at the beach. I couldn't relax, not knowing where she was. I left a note on her door to call my cell when she returned if I wasn't in my room. I went into my room and, completely bored, lay on my bed and easily fell asleep after the afternoon in the sun.

When I awoke, I had momentarily forgotten where I was. It was dark outside, and yet I could hear voices. I picked up my watch and could see that it was after nine. I jumped out of bed, realizing I had yet to hear from Sally. I threw on my clothes and went next door; my note was still attached to her door. Shit! Now I was starting to worry. What if she'd had a medical emergency? What if she'd drowned? What if she was partying in some crack cottage, so far gone she didn't know who she was? I know she hadn't completely abandoned me because her little suitcase was still next to her bed. I made the rounds of the clubs again—which took all of ten minutes in that tiny island village—but she still wasn't to be found.

I went back to the bar by the hotel, which had a nice view of the pool, the Ice Palace, and the wide sidewalk leading to the entire area. I couldn't miss her if she were to walk by. I ordered a beer.

It wasn't long before some older guy sat next to me and started chatting me up. Before he had finished his pitch, his hand was on my shoulder. I shoved it away. "Sorry, man, I'm straight."

"Well, I've heard many variations on, 'I'm not interested,' but that's the best one yet. What an odd choice of vacation for yourself."

"No, it's true—" I started to explain.

"Oh, save it. You're one of those straight guys who allows a few lucky men to suck your dick, right?" he said, then got up and walked away. Was there some kind of conspiracy going on?

It was going to be a long night. It was still only ten o'clock; that place was just beginning to hop for a Saturday night. Where was Sally? Then it hit me: *The Pines*! She had told me I *had* to see it. That must be where she went. I drained my beer and headed down to the pier to catch a water taxi.

The ride over cost about ten bucks and I wasn't sure we were going to make it. The water was rough and the guy was speeding over the waves. All of us crowded in the back were laughing and getting sprayed. I wouldn't have wanted to take that ride after a night of partying.

Just as Sally had told me, the scene at The Pines was quite different. It was almost all guys—hardly a lesbian to speak of—and they were either old or young, hardly any in-between. Also, I'd have prepped it up if I had known the social set was going to be like this; my mother would have fit right in if she were able to forget the men around her were gay. There were a lot of guys that looked to be my age. They either traveled in predatory wolf packs or were arm in arm with silver-haired gentlemen, calmly strolling the promenade, having already captured their prey. The young guys, nothing but high-class hustlers by the look and sound of them, incredibly, had a higher snob factor than the millionaires they were wooing. This place, with its mansions tucked away behind the evergreens and its pristine sidewalks with high-priced boutiques and cafés, was a sight to behold, but totally Skanksville at the same time. Sally had to be here.

I followed a couple of the wolf packs down a lane away from the water and could hear dance music in the distance. Within a couple of minutes, I was outside of the Pavilion, a large, two-story glorified barn, and music was blasting through the windows. This was the hot spot.

As I entered, I was gratified to hear the opening tribal beat of "Grind" starting up, and the whoops and hollers from guys on the dance floor who were excited to hear it. Then I heard the deejay announce, "Even better, guys, tonight we have the singer here, and she's going to perform her new hit for us!" Screams of delight from the fans. Panicked, I pushed my way onto the crowded dance floor and worked my way to the front. There was Sally on the stage in her little black dress, panties still on, grinding her way and "oohing" and "ahhing" over the extended opening rhythms. As I got closer, I could see that her eyes were glazed over, her face sweating. She was wasted!

I didn't want to kill the party, but I was pissed! She had now taken it upon herself to perform for free! I decided to stop behind a bunch of guys in front of the stage, so she wouldn't see me.

As the song went on, she did the memorized moves that Antonio had taught her, but the drugs she had taken gave them even more fluidity, like they were natural body movements, not choreographed steps. Her free hand was roaming all over her body, the crowd egging her on. When she finally got to the climactic ending she was, well, practically giving herself a climax. She was rolling around on the floor, rubbing herself, basically. Really, it was more obscene than if she had been prancing around nude. When it was over, she fell prostrate on the stage floor, arms outstretched with a look of bliss on her face. At last, she rose to massive applause and made her way, stumbling a bit, to the deejay booth. As she was trying to convince him to play another song, I caught up with her.

"Sally, what are you doing?"

"Hey, sugar, you found me!" she slurred. "I met these great guys, I've been hanging out with them at their mansion all day, by their pool."

I ignored her. "Sally, we need to get out of here. You shouldn't be performing for free. I could have gotten you in here for several hundred dollars."

"Well, now maybe you can get me in here for over a thousand." She was leaning against the wall as if trying to hold it up, her head lolling back and forth.

"You are fucked up. We're going back to the hotel."

"No, the guys said I could stay over. They have an extra bed."

"Absolutely not! You have another gig tomorrow and you are in no condition to be partying all night!"

"You don't own me."

"Yeah, I do, actually. I've advanced thousands and thousands of dollars toward your career and until I make it back, I own you." It was probably the worst thing one could say to Sally, and tomorrow she wouldn't remember it, but that night I should not have been arguing with a drunk on drugs.

"You little punk! You dragged me out of my home and I'm giving you everything you wanted and more. And now you want to control me, having me under your thumb, just like all the rest."

"No, Sally, that's not it. I want this to be a big success for both of us, but it's going to take discipline." I grabbed her arm. "Now come on, let's go back to the hotel."

"I'm not your whore!" she screamed, and even the oblivious, sweaty, shirtless guys looked over at us.

"Don't worry, Sally, that's pretty clear to me. You're everyone else's whore." I couldn't help myself, I was at my wit's end. She took a swing at me but, in her state, she only grazed me and ended up punching the wall.

By then a security guard was upon us. "What's the problem here?"

"I'm her manager," I began to explain to his doubtful face, "and I'm just trying to get her out of here. She's pretty fucked up."

He looked at her and then steadied her by holding both of her arms in his big hands and looking into her eyes. "Sally, do you know this guy? Is he your manager?"

She looked from him to me and then back to him. "Yes. Yes, he is," she said quietly, then tears quickly formed in her eyes and spilled down her cheeks. I hadn't seen her cry, or even come close to it, since that Easter morning in church.

The big guy gently wiped her cheeks with his hands and kindly smiled at her. "Maybe you'd better let him take you home. But you come visit us again, okay?"

"Okay." The fight was gone from her at that moment; even she knew she was too fucked up to go on.

The guard helped us out of the club and called the water taxi for us. She draped herself around me and we walked back to the dock. It was still relatively early for a Saturday night, not yet one, so there was only one couple with us on the ride back to Cherry Grove, thank God. Sally was moaning and threatening to barf the whole way, a ten-minute ride that seemed much longer. Fortunately, the couple had a sense of humor about it all. Around there, Sally's condition was probably the norm.

It took no effort to get Sally into bed. In fact, she crawled under the covers, black dress and all, leaving me to wonder what in the hell she would wear for the next day's performance. A bathing suit? I debated getting into bed with her—not to do anything, of course, even though I wanted to, like always—but just to be able to keep tabs on her. Instead, I stayed with her until I knew she was asleep—that didn't take long—and then went to my own room. At that point, I was exhausted myself.

The next morning, I went to breakfast by myself again, choosing to let Sally sleep off her drugs. We hadn't spent any time together—sober, anyway—since we'd arrived on Friday. So much for winning her back into my arms while she was away from ML.

Anyway, I took my time over breakfast. I picked up a Sunday *Times* and leisurely made my way through its many sections. When I got back to the room, it was nearly one o'clock and Sally still hadn't stirred. The performance was at three.

I rapped on the door. "Sally? Sally, you need to get up." Nothing. "Sally? Come on, get up." I knocked again, louder and more persistently.

"Okay." I let out a big sigh, thanking God she was still alive. "I'm up. Let me get ready."

"Are you okay? Do you need help?"

"I'll be all right."

"Great. Well, I'll be right next door. If you need me, just call."

"Okay."

I felt uneasy, but I went to my room and turned on the TV, flipping through the few working channels, trying to occupy myself. An hour later, she emerged and appeared at my door wearing shorts and a black tank top, holding a garment bag. She gave me a weak smile. "Ready," she announced, sounding unconvinced.

"You look great," I lied. She hadn't yet put on makeup, and her skin was taut and red from the previous day's sun, her eyes listless. "What are you going to wear?" I asked, pointing to the bag.

"Just something I picked up on our Fifth Avenue shopping trip." There had been so much, I was at a loss trying to figure out what it could be.

"Okay. Do you need something to eat?"

"Oh, I can't eat before a performance, you know that."

"When did you last eat?"

"There was food at the guys' house yesterday. I was nibbling all day long."

"Uh-huh. I just want to make sure you're not going to collapse on me."

"Nope," she assured me. "Listen, about last night. I'm sorry. I don't know what came over me. When I party, I just want to let it all hang out."

"I wasn't happy about it, Sally. You have to trust me with the career decisions. But your appearance at the Pavilion may bring in a bigger crowd today."

"Was it that good? I don't remember much of it, but I do remember the applause."

"Let's just say you definitely let it all hang out." I smiled. She had come down and seemed humble. We were at peace.

"It won't happen again."

"Okay. Just go out there today and give us a performance, remembering what Antonio taught you."

"Deal." She came toward me and gave me a hug, a real hug. Like between good friends, you know?

Over at the Ice Palace, we went backstage to the small dressing room. The manager came in and introduced himself and gave us the basic rundown of what would happen, how she would be cued, and so on. Then I left her alone to put on makeup and get dressed, as she liked to do that routine by herself.

Out on the long floor, with wide-open doors to the pool area, the afternoon tea dance had started. Because it was a holiday weekend, and the first unofficial weekend of the summer, there were already quite a few people dancing. I got a beer from the bar and found an inconspicuous spot in the center but leaning against the back wall. I wanted to get a panoramic view of the whole crowd to see how they reacted to Sally.

A little after three, the deejay announced that Sally Testata was coming out for a live performance in a few minutes, then launched into an old Pillow Talk song that probably nobody in the room knew but me.

A blond guy and a thin girl with short dark hair and a tattoo of what looked like an electric fence all the way around her bicep stood together in front of me.

"I heard she masturbated on stage at the Pavilion last night," he told her.

"I'd love to see that," she said.

"I know—that is fucking crazy! She almost makes Britney and Lindsay and Paris look normal," he said, referring to some young starlets of varying talents who were going in and out of rehab and police custody that spring. "Sally Testata could be their mother!"

"Sally Testata can be my mama, ooh yeah," the girl said, demonstrating a sucking sound for her friend.

"Do you think she goes that way?" the guy wondered aloud.

"I think she goes *every* which way!"

"You're probably right."

They stopped talking and listened to the song play out. Then the deejay made another announcement and Sally walked out onto the stage to wild applause. She was wearing a big, pink, flowery—I don't know what! A fucking muumuu or something! I remembered her buying it but didn't think she had it in mind for a performance—maybe for serving breakfast on the veranda after she became rich.

As if reading my mind, the lesbian said, "What the hell is that?"

"I have no idea. But she'll probably strip it off at some point and reveal leather bra and panties."

"I sure hope so. That getup doesn't do anything for me."

The outfit, so out of Sally's usual performance element, seemed to pull her out of her act. She looked a bit lost, more like a kind earth mother. "Bombs Away" was playing but she hadn't counted from the beginning and I could tell she started too late with the vocal; she would get lost when the track went into the chorus. Sure enough, the buildup to the chorus began and she was still singing the verse. She looked over to the deejay for help, but what was he to do? So she just stopped singing all together and came in with the repeat of the chorus. Meanwhile, she had completely forgotten her moves, and basically just stood there singing the song.

"She's completely out of it," the blond guy said.

When she finished, the applause was lukewarm at best. Next was "I Still Have What it Takes," but it didn't look as if she or anyone else believed it. Again, she seemed to be concentrating all her efforts on remembering the lyrics, depriving the performance of any kind of energy. The muumuu billowed around her, succeeding in making her great figure entirely shapeless. The response to that number was also lackluster, but as "Grind" revved up, the crowd cheered and shouted as if to help her out, as if to say, "Come on, Sally, give us something!" Apparently, that song, only out for a couple of weeks, and her performance of it, were already the stuff of legend.

She shimmied and strutted a little more, but the dress remained on. "Maybe she got in trouble for the masturbation thing," the girl offered.

"I guess it's possible," the guy agreed.

When the song ended, the reaction was polite but the audience was obviously expecting more. "Is that it?" tattoo girl asked.

As if to answer her, Sally spoke to the crowd. "Thank you all so much. I'd like to close with one more song which is also on the 'Grind' E.P." She looked over at the deejay, who had his hands up in the air, questioning. "It's just the next song on the disk," she told him. This was, of course, unplanned. Sally was nothing if not unpredictable. "This is a wonderful, classic song about growing up, accepting life as it comes to you." The slow piano accompaniment intro came up. A few people wandered out to the pool. "The world changes around us," the earth mother advised, "and so must we." And with that, she stood behind the microphone and sang "Everything Must Change." Several people mumbled to each other and walked away, but the diehards who decided to see her through were rewarded with a rich, meaningful performance, complete with real tears. I didn't fully understand Sally, or even like her much of the time, but I couldn't help loving her.

When that song ended, those who remained shouted and whistled. "She doesn't need to take her clothes off if she does that," the lesbian said, impressed. "I want to take her home with me."

"Really? I don't get it. Her voice isn't that great," her friend said.

"You're so fucking shallow," she said to him with a smile. "Come on, let's get another drink." They walked to the bar.

I'm not sure who I agreed with. I liked her on the standard, but I also saw people walking away. When she was giving a performance, she was able to really sell the dance songs, which were poised to be big hits. As the manager, I had to go where the money was. As her friend, I wanted her to be fulfilled. Which role would win out?

In the end, we gave up our room for Sunday night. We'd both had quite enough of Fire Island. The sea breeze that enveloped us as we rode atop the ferry back to Long Island at sunset was no longer a refreshing escape, but a tonic of reality washing over us. We said nothing to each other, remaining in our own private thoughts for the entire thirty-minute ride to shore. Sally slept on the train and I tried to read but couldn't concentrate, eventually abandoning it for the soundtrack of my iPod.

Coming up from the underground of Penn Station to the grimy danger of Eighth Avenue, I felt safer, more at home. Maybe Sally did too, as she grabbed my hand and smiled at me as I walked to the curb to hail a cab. No more vacations for Sally. Not on my watch.

CHAPTER NINETEEN

▼

There were still many big decisions to make regarding Sally's career. "Grind" was taking off rapidly—faster than "Bombs Away" in its day, looking at all the signs—and we needed to film a video. We also needed to get into the studio and start recording an entire album of ten or twelve songs, and we hadn't even begun the search process for songs. We would want a full-length CD out by late fall, in time to release the launch of a second single, if all was going well.

While I had my hands full calling clubs across the country, writing and sending out press releases, making travel and hotel arrangements, and trying to get radio and television appearances for Sally—not easy that early in the comeback—I had the added burden of trying to keep Sally busy. A bored Sally was a dangerous Sally. I continued to pay her living expenses plus a weekly stipend for spending money—kind of like an advance—until the career took off. Then, after my investment expenses were met, she would get to keep whatever she made, minus my twenty percent. So while I had control of how much money Sally got from me, I couldn't exactly keep her from spending her own money. After the Fire Island weekend, she began to spend more time with ML and, while that irked and frustrated me, it was better having her with him than having her hovering around me in that small apartment with me always horny because she wouldn't put out. As far as I could tell, ML was a decent guy and pretty busy with his own career. In fact, sometimes he brought her along to the studio to sit in the sound booth and watch and listen to him work, which was a great education for her. Whatever substance abuse problems she had were her own, not ML's.

The summer was shaping up to involve a lot of weekend gigs at gay bars in cities like Boston, Hartford, Philly, Baltimore, and DC, often at Gay Pride events, especially in June. Of course, she'd be rolling down Fifth Avenue in New York's parade at the end of June. After the song release parties and the Fire Island weekend, I was doing a lot of praying because there was no telling how any of those gigs were going to go over. In addition, these smallish gigs barely made any money, especially the ones that involved travel and overnight accommodations. The idea was that the live shows would promote the single, which would then promote her career, which would then finally lead to bigger venues and more money.

The first week of June, I had scheduled a meeting between the two of us and Gus Vanderwall. Technically, I was paying Gus to be a promoter, but he had been in the business for a long time and had managed and produced many acts along the way as well, so I welcomed his advice, even if it meant his taking a larger role in the process.

He welcomed us into his office and we took a seat on the couch and he sat at the chair on the side of the glass table. His first move—a bad one—was to offer us a drink. Sally asked for a gin martini on the rocks with three olives, hold the vermouth, and I, trying to set an example, requested a ginger ale. My example was lost on Sally, who made no comment. Gus got up to make the drinks. After he handed them to us, he gave us incredible news. "I can hardly believe this myself, but in the issue of Billboard that comes out tomorrow, 'Grind' has debuted at forty-seven on the Club Play chart." Sally squealed with delight and I shouted, "Sweet!" Gus continued. "Even with my excellent track record, getting a song out and getting enough airplay to chart within three weeks is an extraordinary accomplishment. It says a lot about the song and a lot about you, Sally. We have a terrific product."

She grimaced at his poor choice of word, perhaps her least favorite word, but a big swallow of gin seemed to help matters. "This is beyond what I could have hoped for and I can't thank both of you enough," Sally remarked. She leaned over to kiss my cheek.

"Greg requested this meeting so that we could all discuss the very crucial next step. The appearances and my continued promotion will keep this song climbing, but we're already behind on a plan for the follow-up. Certainly a video of 'Grind' must be filmed immediately, and work on a CD must begin."

This was a relief to me because it would keep Sally's hands full with projects for the next couple of months, at least. "What did you have in mind, Gus?" I asked, although I knew because he and I had discussed it. However, I wanted him to deliver the dicey proposition to Sally himself.

"Well, Sally, here's what I was thinking. You have created a sensation with your live performances so far. You seem to be fearless. Because 'Grind' is going to be a tough sell to mainstream radio anyway, we have a chance to do something that has never been done before."

"What would that be?" Sally asked, peering over her glass.

"Well, what about an extended-length video with nudity?"

Sally stood up. "You've got to be kidding me! How would that ever get play on MTV or YouTube?"

"That's just the point. It wouldn't. Why compete with all that? We would create an entirely new genre. Rather than those 'accidental' releases of sex tapes of Pamela Anderson and Paris Hilton, we could put it right out there as an artistic product."

"Pornographic music videos? That's your idea? You've just met me and this is what you present me with? I think it's time for me to leave." Sally picked up her purse and started to ease her way past my knees.

"Sally, wait, please wait," Gus begged. "We don't have to do that, I just thought I would ask. I only asked because you seem perfectly comfortable with using nudity in live performance."

Sally turned and faced him, her body rigid with rage. "That is *my* choice, not yours or any man's. And I did it to make a point."

"What point was that, Sally?" Gus asked in a patronizing, grandfatherly way. Even I wanted to smack him.

"The point was that I was roped into singing a pornographic song and I thought, *They want porn, I'll give 'em porn*—when I want to, on my terms. I knew the music industry was becoming inseparable from the porn industry for female singers, so I thought I'd ratchet it up a notch. But I'm doing it in front of gay men. It's outrageous but it doesn't turn them on. But as soon as it is marketed as a porn video, it becomes something for scum like you to leer at and beat off over. That is not a career move for me." A respectful silence followed Sally's passionate speech. Of course, I knew the other reason Sally did outrageous things on stage—because she was smashed out of her mind—but I decided to let that go for the moment and let her have her rallying cry. Sally glanced over at the photos on Gus's wide desk. "How can you have a daughter and suggest that to me?"

Gus was caught in a rare moment of what I would call embarrassment, his tanned face turning a shade of deeper red. "You are right, Sally. I just had to ask. It's business, no offense was meant."

Sally slowly came back to the couch and plopped herself into its deep, soft leather. "I don't see why we can't push 'I Still Have What it Takes,'" she said, to me in particular. "That way we'd make a songwriting royalty on the song."

"Well, that song is on the EP, of course, and as of next week both songs will be available for download on iTunes. Keep performing it live and we'll see how it sells," Gus answered. "The fact is, 'Grind' is already shaping up to be a big hit this summer. We can't very well abandon the ship now that she's left the port. The question, how can we best promote it?"

"We can make a sexy video without making it pornographic," I said. I wondered if that was true.

"I actually have an idea," Sally said. I tried to look expectant, but was dreading what she'd come up with. "And it would be very inexpensive." She then described to us her concept, which would involve a close-up of just her face, with slicked back hair and wearing bright red lipstick, singing the song. That's it. "And ML has a friend who has done independent films, and he'd probably do it for not much money."

Gus and I sat there for what seemed like minutes, although it was probably only about ten seconds, our jaws slack as our minds tried to comprehend the bizarre idea. "Was that ML's idea or yours?" I asked.

"What difference does it make? ML thinks I have a very sexy mouth." ML was right about that, but she had other attributes as well that she had been only too willing to show off on the live stage.

"It sounds a little too French cinema for my taste, Sally," Gus said.

Sally looked at me. "Are we on his payroll or is he on ours?" Jesus Christ, Gus was a giant in the industry and she was slapping him around in his own office!

"I am on yours," Gus said with a tight smile, standing. "I'm afraid I'm going to have to call an end to this meeting. I don't have all day to offer advice to someone who doesn't want it."

"Nor do I have all day to sit around listening to it," Sally said, extending her hand. "But it was so nice to finally meet you, Gus. You are every bit the legend I expected." I think she was being sarcastic, but Gus just shook her hand like a professional.

"Sally, I will continue to do my job promoting this song. You continue to do yours and we'll all be fine."

"I'll meet you outside in a minute, Sally," I said. "I just have a few matters to clear up with Gus."

"No problem." She nearly slammed the heavy wooden door on her way out. "I just want to apologize—" I began.

"You have a loose cannon there," Gus said, pointing at the door. "She ought to be thankful she still has tits and ass to peddle and a song that will market that, because she doesn't have much else. I've had gangster rappers show me more respect."

"Gus, you've done a great job and this song is going to be a big hit. I just need to finesse her a little bit."

"I don't think she can be finessed. She has too much opinion for her own good. Her career is going to sink a second time, faster than the first. Don't let her take you with her. If she doesn't toe the line and starts sabotaging things, you have to dump her. It's a business, my boy, business."

"Understood." I knew all about business, but the reason I sought out Sally for this venture was because of the fun of music. Now every decision was like navigating a faltering plane onto a runway, with the potential for salvation on the one hand or for disaster on the other. I just had to remind myself of lucky number forty-seven. We were forty-seven! And it was just the beginning.

* * *

"One of the top executives in the entire music industry thinks I'm no better than a porn star!" That's the greeting I got from Sally later that evening when I walked through the door. She was pouring gin into a glass of melted ice. Clearly, it was not her first drink. "I told you I didn't want to do that song!"

"Sally, please. It was just a suggestion. He respects your refusal."

"He's going to respect more than that when I'm finished with him."

I couldn't help but laugh at that proposal and her near-hysterical state. "I think it will be a while before we can take on Gus Vanderwall. And right now, he's doing a good job. We're on the charts!"

"But at what price?"

"Believe me, I can tell you what price. It's a price that hasn't been reached yet."

"Money! It's all about money for you! What about my dignity?"

I didn't really have an answer for that, but her live performances certainly hadn't helped matters. "We'll have a big hit and then you can do what you want. You'll get respect."

"Yeah, well, let me know when we have enough to buy it back." She went to her room, gin in hand, and slammed the door.

I needed to talk to somebody about all of this and yet everyone I knew in New York was on my payroll one way or another. Except Marcus. Our last meeting hadn't been great but he was my brother, after all, and in the business. Maybe he could help. To my surprise, he was home and told me to drop by.

When I got there, he ordered Chinese food and we got comfortable on his leather sofa. I began telling him of Sally's erratic behavior and what had happened at Gus's office and even the good news about "Grind" hitting the charts. At the end of it all, I finally asked him, simply, "What should I do?"

"I think you need to come up with an exit strategy. If the song's a hit, you can sell her to one of the major labels. You'll have a track record and can find other talent."

I was shocked by his cold assessment. "But you two get along so well."

"What does that have to do with anything? Sally is a lot of fun. Buy what you have is a very volatile stock. Unload it."

"I can't do that."

"You can't solve everyone's problems. She obviously has a lot of issues. I don't see a long career there unless she cleans up her act. Now."

"Maybe she's really uncomfortable with 'Grind.'"

Marcus dismissed that with a wave of his hand. "It's her job and she's under contract. If she wants to enjoy the money from it, she has to promote it. Nobody told her to take off her panties." He was right about that.

"Okay, I'll try to keep her to business and do what I can this summer. Hopefully, the song will be a big hit and that will solve a lot of the problems. Do you want to ride on the float with us for Gay Pride?"

"That would be fun. I might have to ditch early, though, because I'm working the pier dance later that night."

"Cool." We finished our meal talking about other things while half watching a dumb reality show about models. Watching those beautiful women backstab each other for the privilege of having a brief career of men ogling them, I suddenly had some understanding of Sally's anger.

CHAPTER TWENTY

▼

By the time Gay Pride in New York arrived at the end of June, "Grind" had already moved up from forty-seven to thirty-five to twenty-five on the Club Play chart, and the extended seven-minute mix, where we had added in Sally's improvised dubs from her Barracuda performance, was flying out of the stores in urban centers. Digital sales of the radio-friendly mix were also good: We might make the coveted Hot 100 on sales alone, as radio airplay was still not what we'd hoped for. Programmers were still skittish about the lyrical content.

I had to do some negotiating with Sally, who had remained immovable on getting ML's friend to shoot the video the way they wanted it. In order to agree to that, I had her promise that she would go back to a skimpy dress for live performances—no more flowing pink muumuus. But I also told her no more nudity, which I thought made me some kind of moral leader. She did several gigs in smaller cities from Boston to DC during June.

She had a couple of good points about her friend doing the video: It was inexpensive and was shot in one day and we needed to do something that was PG-rated enough to get on the music video channels.

The director's name was Hazelnut, believe it or not, and he wore a red sweatshirt, a Yankees cap over gnarly dreadlocks, and baggy jeans that somehow were staying on although they were belted around the thighs, his skinny ass clothed in blue-and-white-striped boxers. But he was all business. ML was there for the shoot but, as usual, it was hard to get a word out of him. He stood on the sidelines sucking on a straw and smiling and saying, "Yeah," when he liked something—that was about it. We were filming in a studio in some god-forsaken part of Queens and there was a small crew of three besides Hazelnut. Sally and I were the only white people. I was in a button-down Oxford, khaki trousers, and boat shoes: Could I have been any whiter?

The shoot was actually kind of fun and the guys seemed to like Sally. She was thrilled because she only needed to wear jeans and a tank top. It was all about makeup and hair from the shoulders up. She looked like a cat with all that eyeliner, but with the lipstick and the usually fluffy hair pulled tightly behind her head, the effect of the close-up on her was startling. When she began lip-synching the words to the camera, it was a performance without the distraction of her body but every bit as sexual. It reminded me of an old Barbara Walters interview I'd seen in one of my communications classes, of her interviewing Monica Lewinsky. Every time Monica spoke, the camera did an extreme close-up and she was wearing that wet lip gloss. You know they'd wanted every man in America to be thinking about the blow job she'd given to the president. That's what this video was like: It allowed Sally to be sexual without the audience having to see her tits or ass. And the glare of the close-up showed the lines on her face with glamour but without apology. She was a sexy older woman. A twenty-year-old pop tart couldn't have pulled it off.

As well as everything went, before leaving at the end of the day, I pulled ML into a small side room to talk to him.

"What's goin' down?" he asked me, adjusting the plastic stirrer between his teeth.

"Look, ML, I appreciate what you did here, pulling all this together—and I hope it works—but I need to be in control here."

"You trippin', man. You're in total control."

"I know everybody wants to be part of Sally's ride to the top, but I can't just bring everyone onto the payroll. You know?"

ML glared at me and let me sweat it out for a few moments. "Listen, homeboy. I ain't the playa here. I ain't makin' no scratch off this. What you got today was off the hook and it cost you next to nothing. I did this to respect my girl, which is more than can be said for you and Vanderwall."

"Wait a sec, ML. Don't lay that on me. I want the best for her so that she'll come out of this and never have to clean houses again. What are you in it for?"

For the first time, ML almost came out of his comatose delivery. He poked his finger into my chest. "Do I have to be in this for something? Look, dude, Sally and me, we just kickin' it. She's a dime piece, for sure, but she got heart. She got a mind. She's good people."

I was feeling closed in in the vocal booth I'd chosen for our tête-à-tête. "I'm sorry. It's not you, ML. I just worry about her. I want everything to work out right."

"Maybe you should listen to her."

"Well, I did today, didn't I?"

"Word up. And you'll be glad you did."

We left the booth on that unsteady truce. Sally was waiting patiently with a serene smile on her face, as if she enjoyed seeing her guys discuss her business.

Anyway, the shoot was done in a day, and then Hazelnut edited it in another couple. I got a couple dozen DVDs made and dropped it off to Gus for him to begin pitching it to cable channels. He scowled when I told him I did it her way—"She's gonna ruin, you kid"—but took the disks and promised to see what he could do.

As for the June gigs in cities within driving distance, they ran the gamut: One night there were hundreds packed into Avalon in Boston and the next night had Sally singing on top of a black box to a dozen drunks in an Albany dive. It was a scrappy way to make a living—a few hundred here, five hundred there—but slowly it was adding up. Sally's reputation that "she might do something" preceded her wherever she went, but she managed to put on a sexy, professional show, using Antonio's dance moves but not getting lewd in the process—just as I'd asked. She was getting some press in the local gay papers as well.

* * *

The Gay Pride Parade was a different matter. The day before, she was a wreck, nervous about everything, second-guessing her outfit, worrying about the other two performers on the float. Had I known Sally's hit was going to take off so quickly, I'd have sprung for her own float. As it was, she had to share the stage with—of all people—Olive Martini and Juan Encantilla, a muscled-up, good-looking guy who had managed to get his photo in a lot of second-rate publications but who had failed to dent the dance charts, thus far, with any of his three attempts in the last year. He must have had one hell of a patient manager. Sally deserved better than that carnival act, and I told her so, assuring her that she would be the belle of the float, winning over the crowd on her talent.

For some reason, she didn't seem to be hearing me. That gig seemed to her more important than all the rest. And it wasn't only the parade. She had an interview after the parade on KTU, one of the hottest dance stations in the country. It would be the debut of "Grind" on a mainstream station. The fragile sobriety she had maintained while on the road was threatening to crack again.

The next morning, Sally was up long before I was. She was in the shower a long time, then padding back and forth between the bedroom and the bathroom. As I roused myself, she noticed me watching her frantic movements. "I need to see ML before the parade."

"He'll be there," I reminded her. While the three performers would have seats on a raised platform on the back of the float, there was a section for seating at the front of the float for about ten people, the singers' entourages, if you will. ML, Marcus, and I were to be Sally's guests on the float. That damn Eddie Pearl would be there, representing Olive Martini.

"I know, but we're going to have breakfast and he'll calm me down. No offense."

"None taken." I had come to terms with the fact that I couldn't give Sally what she needed, whatever that was—God, drugs, or a big black dick. "Do what you have to do, but be there on Fifty-first Street at noon, sharp."

"Haven't I been a good little girl all month?" she cooed *a la* Marilyn Monroe.

"You have, and you see how much that has helped to build a hit."

"We've only just begun," she sang.

"Hey, record that. That could be the start of another hit song."

"It's already been a hit, silly."

Maybe I needed to broaden my musical horizons. Sally was soon off, wearing shorts and a T-shirt but carrying the little black dress and shoes in a garment bag. That gave me a couple hours to leisurely have breakfast and make a few phone calls.

By the time I got to Fifty-first Street, Sally was already there. They were conducting a sound check, so each performer was singing a line or two into the mike. Olive was decked out in her usual green, wearing a hat that looked like a leaf. Juan Encantilla was shirtless with tight pleather pants: His body was his whole act, in my opinion. He didn't look too happy about having three male Splash dancers on the float with them, wearing nothing but g-strings, stealing his fire.

I took a seat next to ML. "I hope you were able to calm her down," I said to him.

"I ain't spoken to her. I just got here," he said.

Shit! She had lied to me! That means she had met up with her dealer. I looked up at her and she gave me a happy wave. She was full of energy, all right, already coked up.

"ML, we have to do something about her addiction problem," I whispered to him.

"I've talked to her about it."

"And?"

"And what? You know how she is. That's why she can't move in with me. I can't commit that much, not with that shit hanging over her head."

"I see what you mean."

We were supposed to be going down Fifth Avenue by one o'clock, but it was closer to two by the time we finally got out there. We were on gay time, someone said. One of the first crowds was in front of St. Patrick's Cathedral and there were many picketing people lined up there. Thank God, Sally wasn't at the mike. It was Juan, whose song was more sleep-inducing than offensive.

Sally's first performance came somewhere in the thirties, where the crowds were thinnest, but she managed to have the audience dancing on the sidewalk. In fact, many were doing some kind of grinding motion and I wondered if Sally's song would start a whole new dance craze. The spotlight rotated back to Juan and then Olive, who would be repeating her one hit song from last year, *ad nauseum*.

By the time it was Sally's turn to sing again, we were between Fourteenth Street and the turnoff onto Eighth Street and the crowd was thick and very gay-friendly. Juan managed to work up the throngs by suggestively peeling down his pants and showing his ass during his song. He wasn't about to let the dancers get all the ass time. Not to be outdone, Sally got to the mike and as the intro was playing, she announced, "Juan, you're awfully pretty, but I'm the only one on this stage with one of these! I dedicate this song and dance to Gus Vanderwall!" Off came the panties! Horror-stricken, I looked at the reaction. Onlookers were screaming, most of them approvingly, but several parents quickly covered their kids' eyes or turned the strollers away from the street. Behind me, I heard ML mutter, "Damn!" Eddie Pearl was howling with laughter, those fucking teeth shining in the midday sun. She began to dance and sing, but she wasn't far into it before two cops bounded up onto the float and each grabbed one of her arms. One of the cops was a woman, and she grabbed the panties and ordered Sally to put them on, which she did. The track continued to play, but there was chaos on the street as hordes of gays continued to cheer. The cops had ordered the float to stop and they were guiding Sally off of it; apparently, she was being arrested.

I leaned forward and caught Marcus's attention. He was seated at the end of my row. "What do I do?"

"You'd better go with her," was all he said.

I grabbed her purse and garment bag and ML and I followed the cops, who were whisking her down Ninth Street as fans shouted encouragements to her. I looked back at the float, which was lumbering along again and letting the track play out. Marcus, never one to miss his precious parade, smiled and waved at me from his perch. God forbid he should help me out. The cops put her in a squad car and the woman asked if I was carrying her stuff. I told her yes, and she took the bags from me.

We followed on foot to the precinct on Tenth Street. By the time we got there, Sally had already been booked and charged with indecency and possession of a controlled substance—they had found a small bag of cocaine in the purse that I had handed over to them. Sally would be added to the list of arrested celebrity bimbos that summer—except that she was old enough to be the mother of the others and I, for one, knew she was no bimbo. I could already hear Gus Vanderwall snickering in his office, "I told you so."

Sally ended up spending a couple of hours in the slammer while I tried to make some calls to secure a lawyer. When it became clear there would be no visitation allowed, ML said to me, "Look, I can't take this shit no more," and walked out of the precinct.

Early that evening, after I had posted her bail, Sally sauntered out to greet me, remarkably unfazed by it all. And she was sober.

CHAPTER TWENTY-ONE

▼

Despite the stresses of the day, I managed to get her over to KTU for her nine o'clock interview.

I accompanied her into the station and sat outside the booth so I could give her visual encouragement, if needed. Sally sat in one booth and Gina Ferrara, the deejay, sat in the other. They saw each other through the glass but communicated through microphones and headsets. Kind of weird.

After some introductory banter and a few laughs, Gina asked her, "Is it true, Sally, that you've done some naughty things on stage?"

"There were a couple of isolated incidents early on, but I've tried to be a good girl ever since."

"Were you a good girl today?"

"Depends on your definition. Whatever I do onstage is what I want to do. I've been around this business long enough that I'm not going to let anyone else tell me what to do. We girls have to stand up to the men who run this business, you know?"

"I hear you, girlfriend. But has it been that bad? Your manager over there, he seems like a sweetheart." Thankfully, the drug part of Sally's arrest hadn't yet gotten to Gina Ferrara.

"Greg? Yeah, he is." Sally gave me a wink. "But I've had to educate him in the ways of the music business a little bit." I rolled my eyes but, okay, this was probably playing well for her audience.

"Is it true you dedicated your, um, performance today to Gus Vanderwall? What was that all about?"

"Well, we just came out with the video for 'Grind' and I had to beg Greg to do it the way I wanted it done and it's very sexy but unexpected. Gus Vanderwall wanted me to do a seven-minute pornographic video; he said it would be a whole new market. So my performance today was a little bit of "Take that, Gus!'" Jesus Christ! Gus Vanderwall had gotten her this very interview!

Gina Ferrara's eyes widened. "Really? Gus Vanderwall? I read somewhere that he has a teenage daughter who wants to get into the business." Gina had stumbled onto a scoop. The switchboard in front of Gina was already lighting up.

"Well, I didn't know about that, but I did see her picture in his office. She's a pretty girl and I wish her luck. I hope he doesn't book her in the strip clubs."

I motioned through the glass for Sally to cut this line of dialogue, running a finger across my throat. Both Sally and Gina saw me and smiled. Gina went on. "How did you react to his suggestion?"

"Oh, believe me, no woman has ever talked to Gus Vanderwall like I did. He basically kicked me out of his office."

Gina laughed uproariously. They were becoming fast friends. "Wow, Sally, you are something else. Tell me, isn't Gus promoting your first single, which we're going to hear in a minute?"

"Yes, and he's done a good job of it. But he should stick to the music and trust that the artist knows something about how to market his or her image."

"He's been successful at this for a long time, though." Gina knew where her bread was buttered.

"Uh-huh. And I wish him continued success. But I know only too well that success can be very fleeting in this business."

"Tell us a little about how you managed this comeback."

Sally went on to give an abbreviated version of the whole adventure, from my discovery of her in Scranton to her current ride up the charts. At last, Gina brought the interview to a close and said, "Now we're going to hear Sally's comeback smash, 'Grind.' And look for her July sixth at Key West in Philly. Thank you, Sally Testata!" The familiar beat started pumping over the sound system. Gina took off her headphones and came out to shake our hands, Sally having come out into the hallway. "I think you made some waves tonight, Sally," she said.

"No doubt," I agreed.

"Thank you so much, Gina. Hopefully, we'll meet again when the next hit is climbing the charts," Sally said. "By the way, don't be shy about playing 'I Still Have What it Takes.' We wrote that one."

"I'll see what I can do," Gina said, which in this business meant no. "Good luck to both of you."

By the time we got into a cab and I turned on my cell phone, I'd already had a message from Gus: "I am ending my services with you as of now. I will send you a bill." That was it. I relayed the information to Sally.

"We don't need him," was all she replied.

"Sally, you need to rein it in sometimes. You're going to get yourself into a lot of trouble."

"No more trouble than I've already had."

We rode silently the rest of the way to Midtown. I was contemplating my next move, where I would find another promoter, and wondering if Gus had given us enough momentum to keep us climbing for a while.

On Monday morning, Sally Testata had the unique distinction of having three mentions in different *New York Post* stories. First, there was the article about her arrest. She was nowhere near as big a star as the Hollywood trio of Paris, Lindsay, and Britney, but the article lumped her in with them as being part of a summer epidemic. She also had the added distinction of the indecency charge and, as I predicted, her age—she, above all, should know better, it was implied. Then her name popped up in a general article about the parade coverage; her arrest was the biggest drama of the day in a parade that had long ago lost its ability to shock. Finally, she was mentioned in a Page Six item regarding her KTU interview implicating Gus Vanderwall as a sleaze who tried to push Sally into pornography.

While this ocean of free publicity would surely stir up something, we had no time to think about it. Before we had even finished our morning coffee, reading the papers and watching the events unfold on New York One, the apartment buzzer was sounding.

"Oh, no, the press is coming right to our doorstep now," I said. We had a sublet, so I was wondering how they had found us. I spoke into the intercom. "Yeah?"

"It's ML." I looked at Sally to get her okay and she just shrugged. I buzzed him up.

ML came into the apartment dressed in jeans and a tank top, with a baseball cap on backwards. "How come you don't return my calls?" he asked Sally, throwing his arms up in the air.

"Oh, sweetie, I didn't know you called. I think my phone has been on silent since the radio station." Sally made a move toward her bedroom to retrieve the phone.

"Forget it," ML said. "Look, boo. I need a break from all this shit goin' down."

I turned away, pretending to busy myself with tidying up the kitchen.

"Need a break?" Sally asked. "Babe, things are just heating up. We're gonna do well."

"Do your thang, girl, you'll make your bling," ML said. "Look, I don't like that phat pocket peckerwood Vanderwall any more than you do, but in the biz, he is trump tight, no touchin' him."

"So you can't be seen with me, is that it?"

"I just gotta lay low for a while, 'til this all blows over."

I felt I had to add something. "ML, we need you around for a while, while things are crazy out there."

"Yo, motherfucker, what do *you* have to do with any of this? This is between me and my girl. Shit, man, all you think about is your game, gettin' your dough." He cackled and turned back to Sally. "Didn't this punk want me outta the picture just last week?"

"Yes, he did," Sally said, trying to play along with a fake laugh, but she was wiping away tears.

ML stepped toward her, held her by the shoulders and looked into her eyes. "Salsa, you be strong and do your thing. I'll be watchin' and cheerin' you on, but I just need to do my own thing for a minute, okay?"

"Okay," Sally managed to hiccup. ML pulled her into a long embrace, then pushed himself away and headed toward the door.

"One, four, three, Salsa. You go out there and kick ass!" He gave her a thumbs-up and headed out the door.

I ran after him down the steps. "ML! ML!"

He stopped on a landing and turned to face me. "Whatchu want?"

"You're a good guy, ML. I just …" I searched for the right words to say. "I just wished you'd waited a bit; she really needs you right now."

"No," he said, pointing at me. "*You* really need me right now. You in over your head and the shit is comin' down and you can't handle her. You thought you had it all, and you ain't."

"I got a song on the charts. That's pretty damn good," I said.

"And I give you props for that. But the game ain't over yet." He started to walk away.

Desperately, I called out, "ML, what do I do?"

"You best call that oreo."

"Oreo?"

"You know, Antonio Motherfucking Grant. Uncle Tom will set her straight."

* * *

Sally took a couple of sleeping pills and stayed in bed all day, occasionally waking up in a crying jag, then falling asleep again. I unplugged the phone and fielded calls on my cell phone, which is what I used for business anyway. And, man, did the calls come in!

The calls were no longer just second-rate clubs looking to book a D-list celebrity—although those came in, too—but now there were requests for interviews, print, radio, and even television. They didn't so much want to talk about Sally and her personal demons—they wanted dirt on Gus Vanderwall! You see, outside of gay dance club circles, Sally was still pretty much an unknown. But Gus Vanderwall had a thirty-year career as a producer, manager, and promoter. He was never content just doing work behind the scenes, but was a charismatic newsmaker himself. He was like the Donald Trump of the music business. It looked as if Sally's little ill-thought comments were threatening to bring him down.

Sure enough, that night on the news, about ten minutes into the broadcast, the story came on:

> Dance club singer Sally Testata was arrested on charges of indecency and cocaine possession at yesterday's Gay Pride Parade in Greenwich Village, but that seems to be just the tip of the iceberg. Testata revealed in a weekend interview on WKTU that well-known music promoter Gus Vanderwall urged her to go into pornography to boost her singing career. This has caused outrage among many women in our area, and we now go to our correspondent Tucker McElroy in Times Square.

McElroy then asked several female passersby on the street what they thought of the controversy. One woman said, "I'm not surprised. The men running the music business have already turned it into pornography. Maybe this will be a wake-up call."

Another said, "He ought to be ashamed of himself. Is that how he's going to market his daughter?"

Still another offered, "Sally Testata is no role model, but she's a brave woman to stand up to that pig and the male exploitation of women in the entertainment industry."

The story then went back to the anchor behind the desk, who then said, "Gus Vanderwall would not appear on camera but he issued the following statement:

> Sally Testata is a very troubled woman with possibly serious drug and psychological problems. These things must be taken into account when evaluating her statements. In a meeting to discuss her career, we talked about several options. At no time did I suggest pornography as an appropriate career choice. I have always been about discovering and promoting musical talent. Miss Testata's statements have been extremely hurtful to me and my family. I no longer represent Miss Testata, but I wish her well.

The anchor then went on to another story, but Sally, whom I had roused when the story began, threw a pillow to the floor. "That fucking liar! That's slander!"

"Sally, you are the star of the day!" I shouted.

"I don't give a shit about that. I want his head on a plate!"

"Hold on, hold on. We need to think about what to do next. We don't even have a lawyer." I hadn't secured one while at the police station but since this morning's news, several had called. Perhaps that would have to be my next hire.

"Then let's get one," Sally commanded, reading my mind.

It became obvious that we needed one as the evening wore on. The tabloid shows like *Entertainment Tonight* and *Inside Edition* were also running the story, focusing on the Gus Vanderwall angle. By the next day, columnists were weighing in on the issue, most of them saying that the music industry had gone too far in pushing female singers to be sex objects and that it took an older woman like Sally Testata, who had nothing to lose with her career, to speak out about the issue. Even worse for Gus, a singer in her thirties, who had had a couple of minor hits about ten years before, came forward and said that Gus, as her manager, had touched her inappropriately and had coaxed her, eventually, to do a layout for *Penthouse,* which she claimed ruined her career as a serious singer. There were rumblings that more famous and semi-famous women would come forward with opinions on the issue in general, and perhaps on Gus in particular. By Tuesday evening, I had retained a celebrity lawyer, Joel Feldman, and by the evening news, he'd already released a statement to the press:

> Sally Testata will not be speaking at this time, but
> is recuperating from a very stressful weekend. As for
> Mr. Vanderwall, he is in no position to judge her
> alleged psychological or drug problems, and we will
> take whatever legal steps we need to make to ensure
> that her character is not impugned. As for Ms. Testata's
> statements regarding Mr. Vanderwall urging her to
> do a pornographic music video, I have every reason
> to believe in the veracity of her statement, and will
> be willing to further discuss it at the appropriate time.

Unbelievable! It was turning into a three-ring circus and we might all—outside of Gus—come up winners!

The story had legs for the whole week, with the whole social issue being brought up. Best of all, when I checked the charts on *billboard.com* on Thursday—which would be officially published on Saturday, giving data through the previous Tuesday—I saw that "Grind" had shot up to number nine on the Club Play list and debuted at number ten on the Dance Sales list, the highest debut on that chart in four years, according to the "Chartbeat" column. Most of that had to have been just from the spike in interest from Sunday to Tuesday, after the interview, parade, and succeeding news stories, so better chart news was sure to follow the next week. In addition, the news stories had created interest in the offbeat video, which, thankfully, Gus had sent out prior to the weekend. It was now getting play on the major outlets like MTV and FUSE and LOGO, not to mention a bit of it would be shown every time a news story played. YouTube views were going through the roof! Infotainment commentators would weigh in on the video with comments like, "Well, this is pretty sexy, don't you think?"

In the meantime, our dumpy walk-up apartment was no longer providing the security and privacy we needed, so, at the urging of Joel, we moved into a two-bedroom suite at the Sheraton in midtown—at the rate of twenty-six hundred bucks per week! I asked Marcus if we could stay at his place, but he flat out refused, saying he didn't need that kind of publicity. I had Sally's cell phone temporarily disconnected; I had to keep a close watch on her and didn't want her contacting her dealer. That meant that, for a short time, only the business-related people or friends and family could reach us, through my cell phone number. God, when would the big money start rolling in?

Chester Sweethouse called, clearly anticipating his royalties flowing in the coming months, urging us to listen to a new sex-drenched anthem. Sally politely told him to send it along, that we were listening to all kinds of stuff for the album, but that she was considering something different for the next release. Given her track record on decision-making in the last couple of weeks—the arrest notwithstanding—I was content to let her call the artistic shots for the time being.

Eddie Pearl called, having had my business card, and wanted to speak to Sally but I firmly told him she wasn't available. "Come on, I know Sally, and I know she's holed up in that hotel suite with you."

I was finally getting fed up. "Eddie, you have no business talking to her right now. I am handling her affairs."

He laughed loudly. "You are in over your head, kid. She might want a word of wisdom from an old friend who's been in the business for thirty years."

"Maybe if you'd had a little more wisdom a few years ago, you wouldn't have to be going through me right now," I told him. This business was giving me a new set of balls, fast.

"Listen, you little son of a bitch, you hit the lucky jackpot your first time out, but your kind can't handle it for the long haul."

"If the long haul means a one-hit drag queen is my ticket to the big time, you're probably right." I hung up. That would keep him out of my hair for a while.

Antonio Grant called from LA and I let him speak with Sally. I tried to listen at her door, but she seemed to only offer him one-word answers in a little-girl kind of voice.

Rick and Pete called, too, from their respective post-graduation perches. Pete, as predicted, had taken the job at his friend's company in Florida. Rick, just as he said, had opted to go back to Pittsburgh and live with his parents while he figured out his next move. He was coaching a Little League team and working at a sporting goods store. I had expected bigger things from him. Anyway, *now* they both knew who Sally Testata was! It was great catching up with them and, as Rick put it, he couldn't believe I'd "made it big with that old, drunk broad at Fat Bo's."

About the only person who didn't call was my mother. Of course she knew what was going on; she was a news junkie. So far, in all the stories, my name had hardly come up at all—which was fine with me—because Feldman had taken on the role as spokesperson as soon as the shit started to hit the fan. I imagined her sitting in her wingback chair reading the newspaper and then gazing over the top of it, lost in thought, wondering how she could play this latest development to her own advantage. I debated calling her because Sally had the gig at Key West in Philadelphia after the Fourth of July. I had booked her there a couple of months ago, kind of as a favor for Ron, the friendly deejay I'd met there in February. Now, Sally's career was the hot moment, and I could see that the scheduled gig had turned out to be like handing Ron a winning lottery ticket. The club would make a fortune and have us for the small fee of a few hundred dollars.

Feldman had advised us to cancel the remaining summer gigs—to the tune of a loss of thousands of dollars—and wait until after Sally's court appearance, scheduled for September eleventh, oddly enough. I begged him to consider the financial loss, but he insisted that her laying low and going the rehab route would help her in the public eye and with the judge as well.

"But Joel," I begged. "This is going to kill me. Financially, I'm bleeding like a stuck pig. The hotel, twenty-six hundred bucks a week." I was not crass enough to mention his sizeable fee, a three thousand dollar retainer and seven-fifty an hour. He had racked up many hours that first week alone. I'd have to see my accountant. My half mil was rapidly disappearing. I, like Chester Sweethouse, was desperately awaiting royalties to save my ass. "How much is rehab?"

"Oh, I don't know. For six weeks, anywhere from twelve thousand on up, I guess."

"She can't afford that."

"Uh, she is an employee of your record company, isn't she? I believe that would be your expense."

I buried my head in my hands.

"You have to decide if you want a one-hit wonder or a long-term prospect," Feldman said.

"I think she'll be fine. She's excited now that the song is climbing the charts and she has a fight on her hands."

"If you say so."

Philadelphia was shaping up to be big testing ground for Sally's future: all or nothing.

CHAPTER TWENTY-TWO

▼

The Fourth of July was on a Wednesday that year, but we were actually going to Philly for Friday the sixth, after the holiday. What normally would have been a slow holiday weekend in any large city promised to be a buzzworthy one for us because when the new *Billboard* charts came out on Thursday—a week and a half after the historic Gay Pride Parade publicity—"Grind" had leaped to number one on both the Dance Club Play and Dance Sales charts, making it the fastest-rising number one song on those lists in years. Better yet, on the all-important Hot 100, which combines the top airplay and sales from all the charts, the song debuted at sixty-five. All of the publicity had fueled a boost on urban radio formats, despite the racy lyrics. "It's okay for male rappers to sing about sex with bitches and 'hos, but if a woman does it, it's too risky," Sally had wryly observed. In our case, money and headlines talked.

On the tabloid shows, there had been talk about what Sally Testata should do next, whether to ramp up (that's what they wanted; they were dying to interview her) or go the rehab route—just what Feldman had recommended—but I had yet to discuss it with Sally. The real heat of the story was focused on Gus Vanderwall. A couple dozen women began picketing outside of his midtown building, carry signs like "We Don't Want to See Yours, Gus—Why Do You Want to See Ours?"' and "Naked Women—Music to Gus Vanderwall's Ears." There seemed to be a belief that Sally's lewd stage behavior had been created and promoted by Gus, a belief that Feldman did not make any effort to refute. In any case, Gus, with his billions, was probably off on an extended holiday vacation to escape the glare and could not be found anywhere to respond to the stories.

Of course, television talk shows had been clamoring to get Sally on the air that week. The hens from *The View* were particularly insistent. Joel Feldman, exercising his new role as attorney/publicist/protector, insisted that Sally lay low. Privately, he told me that we could not afford to have Sally run her mouth off on live TV and risk alienating viewers or, even worse, swaying a judge, never mind offending more people in power.

Holed up in the Sheraton, Sally was furious about the turn of events. "Doesn't he know that I staged that event and got us more publicity than we could have ever dreamed of? We should be jumping on this!"

From a purely financial point of view, I couldn't agree more. But Feldman, with his years of experience in the business, had convinced me of the long view. "If it wasn't for the drug arrest, I think we'd be on top of the world and the protest would have meant more."

She waved me off. "Yeah, yeah, that was stupid. But I was nervous, knew what I was going to do. I needed a boost."

"Well, that boost could still land you in jail. That's Feldman's concern: that you appear contrite until you go to court."

"Contrite! I've never been contrite in my life."

Still, despite her complaints, Sally managed to keep herself in check during that long week and I somehow managed to keep her from doing live call-ins on shows like *Larry King* and morning television chatfests.

Given that Key West in Philly would be our last gig in a while, we did grant a well-orchestrated telephone interview for *The Philadelphia Inquirer*, which was running a feature on Sally in its Friday entertainment section to coincide with her gig. The most controversial thing she said was, "You never know what you'll get when I'm on stage." Even I was quoted for the first time, saying things like "'Grind' is a hit for the summer but Sally is a star for the ages," and, "We're currently looking at all kinds of offers." That was true, in a sense, but I didn't reveal that the offers at that point had been for a spread in *Playboy*, a reality freak show on MTV, male strip clubs, and more gay dives across the country—all of which we refused. The only offers we considered—Feldman, at the price I was paying him, was now part of the decision team—were fairly lucrative gigs in Atlantic City or Las Vegas, but we wanted to hold out and see how big the song would become, thus upping our price—and we also wanted to see how Sally held out on her sobriety.

Sally read the article to me over dinner at a small restaurant in Center City a few hours before the gig. We were less than a mile from my parents' house and, no doubt, my mother knew I was in town, but she hadn't called—not that I'd have answered her call—and I had no intention of calling her. Sally was basically pushing the food around on her plate.

"Aren't you going to eat?" I asked her.

"I want to look good in that dress, not all bloated."

The fact is, she had lost the weight and was looking better than she ever had. "Okay," I said. I moved on to an even touchier subject. "Sally, what do you think of this rehab idea?"

"I don't need rehab. If I had a drug problem, don't you think I'd be doing them every day?"

"I guess so. But Joel thinks we should nip it in the bud before it gets to that point and it would also help your case with the judge if you can show that you're proactive in helping yourself."

"Feldman, Feldman, Feldman. I'm sick of fucking Feldman. Christ, these people come into your life for a week and they want to take over. Have some balls and dump his ass!"

"This is bigger than what the two of us can handle at this point. We need someone savvy and powerful in the industry to get us through this rough spot."

"I'll say it's a rough spot. We're number one and we have no gigs and no television." She had a point.

"He's thinking long term."

"Of course he is. That's how he stays on the payroll."

I didn't have the answers. I just wanted to sail through that night's gig so I would have a little time to think about the next step.

Key West was located right in Center City and attracted a diverse crowd. As soon as we arrived, we saw Sally's blown-up photo on the window, advertising her appearance that night. It was not the ideal place for a show; as I've said, Sally's appearance turned out to be more of a favor for Ron and the owners than anything it could do for us. The problem was, there were several rooms over three floors of space: a pool room, a big bar with male strippers, a piano bar, and the dance floor, which was on the small size—nowhere near as big as Splash. It would be hard to get all the fans into one room for a performance. However, they did a good job of putting together a little stage on one end of the dance floor and Ron proudly showed us the lights they had put up especially for the performance. They gave us the third floor loft—apparently used as a make-out spot—to use as a dressing room.

We arrived about an hour before the show and there was already a line at the door. The crowd erupted into applause as they recognized Sally. She waved and shouted out a thank you and promised to sign autographs after the show. It was then that I realized there was hardly any product to sign: Of the original ten thousand EPs pressed, at least a couple thousand had been sent to deejays and radio stations across the country; anything left over had to have been sold by now. In fact, the distributor had been calling for more copies. I guess I'd have to order another quick pressing after the holiday and get them out. More money.

Sally wanted to order a gin and tonic, "just to relax," as she put it. I absolutely forbid it. She sulked in her chair. Finally, Ron came in and told us it was fifteen minutes until show time. Hearing the mob scene outside of our dressing room, Sally at last slammed her hand on the dressing table. "I can't do this without a drink!" She really did need help.

"Will one drink calm your nerves?"

"Yes, that will do it," she said, almost begging.

"Okay, I'll be back," I said, heading out the door.

"Make it a double!"

When I returned, fighting my way through the crowd, Ron told us it would be five minutes. I had good slug of gin in a small glass for Sally, who remained in the tiny bathroom. "Come on, Sally," I said through the door. "I have your drink. We're almost on."

"Just a sec." A minute later, she came out looking pleased as punch. She downed the gin in two quick gulps.

A bouncer-type came in to escort Sally to the stage. As they stood at the door ready for her entrance, I tucked into the bathroom for a quick piss. As I was doing my thing, I heard Ron announce, "Straight from New York with her brand new number one song, Pennsylvania's own superstar, Sally Testata!" The crowd thundered its approval—shit, it must be packed out there. I finished and went to wash my hands. Just as I was about to turn on the faucet, I noticed a few stray flecks of powder on the top of the sink. Goddamn it! How and where did she get the shit?

I raced into the room just in time to see Sally step onto the stage. I prepared for what I thought might be the final disaster. I made my way over to Ron in the booth just in case there was a problem with the music. The intro to "I Still Have What it Takes" was already playing and I was already praying.

At least she started singing in the right place: *I'm gonna rise to the top ... Even if I have to stop—and smell the roses ..."* The performance was accurate, if not exciting. Fortunately, the crowd—probably just thrilled to have a celebrity in their midst—was on her side and several called out, "We love you, Sally!" after the song.

Sally improvised some patter. "I love you all. This comeback could not have happened without you all behind me one hundred percent." She quickly surveyed the crowd of mostly young men in front of her. "I'd like to have several of you behind me right now, come to think of it," she cooed and bent over suggestively. Everyone hollered approval and, "Take 'em off!" Her reputation preceded her.

"No, I'm not taking anything off tonight," she said. "I wouldn't want to do anything to give Gus Vanderwall pleasure!" More screams of approval. "However, I want to show you that you don't need to take anything off in order to be sexy—just like in my video." She gave a look to Ron up in the booth to signal the start of "Grind.'" As the groove began, her free hand started traveling up and down her body, teasingly between her legs. At the same time,

Ron was playing the provocative video on the big screen behind her. So far, so good: She was becoming the pro I knew she could be. The dancing was sensual but not over the top. As the song went on, she made the right moves. She forgot a couple of lyrics, but nobody seemed to care. As she got to the end of the song, she went down on her knees and thrust her hips forward and back to the rhythm. Then she fell to her side and I thought, "What now?" It was hard for many in the crowd to see her lying down, not the best move on her part. But wait. She wasn't getting up. Her arm with the mike still in hand lay outstretched under her, as though the Statue of Liberty had toppled over. She began to convulse and vomit on the stage.

"Oh, my God! Call nine-one-one!" I cried, and urged Ron to turn off the music. People were gasping and screaming as two security guards pushed their way to the stage. Ron made some kind of announcement about clearing the area for paramedics as I, too, moved toward the stage.

She was moaning—therefore breathing—but her eyes were rolled back and her head was a dead weight as I sat down and placed her head on my leg. "Come on, Sally, hang on," I pleaded.

A long ten minutes later, the EMTs had arrived and she was carried away, still unconscious, to a waiting ambulance. Paparazzi were already there, snapping photos. I rode with her to a nearby hospital. She regained consciousness in the ambulance and I joked with her. "Sally, you know how to make a lasting impact." She offered a weak smile in return.

I walked alongside as the medics wheeled her down the hall to the emergency room and waited until they moved her to a room where she would stay for observation overnight.

I waited outside her room for a moment, until a nurse with a clipboard emerged. "We'll be calling her father."

"Is it that serious? Is that necessary?" I asked, incredulous.

"It's protocol to call the next of kin when someone is admitted to the hospital."

"Well, what is wrong with her?"

"I can only discuss that with her or a relative or legal health care proxy."

"This is bullshit! I brought her here!"

"Sorry, Mr. Bounder. Those are the rules."

I went into Sally's room but she was asleep and was hooked up to IV bags, so I decided not to bother her. We had planned to drive back to New York after the gig—after all, we already had a very expensive suite at the Sheraton, why stay anywhere else? Even if I'd wanted to stay at my parents' house, it was much too late to wake up my mother and have a midnight rendezvous. I was able to get a room at the nearby Center City Holiday Inn.

The next morning as I got ready, I listened to the deejays talking and joking about Sally's collapse. Everybody suspected—rightly—that it was drug-related, but thank God there were no drugs found on Sally's possession. The *Inquirer* ran a front-page story, complete with a photo of Sally being put into an ambulance. Surely this would be a national story as well.

I knew my mother would be looking over those tabloid stories with great interest as she sipped her morning coffee. I don't know what possessed me—boredom?—but I decided to pay my parents a visit while I was in town. Normally, I could just walk into the house—I still had a key—but under the circumstances I decided to ring the doorbell.

After a nerve-wracking minute, the big door opened and there stood my mother, dressed in a colorful kimono and jewel-encrusted sandals, not yet dressed for the day but the hair and makeup flawless.

She seemed utterly unsurprised that I was standing in front of her. "I'm having coffee in the garden. Would you like some?"

"Sure. Thanks." I followed her into the great parlor room, through the hallway past the dining room, into the kitchen and beyond, out the back door. As I had predicted, the *Philadelphia Inquirer* was opened to the exact page of the story about Sally.

"Your father is at the country club. It's a rare morning of leisure for me." Although my mother kept herself busy with appearances and social activities, it all seemed like leisure to me.

She poured me a cup of coffee from a carafe and gestured toward a few cinnamon rolls on the white, corrugated metal table. Surely she wasn't expecting me? "Have you perhaps bitten off more than you can chew with this Sally woman?" she began.

"We have a big hit on our hands," I said, sidestepping her question.

"Yes, so I've read. Having heard it and seen her performance at the Barracuda Club, I can't imagine why."

We sat in silence amid the shaded greenery—there is no sunshine in Philadelphia, the buildings are too close together—each of us perhaps contemplating our next strategic move.

"So what next for Miss Sally?" she asked, at last. "She appears to be out of commission for a while."

"Yes, well, it's all for the good. She'll be in better health for the fall tour and recording project." Secretly, doubts were creeping in for the first time.

She breezed into the kitchen to fetch more half and half and some fruit, casually saying over her shoulder, "How's the money holding out?"

"Well, obviously there will be a lot coming in."

Mother returned and set the things on the table. She became serious. "Your father remembers what it's like to start a business. He lived in poverty as a child for years while your grandfather started Bounder & Lightning. And your brother, I suppose, knows what it's like to start a business. He has done well," she conceded. She sighed. "And you have done well on your first effort. You seem to have the Bounder knack for business. But one hit does not make a career—for her or for you. If you really want to make a go of this, I suggest dropping her after your deal is complete and moving on to an artist who isn't so flash-in-the-pan."

"I can't do that to Sally."

"You are young. Eventually you will learn that a good businessman learns not to mix his feelings with the business."

We had a number one song, but suddenly everyone else was the expert in business. "Thank you, Mother. I must get back to the hospital and see about Sally." I rose and kissed the top of her head.

"Of course," she said condescendingly. "I just thank God your name has not been in most of the press coverage."

"I'll try to keep it that way," I said, leaving her behind to nibble on her roll.

* * *

When I arrived back at the hospital, I stopped suddenly in the waiting area: Rolf was having a cup of coffee and reading a newspaper. He gave me an icy glare.

"Rolf, good to see you," I said in my best salesman's pitch, although he wasn't buying. "Why are you here?"

"The question is, why aren't you here?"

"Well, after Sally was brought in last night, she was sleeping and I didn't want to disturb her, so I got a hotel room nearby and stopped in to visit my mother," I lamely explained.

"Nice." He went back to his newspaper.

"So how is she doing?"

"Maybe you should ask her father. I brought him down here last night while you were living it up at the Ritz Carlton."

"It wasn't the Ritz Carlton and I was not—"

Rolf held up a hand. "Save it, asshole."

I walked down the hallway toward Sally's room. Just as I was arriving, Charlie Teskewicz was coming out. He looked even older and more tired than he had on that winter morning so long ago. His being up all night certainly hadn't helped.

He looked at me and tears glistened in his eyes. "She's all I got," he said to me in a hoarse whisper as a tear spilled down his cheek.

"I'm sorry, Mr. Teskewicz," was all I could say, and I meant it. He just nodded his head and walked away. I would never forget that sad, tired look on his face.

I slowly and quietly entered Sally's room. She was propped up in bed, a serene look on her face. She was still hooked up to a couple of IV bags but the color had returned to her cheeks.

"Hey, Sally. How are you doing?"

"Hey, sugar. I'm okay. They just want to keep me here until Monday to make sure I'm rested and up to par with all my vitamins and minerals."

"Did they say what the problem was?"

"Well, nothing we couldn't figure out ourselves: malnutrition brought on by a touch of anorexia; exhaustion. Obviously, the drugs didn't help."

"Your father seems really worried."

"Yeah, I've never seen him like that. Even during my mother's illness and after her death, he never showed any emotion. Either in shock or didn't know how. But now maybe it's sinking in to him how fragile life is and that he doesn't want to lose a daughter."

"Nobody's going to lose you," I said to cheer her up. "After Monday, you'll be good as new."

"Of course I will. And we have a hit song to promote, right? We have to re-book some of those shows; this is no time to be laying around. We have a number one song!" Somehow, a role reversal had taken place and Sally seemed to be trying to cheer me up.

"That's the attitude," I said, and gave her a soft high-five on the hand that was not hooked up to IV tubes. "So, um, should I stay over until Monday?"

"Oh, gosh, no," Sally told me. "You go on back to New York. I told my father and Rolf to go back to Scranton. I'll be fine. Antonio called and said he'd be here on Monday when I'm discharged."

Smooth Antonio was suddenly back in the picture. "He doesn't need to do that. I can be here, I'm not on a schedule." It would make my life easier not to have to hang around in Philadelphia for two more days, but my jealousy was taking hold at the thought of Antonio perhaps trying to woo her back.

As if reading my mind, she grinned and said, "You're jealous. Don't worry, Antonio's going to have to work hard to get me back."

"And don't forget, you're on the rebound from ML and very vulnerable from all of this," I said, indicating our surroundings.

"I hear you," she said. "Although, Antonio really has his act together now. I could do worse."

We had about fifteen more minutes of conversation and then I leaned over to give her a hug and say good-bye. "I'll be home waiting for you on Monday. Don't hesitate to call if you need anything."

"Okay, tiger. You just keep that song number one and we'll have every-thing we need."

* * *

I got back in New York on Saturday night and got a good night's sleep. On Sunday morning, I went for a long run in Central Park, my mind racing with thoughts. There was so much to plan. I had a big hit; no promoter; an expen-sive, high-powered attorney; a big hospital bill on the way; and a troubled star with no shows in sight until a homecoming gig in Scranton in September. Maybe Antonio *would* be good for her, to keep her emotional life in check while I took control of the career.

When I got back to the hotel room, I called and left a message for Anto-nio. Within a couple of hours, he returned my call.

"Antonio, I just wanted to thank you for picking up Sally tomorrow."

"No problem, I'd do anything for Sally. I owe her big-time."

"Listen, I know I acted kind of crazy with that whole ML situation but I just wanted you to know that if you were, you know, interested in Sally again, I'd be okay with that."

There was an uncomfortable silence for a moment—I thought we had been disconnected—and then Antonio burst out laughing. "I bet you would be okay with that! It would keep her occupied, right?"

"I don't mean it like that. I just mean that you would be good for her."

"Maybe so, but if there's one thing I've learned, it's that an addict needs to take care of herself. Nobody else can do it for her. And I certainly don't want to date one."

"Addict? That's a pretty strong word. She doesn't use drugs that often."

"You need to face it. Don't keep enabling her to keep your careers going. She's not going to get better with a two-day hospital stay. She'll go right back to the same behavior and it will only get worse when she has access to more money."

"So what do we do?"

"That's up to her and you. But Sally and I are going to have a long talk about it during our drive up to New York on Monday."

I thanked him and we said our good-byes. I walked over to the window and looked out at the magical city of my dreams, gleaming from my high perch. There was Worldwide Plaza, with its golden pyramid on top, surrounded by new, shining glass towers, lower tenement buildings further west, and the Hudson River beyond that. If I went down to the streets and into the build-ings, no doubt I would find people of all ages and stripes, with problems just like ours. The dream was a compelling façade, but reality eventually intruded. I had done so well so quickly, and yet …

* * *

Sally walked into our suite on Monday afternoon and we hugged. Antonio didn't even come up to say hello. She seemed rested and quiet, perhaps as full of thoughts as I was.

That night, Sally and I were in the suite listening to Gina Ferrara's program on KTU and Gina said, to our surprise, "This one goes out to Sally Testata, who has had a rough couple of weeks since she appeared on my program. Let's hope she gets well soon. She still has what it takes." She then played "I Still Have What it Takes"!

Sally immediately wanted to call in to the station and—to hell with Feldman—I agreed with her. We had Gina's business card, so was able to reach her right away. Gina was very pleased and wanted to have her on the air.

When the song was over, Gina enthusiastically told her listening audience that Sally was on the line. She then began the short interview.

"Sally, great to have you back. How are you feeling?"

"I'm feeling great, Gina. I've had a little bit of down time the last two days. A chance to think."

"Any new thoughts you'd like to share with us?"

"First of all, thank you for playing that song that I co-wrote with Greg Bounder and Chester Sweethouse." It bugged the shit out of me that Chester would share that royalty. "I prefer the message of that song to 'Grind.' Second, I have no regrets about taking on Gus Vanderwall. We girls need to take this business back. The men have made money off of us for too long."

"You got that right. But you know Gus will not go down without a fight."

Our ears perked up. "What do you mean?" Sally asked.

"I'm not at liberty to say." Gina had stepped into the shit big time. She quickly tried to right herself. "Any other news you'd like to share, Sally?"

"Well, I would like to tell your audience that I will be entering rehab this week. I need to deal with some of my issues so that I can come back in a big way in the fall. If I'm going to take on the big guys, I have to be strong!"

I had to give it to Sally. Without even telling me, she was breaking yet more news over the airwaves. I wondered how many headlines could she generate in a month. Were there any surprises left?

After a few more minutes of small talk, the interview ended and Sally hung up. I gave her a big hug and assured her that the rehab would be all for the good—a chance for both of us to look back and take stock before looking ahead.

CHAPTER TWENTY-THREE

▼

It seemed that July that the headlines would never stop. The week after Sally's KTU interview, the tabloids followed up on Sally's announcement that she would go into rehab. Furthermore, Page Six of *The Post* speculated what Gina Ferrara meant by her comment about Gus Vanderwall not going down without a fight. She now became the focus of a small media frenzy, but she too kept her lips zipped.

Antonio found a rural rehab facility in New Jersey and Sally checked in on Monday the sixteenth. She spent the week before that packing up her stuff and watching the tabloid shows for any new wrinkles in the stories. At the end of the week, "Grind" was still number one on both dance charts and had moved up to fifty-five on the Hot 100. The digital download sales had peaked in the first week after the parade, but since then radio play had picked up slightly, which was really more important for ongoing sales and chart position. I needed to press more CDs. I had wanted to press another ten thousand but the distributor wanted at least fifty thousand, assuring me that there would be interest overseas, where hard copies still outsold downloads. I understood their point but, Jesus, that would cost me another forty thousand dollars or so—thankfully, with each pressing, the price per copy went down some. Still, after that and rehab, plus the mounting bills for Feldman and the hotel and my living expenses, my half million was down to less than two hundred thousand by mid-July.

I drove Sally to the Blossom Gardens Clinic on the sixteenth. She was surprisingly strong and determined about what she had to do that day, gave me a big hug and, after check-in, walked with her health care aide through a set of swinging doors without looking back. I felt as if a huge weight had been lifted off my shoulders.

I immediately got to work on a plan. First thing, I would start calling radio stations all over the place to try and get them to play "I Still Have What it Takes." Since I had no other product to work with—after Sally's six-week stint in rehab, she would come out and we'd still have to record an entire follow-up CD, which would take at least six months—I had to work with what I had. Besides, we'd at least have a songwriting royalty on that one, eventually. Next, I wanted to start booking fall gigs, but Feldman told me to hold off until we got an idea of how Sally was progressing.

I also immediately moved out of the costly Sheraton and into a cheaper hotel room downtown—a mere two hundred bucks per night. I needed to get my own place and the Manhattan real estate market was booming. August looked like a good time to buy and it looked like I'd better do it while I still had money for a down payment.

Feldman called me that Thursday and asked me if I'd seen *Billboard*, which had just come out. Oddly enough, with all the work I was doing, I had forgotten to look. He told me that mainstream radio airplay and sales had flatlined the previous week. That made absolutely no sense! Luckily, it remained at number one on the dance charts, which are mainly supported by gays, a fringe market.

Those within the industry—which I was now a part of—had begun a whispering campaign, but it was all under wraps from the general public. But not for long. Gina Ferrara, still being hounded by the media, finally spilled her guts on her own show the following Sunday. She revealed that Gus Vanderwall had promised many big radio stations access to his roster of big stars—*if* they stopped playing "Grind." With that bombshell, she then played the song! So *that* was the fight Gus was giving! I would sue his ass for interfering with my business. And I had paid him dearly to start that business!

The scandal, one angle of it or another, was going into its fifth week. Gina Ferrara was promptly fired by KTU. Its owner stated that Gina Ferrara had acted irresponsibly and that Gus Vanderwall had "absolutely not influenced his or any other station regarding the issue of airplay for 'Grind' since its release." Bullshit!

That week the scandal that had seemed to peak the week after the parade mushroomed again. Gina Ferrara appeared on *The View* and *Larry King Live* to further blab about it. Finally, Gus Vanderwall himself was forced to come out of hiding. He provided the news outlets a videotaped statement filmed at his office:

> I would like to state that I did not and never have
> negatively influenced any individuals or organizations
> regarding "Grind," Sally Testata, or any other artist,
> now or in the past. I have been heavily involved
> in the music industry for thirty years, starting on
> the ground floor and working my way up through
> hard work and long hours. It is unfortunate that a

few individuals choose to spread gossip and outright
lies to destroy my reputation. I will continue the
good work I do on behalf of many hardworking
individuals in this industry, artists who need not
resort to taking off their clothes or possibly
engaging in illegal activities in order to have
a hit record. Thank you.

Fighting words for sure! It was a start, a good opening salvo on Gus's part, but now he would have to come out of his tower and appear on the talk shows as well, as Gina showed no signs of letting up.

And now he'd have Joel Feldman to contend with, who wanted an investigation. He also filed a lawsuit against Vanderwall on Sally's behalf, asserting that he had damaged her reputation. In response, Vanderwall countersued Sally and ScranNY Records for the same charge. Even I was being called by several outlets for a response.

That week, the Hot 100 showed that "Grind" had, in fact, dropped to sixty-one, but that only covered the Monday after Gina's bombshell announcement. The following week would be different. However, despite all the publicity, I noticed that MTV and VH1 were still reluctant to play the "Grind" video, telling me that that kind of music was not part of their usual format, but I knew better. Gus's tentacles were all over that. What station wouldn't play a video by an artist who was causing such an uproar? Thank God for YouTube, where it was still getting thousands of views.

Sure enough, the following week, download sales shot up again and more small, independent stations had started playing "Grind," kind of as a protest against the monopoly of the mainstream music industry, whether they believed Gus or not. Even though the larger stations—influenced by Gus, I had no doubt—were still not playing "Grind" very much, all in all, the small stations and sales were enough to help the song rebound to number eighteen—Sally's first mainstream Top Forty hit! And it was still number one on the dance charts—the boys were grinding away in clubs all over America!

It was now August, and ScranNY Records, of which I was sole owner, finally received its first checks, which covered the first half of the year through the end of June. I got about two-thirds from the sale of the EP, which amounted to about six thousand copies, all of which had come in June alone, making my cut about twenty-four thousand dollars. I also got roughly the same percentage from the sale of digital downloads on iTunes, which sold for ninety-nine cents apiece. However, the number of sales was greater, about ten thousand, so that check was for about six thousand dollars. This tells you why the industry was becoming very concerned that year about the popularity of downloads versus album sales. If a company spent several hundred thousand dollars on a CD, it would have a hard time recouping its costs on down-loading individual songs. And CD sales were on the decline. Considering I had spent about three hundred thousand dollars up to that point, a return of one-tenth of that wasn't much, but I eagerly anticipated getting a much heftier paycheck the following January—if my bank account could hold out that long. And, of course, I had to send off a songwriting royalty payment of about thirty-seven hundred bucks to Chester Sweethouse for his two mixes of "Grind" and one-third ownership of "I Still Have What it Takes," and a smaller check to the writers of "Everything Must Change," since it, too, was on the EP. I had not, however, made that song available for download. And then there were taxes to consider ...

Naturally, I wanted to share all this news with Sally, but when I called Blossom Gardens I was told in no uncertain terms that she was being moni-tored closely to make sure she did not see any news reports concerning herself and that it probably wasn't a good idea for her to see me at that time. And I was paying for the fucking rehab!

In the meantime, I had to do more than sit around and watch the talk shows that summer. I started getting out to the clubs again, hearing what was coming out and trying to promote "I Still Have What it Takes." Although I was not about to get myself in a compromising position with a guy again, I tried to look as hot as possible on my rounds, figuring it would help with the deejays. I left Feldman alone to work his legal magic.

By the end of August, I had found a one-bedroom apartment on the west side in Midtown, which meant a down payment of sixty thousand dollars. My credit was good, as well as my family history, and I had a promising career ahead of me. Still, Grandpa's money was coming to an end. I would move in by September first.

Also, by that time, the scandal of the summer had pretty much died down. I had called Gina at one point to thank her for taking such a hit on Sally's behalf, but she pretty much blew me off. I can imagine she may have been regretful at that point because she had made herself unhireable in the indus-try. Feldman had managed to get an independent investigation into Gus Vanderwall's promoting practices, but it was all behind the scenes and would take many months. And at that point, it didn't look like there was going to be any smoking gun. As I've said, money talks, and few people or industries had more than Gus Vanderwall and the music industry.

As for "Grind," then in its ninth week on the Hot 100, it had already peaked two weeks before at number ten, which would give Sally bragging rights for a Top Ten hit. It was now down to number twenty-five, and also no longer number one on the dance charts, but still Top Ten there. What should have been a bigger hit was, I believe, both started and stopped by

Gus Vanderwall. In retrospect, I've wondered if I should have hired another promoter while it was hot, but who's to say another promoter would have had any effect?

In the meantime, my efforts with "I Still Have What it Takes" went almost nowhere. There was some success on the dance club play chart, where deejays were eager to try any follow-up to Sally's big club hit, but the sunny message of the song was not really what the clubgoers wanted from her. By the end of August, in its third week on that chart, it had inched up to number thirty-eight. Sales, however, were negligible and radio airplay was nonexistent, so there was no hope for it to become any kind of crossover hit.

Better news for me was that I had found a new artist to represent. I hadn't necessarily been looking, but after Sally had been gone for a few weeks and with everything on hold until she came out of rehab, it made no sense for me to sit on my hands. After all, most managers handle more than one artist. Her name was Angelina Velez, and I found her one night when I was walking down Bleecker Street. It was a warm night, and the door to some rock club was open. I heard her passionate voice over a guitar and walked inside. She was singing one of her original songs. The song wasn't so great, but she sounded and looked fantastic. She was just nineteen years old, but real sophisticated, like New York girls are. When I introduced myself to her, she took my card and was very excited—she knew who I was and everything, although "'Grind'" was about as far away from her kind of music as it could be. Angelina was kind of a darker, sultrier Avril Lavigne. As I spoke with her, I was noticing that—I'll be damned—there were straight people all around me. And I could appreciate this music. If I hoped to survive in the business, I had to stretch.

All of this meant that I had a difficult decision to make: Should I keep Sally? Obviously, her efforts with me had peaked at that point. Could I sink more money into a full-length CD and tour for someone who had alienated herself from the powers that be in the music industry? I had very little money left to play with. Maybe our association should end in Scranton, where it had begun. I reminded myself that Sally herself had often said she didn't want to be back in the music industry and she certainly didn't enjoy performing "Grind," which would more than likely end up as her biggest hit.

I poured myself a drink and called Marcus. "You were right. I think I need to let Sally go."

"It will be better for both of you in the long run," he said.

"It's all my fault she's in this mess."

"She couldn't handle it. Maybe she'll get better and figure it out. But you need to move on with your career and not worry about taking care of her."

"Yeah." I tried to imagine my life in New York without Sally. As crazy as our adventure had been, it was ours and all of my associations up to that point had been because of our hit together. Suddenly, New York seemed like a big, lonely place. I thanked Marcus for the reassurance and ended the call.

Sally would be discharged from Blossom Gardens at the end of August. I steeled myself to do what I had to do.

CHAPTER TWENTY-FOUR

▼

I offered to pick up Sally from Blossom Gardens at the end of August, but she said that was all right—Rolf was picking her up and she was going back to Scranton until the gig on the eighth of September. I wanted to see her and find out what rehab was like, but this plan was better: I could put off dropping her until after the gig and wouldn't have to worry about babysitting her in New York, making sure she didn't go off the wagon. I felt guilty, but I had the brains and know-how of Joel Feldman and Marcus—not to mention my mother—behind me. I couldn't let my feelings interfere.

I was certain so many would be thinking, *You bastard. You're dumping her just like Eddie Pearl did six years before!* Believe me, that nagging thought kept running through my head. But seeing how the music industry brought out the worst in her, I agreed with Marcus that perhaps I was doing her a favor.

Although I couldn't tell her until after the Copper Penny gig, I would be by her side at her sentencing on the eleventh, whether I was her manager or not. Until then, I had time to move out of the Sheraton and settle into my own place. I also ended my lease at the apartment in Scranton, but had offered to pay the landlord for September if I could keep my stuff in there until the ninth.

On the eighth of September I drove into Sally's driveway to pick her up. She didn't even invite me in, coming out with her garment bag before I had even turned off the engine. She looked rested and peaceful—fantastic, really. I was beginning to regret my decision. "The place is a dump," she explained.

"Sally, it was a dump when you lived there," I reminded her.

"True, but nothing compared to what my father has done to it."

As I pulled out onto the highway, I told Sally how good she looked. "So what did you learn at Blossom Gardens?"

She let out a musical sigh. "Well, it probably sounds silly, but I learned that I'm okay just the way I am."

"Of course you are!" I said glibly. "But as far as the drugs and stuff, you're cured, right?"

"Cured?" she said with a surprised giggle. "It doesn't work like that. I'll always be an addict. One day at a time." She suddenly started laughing. "You'll never believe what they had me doing as part of my daily therapy!"

"What's that?"

"They put me to work scrubbing and cleaning the kitchens and bathrooms! I told my counselor, 'Shit, I knew this was therapeutic when I did this for a living but at least I got paid!'" Sally continued to laugh, wiping tears from the corners of her eyes.

"That's fucked up," I said. I was not nearly as amused as she was that my good money was being used to put her to work as a custodian.

"Actually, it's not. It's the discipline of work and feeling your whole body in the process. This music business has, I don't know … too much freedom. It can get you into trouble."

So it sounded like Sally wanted to go back to cleaning houses. I couldn't understand it, but it would make my firing her a lot easier.

By the time we arrived at the Copper Penny a little after eight—no late-night gigs in Scranton—there was already a crowd milling around on the sidewalk. There were also a couple of cops standing near the entrance, probably in case Sally tried any of her infamous antics. A life-sized poster of Sally was up near the entrance. We were cheered as we hurried into the club. Despite a big dance hit and a modest pop hit, Sally was still fairly minor league in the music industry and only recognizable on the street because of her bigger-than-life tabloid headlines of the summer. In Scranton, she would no doubt be a star for the rest of her days.

The booking manager and deejay greeted us warmly and I handed the deejay the tracks with instructions for which ones to play and in what order. The club had the same kind of feel as Key West in Philly, three floors of activity and a makeshift dressing room for the rare live guest appearance. Despite the ten weeks of no gigs, this was starting to feel a bit old and amateurish. It might have been fine for Eddie Pearl to make chump change sending Olive Martini to second-rate clubs in second-rate cities, but not for me.

Sally seemed a little nervous, but upbeat. This was her town and there would be several people she knew in the audience. There would also be a few friends of mine from the university, and even Rick was coming up from Pittsburgh to say hello and check out my discovery. Because of the news flashes back in June and Sally's hit, I think my friends assumed I was big-time and that I was making millions. Little did they know. The fact that Sally was now playing the Copper Penny should have been a clue.

Sally did not want to wear her little black dress for this gig. I let her do what she wanted. She opted for one of her older outfits, a flouncy skirt and a button-down blouse open halfway down, with a Lycra halter top underneath, showing ample cleavage. And cowboy boots. Christ! Other than that, however, I was relieved: She did not have a drink backstage.

By ten, when Sally was to go on, the place was jam packed: Who knew there were that many people in Scranton? Space was cheap in Scranton; the Copper Penny was a big club with good sight lines to the second floor stage. When Sally's name was announced, I escorted her to the stage to thunderous applause. I went off to the side, but not before seeing Rolf standing front and center, next to that Tommy guy, her father nearby and Rick near the front also. He gave me a thumbs-up.

Sally started with "Bombs Away" and it went without a hitch, although she seemed slightly nervous. The warmth of the crowd seemed to put her at ease by the end of the song, however. "Wow, there are so many of you out there tonight, so many old friends," she said. "If you all downloaded my song from iTunes when you got home tonight, I could move back up the charts!" She wasn't far wrong. It only took a few hundred sales in a week to make a difference on a chart—much easier said than done. "But before I get to my number one hit, I'll do a song that Greg and I first started writing at a little bar called Fat Bo's, up on the hill!" More applause. "It wasn't much of a hit, but that just shows you how fucked up this country is!" The audience screamed in agreement as she began "I Still Have What it Takes." She started sensually lifting the skirt up her thighs as she pranced around. I caught a glance of Rolf, whose face had tightened up like my mother's, and her father who, oddly, was cheering her on. After our encounter at the hospital, he probably had come to realize that the money to be made trumped a brief hospital stay ... or he was genuinely happy she was healthy again. Sally managed to be sexy without going over the top and the crowd again showed its appreciation.

"Now, for the number one dance song of the summer!" she shouted to the crowds. "We had to fight to get this one heard, didn't we, Greg? This country still doesn't take to a woman being sexual, but we showed them!" That brought tepid applause from that little conservative corner of the world, perhaps evoking memories of her unpleasant arrest and unseemly battle with Gus Vanderwall. This crowd wasn't shouting at her to "take it all off" like they did in New York. This crowd was decidedly mixed, male and female, straight and gay, old and young. They seemed nervous about what she might do.

"Sounds like you don't want a woman to be sexual either! Well, I'll show you!" The music for "Grind" began. She did the sexy dance that Antonio had taught her and started teasing with the skirt again. Shit, I realized that I didn't *know* if she was wearing panties or not! It turned out that we didn't have time

to find out. Rolf jumped up on the stage and grabbed her by the arm and tried to pull her off the stage. What the hell was going on?

The crowd seemed stunned, neither applauding nor booing, as the musical track played on. I pushed my way through the crowd, jumped up on the stage and grabbed Rolf by the arm. "What the hell are you doing?"

"What have you done to her, you son of a bitch?" he snarled at me.

"What are you talking about?"

"I told you to stay away from her. You have turned her into a national joke!" With that, he threw a punch at me, which hit me squarely on the left cheek and sent me reeling, although I managed to stay on my feet. I'm short, but I was a champion wrestler. Big mistake on Rolf's part.

I bent low and ran into Rolf, head-butting him in the torso while I lifted him up from behind the knees. I slammed that big sack of shit right up onto the bar to the left of the stage, which had quickly cleared when the patrons saw us coming. Rolf, though, had me by the back of my shirt as he landed and wouldn't let go, so he trapped my arms as he pulled it over my head. He then kicked me in the stomach with a free foot and I let go, falling back and letting the shirt come off in his hands. Enraged, I pounced on top of him. We were wrestling and punching, rolling sideways along the wide bar, knocking over glasses as we went. I was getting sliced up by cut glass on my bare skin, and he probably was too, but my adrenaline was so pumped up I didn't feel it. I don't know how much time passed, but hands were pulling us apart. There was pandemonium and a siren in the distance and I was being dragged out of the club by two cops.

To make a long story short, I was the one arrested that night.

CHAPTER TWENTY-FIVE

▼

Naturally, the story made the front page of the *Scranton Times-Tribune* and was picked up by the national media as well, although with only passing interest this time around, the only surprise being that I was arrested and not Sally. Even the media was tiring of us, as they had tired of the younger trouble-making starlets that year.

I spent the night in jail and Sally, of all people, came to get me out the next morning. She laughed when she saw me behind bars. Rolf, a beloved local, was not put in jail. However, Sally informed me that he was charged with the same things I was: disorderly conduct, inciting riot, and destruction of property. Enough witnesses had come forward saying that Rolf had landed the first punch. Therefore, I would not be charged with assault. I assumed I would not gain much traction charging *him* with assault.

All of this, in my mind, meant Sally and I were just a bad mix and that I had to break the news to her sooner rather than later. Over breakfast, I stumbled around trying to tell her that I had something to tell her. It didn't take her long to figure out something was up.

"Are you trying to dump me?" She didn't seem surprised. She actually had a smile on her face, which scared me more than it comforted me.

"Well, look at all the shit that's happened. Maybe you were right in the beginning."

"What are you talking about? I had a big hit. I admit, I went off the deep end a few times but I'm better now." She paused to ask for a refill on her coffee. "You know, last night Rolf asked me to marry him."

"What? Are you kidding me? What did you say?"

"What do you think I said?"

That damn Rolf might be the solution to my problems. "Well, yes, I hope. You two seem right for each other."

"Well, that shows you how well you know me after all this time. I said no."

"But why, Sally? You could be back home with someone you love."

"He's holding onto something that's twenty-five years old. And besides, I've had about enough of men trying to rescue me." She seductively bit off a piece of bacon and looked me squarely in the eyes. "You know, you can't just dump me. We had a contract for a year. Binding on both sides."

"Well, that was to protect me in case you wanted to bolt."

"That's not what the fine print says. Your option is up after a year. What about my protection? I'm owed a CD."

"Sally, I've been paying you an advance since March, plus the cost of living expenses, and your rehab."

"I'm a hot property. I'm a household name all over the country. It's going to cost you."

I figured she was bluffing. There was no way she could afford to hire a lawyer. "Have your lawyer contact me."

She grinned from ear to ear, her eyes never leaving mine. "You bet your sweet ass," she whispered. I was in love all over again!

Sally stood up and turned to go. "You'll take care of the check, right?"

CHAPTER TWENTY-SIX

▼

I returned to New York and attended her court appearance on the eleventh. However, she didn't speak to me and I just observed from the back. She got off with a fine of a few thousand dollars and community service and a year's probation. After that, Sally drove back to Scranton and I didn't hear from her for weeks. Technically, I was still her manager, but I could ride out the contract and claim I was doing work. I still had to pay her the two hundred a week allowance/advance, though. Things were getting dangerous: I had less than a hundred thousand in the bank, and I was planning to launch Angelina's career. I was expecting a royalty check from ASCAP any day, based on radio airplay, and while it would be a welcome several thousand dollars, the bulk of my money would still be coming in January, after the fiscal year had ended.

At the end of September, I got a letter from an attorney—Sally's attorney—that was basically a contract to end my previous contract with Sally. I showed it to Feldman. The gist was that she wanted a half million dollars because I would be irreparably damaging her reputation by firing her before the end of her contract; that I had been cheating her out of x number of lucrative bookings by not filling up her fall calendar; and that I had not followed through with a full-length CD, which had been promised in the contract. The attorney had listed a number of clubs, including some in Atlantic City and Las Vegas, that supposedly had expressed interest in booking her. Even Feldman hadn't seen this coming and he essentially said, "Well, we can fight this, which could cost you more in the long run, with legal fees, or you can keep her on and book all these gigs and more, plus deliver the CD, or you can buy out her contract and be rid of her."

"I can't afford any of those options," I whined.

"You will get a big payment in January. And you are young and energetic and have proven yourself a force to be reckoned with on your first project. You will make a lot of money in this industry. I say pay her off."

So that was the end of my business association with Sally. By the end of October, the paperwork was finalized. Feldman had negotiated the buyout down to three hundred grand, but Sally had also made sure that she would have the right to continue to promote her recordings on her own and the right to include those recordings on any future release. That was fine with me; I didn't see what she could do with them that I hadn't tried already.

There was a blip in the media about how she had been dropped by me and ScranNY Records. Only a week or so after that, I noticed a small article in the trade magazines that Blue Sound Records, a small independent jazz and blues label, had signed her. Jazz and blues? What was up with that?

I had taken out a million-dollar business loan to pay off Sally and to help me get started with Angelina. As Feldman had said, one hit record and a lot of media attention buys you a lot of credit. I started recording tracks with Angelina in November.

Around the same time, I received more lucky news: "'Grind" was moving up the charts in Europe, which was much more open to dance music and racy lyrics. I guessed I would have to sink more money into pressings for that. I started to think maybe I could have made a whole lot of money with Sally. How much could a European tour have brought in?

In December, all the news programs had year-end recaps and Sally and the Gus Vanderwall scandal figured prominently in all the stories-of-the-year. She even appeared on a Barbara Walters special, her *Ten Most Intriguing People of the Year*. Sally seemed poised and calm and it was hard to believe that it was her first-ever television interview and that she'd managed to get through the whole scandal without saying a peep on camera. She told Barbara she had no regrets about taking on Gus Vanderwall, even though in the long run it hadn't seemed to damage his career. She said it brought awareness to the increasing use of pornography in the music business and that it had led her to … Gina Ferrara—her new manager! Goddamn, how did I miss that? Asked if she had new aspirations, Sally said that she was recording a jazz album and that a song she had previously recorded was already making a mark on the jazz chart. It couldn't be! I ran to the computer and checked it out, just as I heard "Everything Must Change" coming out of the TV set—it was a clip of her performing it live at some little cabaret club in Atlanta! Sure enough, our recording of it was at number twenty-nine in its third week on the Jazz Airplay chart and moving up! No wonder she wanted that clause in her contract: She and Gina wanted to promote that song!

Sally seemed so content. I wanted her back but it seemed that was out of the question. I would have to make do with Angelina, who was very talented and very beautiful. In fact, she was everything I could want in a client.

But she wasn't Sally.

CHAPTER TWENTY-SEVEN

▼

On Christmas Eve, I was back in Philadelphia for the holiday. Marcus had come too. It had been an eventful year for all of us, what with my whirlwind success and its accompanying drama.

After dinner I went up to my room and, after some hesitation, called Sally. Charlie answered.

When I asked to speak with Sally and told him who I was he barked, "What the hell do you want?" Nice holiday sentiment. However, he called out her name.

"Hello, Greg," she said. "How nice of you to call." I think she was sincere.

"I saw you on Barbara Walters. You were really good."

"I was, wasn't I?"

"Yes. How are things working out with Gina?"

"Great, really great."

"I tell you, Sally, right now you have more money than I do."

She laughed. "But that's the way it should be. I've paid my dues. Are you upset about the settlement?"

"No." I paused. "I think I got off easy."

"Aw," Sally cried. "That's about the nicest Christmas present I could ask for."

"I should have held onto you, Sally, I'm sorry."

"Hey, you made what you thought was a good business decision. And so did I. For once. And if you want me back now, it's gonna *really* cost you."

"Yeah, more than I can afford." I thought about what to say next. "I guess I just called to say good luck to you. That I really wish you well."

"I wish you well, too, Greg. You deserve it, you really work hard. Maybe we'll see each other at the Grammy Awards one day." She, too, paused to consider what to say. "Thank you, Greg. Thank you for everything."

"There will never be—" I started, then a sob clutched my throat. I heard a click on the other end as she hung up. I was crying, for Christ's sake. I don't think I'd ever cried in my life.

After a time, I washed my face and went back downstairs. Marcus was sitting with Dad in the living room watching some old Christmas movie. I went into the kitchen where Mother was putting away the last of the dishes.

"I called Sally," I told her.

"Uh-huh." She seemed unsurprised.

"I just wanted to wish her well. You know, she's doing jazz now."

"Yes, I know. I saw her on Barbara Walters. She seems much more suited to that kind of music. I don't know why she insisted on doing that ridiculous dance garbage. Maybe she'll turn out all right after all."

"I wish you'd have told me that before."

"I don't think you would have listened." My mother smiled. "Well, she may not have turned out all right with *you*. That combination didn't seem to be working. You were right to let her go. You will both do better now. You will learn, as she has: Everything must change."

Indeed. Nothing stays the same. Unexpectedly, I stepped toward her and gave her a hug.

"Now go in there and spend some time with your father and brother. I know this isn't as exciting as New York, but it's home nonetheless." As I released her, I detected a tear in her eye.

She had her youngest back in her arms and, for now, that was enough for her despite all that year's change.

Philadelphia, like Scranton, I guess, had its charms.

* * *

Everything must change, indeed. The music industry had changed so much that year, and the following year would bring tremendous changes to the political and economic landscape.

I had been there at the crossroads, playing my small part, finding some measure of success before those years of tumult.

Still, nothing would be as tumultuous or exciting as my year with Sally, my first year on the charts. The adrenaline of the chart climb had become my drug of choice, my addiction. And Sally? Well, she was simply off the charts, as they say.

From that, there was no easy recovery.

THE END

Printed in the United States
by Baker & Taylor Publisher Services